No Safe An

An evocative and fast-moving tale, set on Skye and the West Highlands before moving to Canada, *No Safe Anchorage*, like its title, swirls with risk and danger. It invokes the spirit of Robert Louis Stevenson whose childhood it portrays. With its sharp use of dialogue and tight, concise description, it also conjures up that writer in other ways, creating an adventure story that is as breathless and exciting as some of that nineteenth-century novelist's work.

Donald S. Murray, author

No Safe Anchorage is a great second novel by Liz MacRae Shaw. We follow the life of nineteenth-century naval officer, Tom Masters, a square peg in a round hole. His childhood experiences, slowly revealed, loss of a close friend and awakening sexuality make for a very strong central character. Neatly woven in is part of the life of Robert Louis Stevenson who might be described as a similarly round peg within his lighthouse building family.

Linda Henderson, author and editor

Liz MacRae Shaw can spin a yarn like few others. The young Robert Louis Stevenson tucked up in bed recovering from a fall, Tom's encounter with the fisher lassies, his fierce and admirable sister, Emma, and other vivid happenings set the scene for the sweeping adventure to follow. *No Safe Anchorage* takes Tom from the Hebrides to Canada and along the way he forms relationships, good and bad, with a wide span of characters.

Jenny Salaman Manson, writer and editor

No Safe
Anchorage

Liz MacRae Shaw

No Safe Anchorage

Liz MacRae Shaw

**TOP HAT
BOOKS**

Winchester, UK
Washington, USA

First published by Top Hat Books, 2017
Top Hat Books is an imprint of John Hunt Publishing Ltd., Laurel House, Station Approach,
Alresford, Hants, SO24 9JH, UK
office1@jhpbooks.net
www.johnhuntpublishing.com
www.tophat-books.com

For distributor details and how to order please visit the 'Ordering' section on our website.

Text copyright: Liz MacRae Shaw 2016

ISBN: 978 1 78279 706 7
978 1 78279 787 6 (ebook)
Library of Congress Control Number: 2016951869

A CIP catalogue record for this book is available from the British Library.

Design: Stuart Davies

Printed and bound by CPI Group (UK) Ltd, Croydon, CR0 4YY, UK

We operate a distinctive and ethical publishing philosophy in all
areas of our business, from our global network of authors to
production and worldwide distribution.

CONTENTS

Also by Liz MacRae Shaw – *Love and Music Will Endure,* an historical novel based on the life of Mary MacPherson (Màiri Mhòr nan Oran), the nineteenth-century Skye-born poet and political campaigner. Published by The Islands Book Trust, 2013, ISBN: 978-1-907443-58-9.

Preface

I was inspired to write *No Safe Anchorage* by the story of my great-great-great grandmother who lived on the tiny island of Rona, off the coast of Skye in the Inner Hebrides. For many years, she kept an oil lamp in the window of her house to help seafarers in the treacherous waters. She was visited by Captain Otter, who conducted many surveys of Hebridean waters and had a distinguished naval career. He was so impressed by her dedication that he wrote to Allan Stevenson, engineer to the Commissioners of Northern Lighthouses in 1851, recommending that she be paid for the oil needed for her lamp. Coxswain Richard Williams who served under Captain Otter is buried near the remains of an ancient chapel on the Scorrybreac shore, near Portree on the island of Skye. All three appear in my story. As it is a work of fiction, I have changed some of the details of events while remaining true to the spirit of their characters. For example, Janet MacKenzie probably emigrated to Australia rather than Canada.

Robert Louis Stevenson also appears in the book, both as a child and an adult. He certainly traveled to various Scottish islands with his father, Thomas, who was busy building lighthouses. Although there is not a specific reference to Louis visiting Rona, he became familiar with the Highlands in his youth and their influence permeated his later writing. One of the first books I remember being given as a present was, *A Child's Garden of Verses*. Behind the simple joy in childhood pleasures in these poems lurks the sadness of a boy who was often ill and confined to bed. *The Land of Counterpane* is especially poignant and is alluded to in my story.

I should like to dedicate my book to these people who have inspired me. I should also like to give special thanks to Linda

Henderson who edited my manuscript with shrewdness and sensitivity. My husband, Steve, has been an invaluable support in both the technical and creative aspects of writing this book. I am grateful for the efficiency and professionalism of John Hunt Publishing.

—Liz MacRae Shaw

Chapter 1

Bournemouth, 1886

No sign yet. He peered through the window down the quiet road, the hushed houses standing to attention behind their prim hedges. He sighed as he felt a hankering for Edinburgh's humming gray stone tenements.

Ah, was that him approaching? A young man stalked along the leafy road. Pernickety as a wading bird probing stones he stopped at each entrance, cocking his head before pottering on. He reached the right gate and screwed up his eyes at the ivy-draped walls. Starting as he noticed the model of the lighthouse by the gate post, he nodded at the name *Skerryvore* on the wall and scurried up to the front door. The bell clanged. It sounded through the house, but he seemed too agitated to wait for an answer. He darted past the French windows toward the side of the house where the lawn sloped down into a steep gully, glossy with rhododendrons. His steps faltered.

Louis decided it was time to rescue the poor fellow and strolled out of the side door. The man jumped as he heard the hinges creak.

"Ah, Mr. Ferguson? Do come in this way. You found my retreat without too much difficulty?"

The man stood dumbstruck until Louis walked up to him, holding out his hand.

"Er . . . yes indeed, sir. Thank you for agreeing to see me." He lunged at Louis's hand as if it were a flailing rope on a storm-battered ship.

"What do you think of my home-away-from-home? My miniature Scottish glen, my wife calls it." He grinned. "Though what does she know as a mere American? Still she's done miracles. Planting trees and making paths with seats where I can

1

recline and think deep thoughts. Do come inside."

He led Ferguson into a large airy room fitted out as a study, with a glowing fire in the grate. Apart from a desk and a hard chair the only furniture was a well-worn armchair and a daybed. The russet oriental rug in the center of the room had nearly disappeared under heaps of books, craning toward each other like half-timbered houses across a narrow lane. Landscapes were displayed on the walls—mountains, waterfalls, and sea cliffs. Among them was a portrait of Louis. It showed him walking toward the corner of a drawing room. On the opposite side of the picture was the suggestion of another figure, indicated by a swirl of fabric and a pointing bare foot. Louis smiled as he noticed his visitor staring at it.

"Your accent sounds American, Mr. Ferguson, although your name suggests Scottish forebears."

"Well, I do believe so, although I have Irish and German ancestry, too."

Louis gestured for his guest to take the armchair while he lowered himself into a seat behind a desk laden with books and papers. He shrugged a blood-red shawl over his shoulders. "I apologize for looking like an ancient crone with this decrepit old thing. It's called a poncho, I believe. But I find the summer wind a little chill, even this far south. Fire away with your questions." He folded his arms and ran his fingers over the nap of his black velvet jacket. Tilting back on his chair he perched his feet on the edge of the desk.

He watched as Samuel Ferguson shifted in his seat. Drawing out a notebook and pencil from his jacket pocket, he stroked his sparse moustache, "Well, our readers are eager to know what inspired you to write *Kidnapped*. It's a very different work from *Dr. Jekyll and Mr. Hyde*, if I may say so. Are you perhaps returning to adventure stories like *Treasure Island*?"

"Back to the boys' yarns, you mean?" Louis replied sharply.

Ferguson flushed. "I didn't mean to suggest that *Kidnapped* and *Treasure Island* were merely children's books. The action appeals to young minds, of course, but there is also a subtle portrayal of character."

Louis shrugged, "Forgive me for being peremptory but I'm a little sensitive on the subject. Some critics dismissed *Treasure Island* as only a boys' book. When it was successful, they changed their tune. To answer your question. I've long wanted to write a story set in my homeland but it was only after traveling abroad that I felt able to do so."

"May I ask you about your choice of title? You see, sir, as an American, I may have misunderstood the meaning of this word. I've always taken *kidnapped* to mean someone who's been taken prisoner so that his family has to pay a ransom to release him. What you describe is something different. David Balfour is captured in order to sell him into servitude. Now, the abomination of slavery stained our nation until recent times. A Negro could be bought and sold as if he were a beast of burden. But I hadn't realized that white men could be treated like that in Europe, or at least not in recent history."

"Mmm . . . an interesting point. I don't think it happened regularly here, but there were certainly stories of poor Highlanders being bundled aboard a ship with the connivance of a landlord. It was kept secret of course, like the rest of the terrible treatment meted out after Culloden. I've always known about it, but for the life of me I couldn't tell you where I first heard of it."

Ferguson nodded and scribbled some notes down. "Again, if I could ask you about the historical background which will not be familiar to American readers? In the States there was, and is, a gulf between Yankees and Southerners. It seems to me that your heroes, David Balfour and Alan Breck Stewart, represent a similar divide between Lowlanders and Highlanders."

"Aye, you're right. They have opposing virtues—Highland courage versus Lowland caution."

"You're from the Lowlands yourself, I believe, and yet your

portrayal of Alan is very sympathetic. How did you achieve that?"

Louis leaned forward and flicked a hank of hair behind his ear while he considered the question.

"I congratulate you, Mr. Ferguson. You've identified something I can't explain. My family are Lowland Scots through and through. Practical, no-nonsense sort of people who built lighthouses. Even my old nurse, Cummy, was from Fife and fiercely proud of it. So where did the Highland influence come from?" He cleared his throat. "Yet coiled deep within me in bone and blood is this knowledge of the Highlands. Imagination can't be tied down. As a writer I have an idea. I warp the loom but the weave of the cloth comes from dreams beyond my control. I was often ill as a child and when I was delirious my visions would melt into reality so that the two couldn't be distinguished. If I were being fanciful, I would say that my inspiration comes from hidden creatures, colored brown-gray like sealskin."

He looked sideways at Ferguson who was sitting motionless, creasing his brow and sucking his pencil. Louis's shoulders heaved but his laughter turned into a fit of coughing. He slammed his feet back on the floor and groped in his jacket pocket. Hauling out a handkerchief, he turned away to spit out blood-speckled phlegm.

Ferguson leaped to his feet, looking alarmed, "May I help in any way? A glass of water perhaps?"

Louis shook his head, "It'll pass. Just give me a minute," he gasped, wiping his mouth. He could see Ferguson peering at the portrait again, especially at the partial figure at the edge of the canvas. As the coughing subsided, he said, "It's Fanny. She told John Singer Sargent that she was only a cipher and a shadow. He took her at her word and put only part of her in the picture." Ferguson looked sheepish.

"You must think me a queer fish altogether, with these strange ramblings," Louis said.

"Not at all. I'm honored that you should share your thoughts with me."

"It's a strange sensation. There's a presence there, images just out of reach. A wild sea, a galloping horseman, a fire in the darkness. The stuff of nightmares dissolved by daylight." He sighed. "It's beyond my ken but I tried to show the pride of the Highlander and the canniness of the Lowland mind."

"Will you write a sequel? There is surely more to be told about the two men."

"I hope so although maybe not—"

He started coughing again and the inside door juddered open. "What's going on? I heard you spluttering for breath. I only agreed to that reviewer coming if you didn't get overexcited," a woman scolded.

She glowered at Ferguson. "Have you been exhausting my husband? You know he has delicate health?"

Ferguson jumped up, his notebook dropping to the floor.

"Fanny, my dear, this is Mr. Samuel Ferguson, a compatriot of yours. He's innocent of all charges of upsetting me. It was my laughing that brought on the wretched cough."

"Pleased to meet you, Mrs. Stevenson," Ferguson stuttered. The woman continued to frown.

"Mr. Ferguson has been admiring your beautiful garden, Fanny."

She made no reply but moved to stand beside her husband, chafing his arm.

"Your husband told me how you have turned the garden into a miniature Scotland."

A clock on the mantelpiece chimed the half-hour before she replied, "I wanted it to be somewhere where he could feel inspiration." Her ruffled feathers seemed to be settling. "I've planted fruit trees and tiger lilies, too."

"And there's a dovecote, kennels and stables, too. A veritable Noah's Ark." Louis squeezed his wife's hand. He smiled to himself, thinking how the three of them formed an ill-assorted menagerie. Fanny with her dumpy figure was a bustling hen. Samuel Ferguson in his ill-advised tweeds with their startling scarlet and emerald check was an exotic but timid wader. What about himself? With his spiky limbs and bony head he feared that he resembled a pterodactyl, or more generously, a hunched gray heron.

Ferguson bent to retrieve his notebook. He scanned Fanny and Louis anxiously. Fanny's expression was disapproving but Louis winked at him. Ferguson opened his mouth to speak but his nose twitched and he let out a trumpeting sneeze. As he scrabbled in his pocket for his handkerchief, Fanny screamed, "You've brought a cold with you. How could you? Louis must be kept away from germs."

She lunged at him, dragging him toward the door. Louis huddled his shoulders deeper into his shawl, shaking his head as the reporter was hustled outside. Ferguson tripped over the step as she crashed the door behind him.

"Well, my dear, you defend me as well as the geese that warned the Ancient Romans of invaders," he said as Fanny returned. "I have only one concern. I heard a clatter as Mr. Ferguson beat his retreat. Naturally I hope he didn't hurt himself, but I would be even more worried if he knocked over the model of the *Skerryvore* Lighthouse. Papa would never forgive me if that monstrosity was damaged."

Chapter 2

Thirty-Two Years Earlier . . . HMS *Comet*, October 1854

The oil lamp swayed from its hook on the ceiling, casting a flickering light over a row of glinting instruments. Henry Otter raised a hand to steady it until it glowed, an Arctic sun above the white expanse of the charts. He bent down to peer more closely. How he loved the swell of the Hebridean names on his tongue: Tianavaig Bay, Suisnish, Flodigarry. What was in a name? These ones were an incantation to the wild places on the edge of the world. A prayer to the Hesperides, the daughters of the Evening Star. Names to some men meant fame. The explorers tramping over unknown continents gained immortality by christening newly discovered rivers and mountains. To others names on a map gave power. After sending surveyors to map the Highlands, King James IV learned enough of the topography to dispatch an army to tame the people there.

But it wasn't immortality or power that mattered to Henry. What inspired him was creating accurate charts that enabled seafarers to sail their way safely. Over the centuries, anonymous sailors had named coastal features so that those following them would recognize the landmarks. Henry's eye landed on the settlement of Staffin, north of Portree. It was named by the Vikings and meant "Place of Pillars." He imagined the Viking captain standing at the prow of his longboat as it lunged through spray-spitting seas. What relief he would feel when he recognized the strange contorted mounds and stacks of the Quirang near Staffin and knew that he was heading northward. Henry saw himself and his crew as heirs to that tradition of naming and mapping. They recorded those ancient names and added details about the configuration of the coast, the nature of the seabed, and the depth of the channels. As he ran his finger along the black line of the Skye coastline, he thought about how charts, as well as being useful, had a modest beauty with their neat rows of figures guiding the helmsman along his way. How much labor those soundings represented. Sailors in small boats, often huddled against the lashing of wind and rain had endlessly cast a lead weight on the end of a marked line to record them.

He straightened up with a grunt of satisfaction. The surveys of North Skye were complete. They had made good use of the light summer nights. Tomorrow *HMS Comet* would leave Portree to begin work on charting the herds of smaller islands. A quick stretch of the legs, he decided, and then to bed. As he plodded along the deck he breathed in the night air.

What was that? Something flashed out to sea. A dim star? No, it was much too low in the sky and there was too much cloud for stars. But something was shining, making a tear in the darkness. As he reached into his pocket for his spyglass, he realized that he wasn't alone on deck. "Ah, Lieutenant Masters, you've younger eyes than me. Where's that light coming from?"

"It looks as if it's from Raasay, sir."

"No. It's too far north. It must be on Rona."

"You're right. Is it coming from a building? Well, there's a mystery to uncover. Go and find out tomorrow."

Later as he lay in his bunk, Henry visualized the two smaller islands that stretched along the flank of Skye. Skye reached out over five peninsulas, like the outstretched wing of a sea eagle. Raasay was a thin sliver to the east. It crumbled away northward into scattered skerries, steppingstones to its smaller neighbor. Rona was a rocky outpost with two deep bays on its western side, chewed out by the sea. So the light must come from one of those harbors, but which one and why? Surely there were only a few poor fishermen living there?

Well, he would have to see what Tom Masters could find out. The fellow's fair curls and boyish smile made him very successful in getting information from local people, especially ladies, even when they knew little English.

Tom reported on his mission the next day, "Sir, the light comes from a house on the beach at Big Harbour. A widow called Janet MacKenzie lives there. I don't know why she keeps a lamp lighted in the window. My interpreting skills ran out, I'm afraid."

"Never mind. We'll pay a visit to this widow before we embark on the next stage of the survey."

So an hour later, at the top of the tide, they steamed across to Rona on a strong swell, nosing the *Comet* into the outer rim of Big Harbour. Tom had hired a local fisherman as a pilot, a spare man, his cheeks reddened and his blue eyes watery after years of scouring by the elements.

"Treacherous rocks there," Henry said, "They must have wrecked a few boats in their time."

"Aye," the pilot replied. "But I know their ways." He seemed disinclined to say more. Henry didn't know whether it was because he had little English or if he was taciturn by nature. So he left the man in peace to gesture to the helmsman what line the ship should take. Henry always felt tense when he wasn't in command. He only breathed more easily once the ship was anchored well clear of the rocks that stoppered the inner entrance. A boat was lowered over the side and coxswain Richard Williams rowed the captain and the lieutenant to the beach.

"Brush yourself down," Henry ordered Tom as they jumped on to the shingle. The captain knew that the younger officers were irked by his insistence on immaculate uniforms. But it was too easy to let discipline slide on a survey vessel in remote locations. He rubbed wet sand from his own trousers and smoothed down the lapels of his jacket before looking about him.

"That must be the house," he said, pointing at a building roosting by itself on the beach among the rocks, "Quite substantial too, two floors. Not the usual black house."

As he rapped on the heavy front door, he could hear scuffling noises from inside. It was opened by a mouselike young girl. "I'm Captain Otter of the Royal Navy. Is your mistress in?"

The girl's eyes opened wide and her nose started to twitch as if she was about to burst into tears. There was a rustling behind her and a tall, slender figure in a black gown appeared. Henry saw a face as weathered as a wooden carving and felt the gaze of her eyes, gray as wintry seas, "I'm Mistress MacKenzie. Would you gentlemen like to step inside?" Her voice was cool and deliberate.

They followed her stiff back into a parlour at the front of the house. She gestured for them to sit on a well-polished settle while she perched on a hard chair. The room was spare but snug. A woolen rug lay in front of the fireplace and a tall press stood in one corner. What drew Henry's eye though stood in front of the small window overlooking the sea. The glass was almost completely obscured by an elaborate lamp wedged onto the stone sill. It wouldn't have looked out of place in an Edinburgh drawing room. It had a wide brass base and a tall chimney topped by a glass globe that reminded him of a fortune-teller's crystal ball. He had to clench his hands together to curb his eagerness while they waited for the flustered maid. She scampered in eventually with a tray of tea things, clattering the cups as she served them. The widow remained silent and composed.

"Madam, I instructed Lieutenant Masters here to discover who owned the light we could see from Portree Harbor."

She nodded. Her eyes beneath the stiff widow's cap had the unblinking stare of a ship's figurehead.

"You are performing an invaluable service for seafarers."

Again the fixed look and the eventual nod. Henry was beginning to feel uneasy and wishing he had left Tom Masters to make the visit on his own. He knew that his height and his burly form could make people apprehensive. But he didn't sense any fear in this lady. He tried again. "May I ask you what prompted you to provide this service for passing ships?"

This time the silence was even longer, "I've put the lamp in my window for many a year but not in the summer when the light is good."

Henry hesitated, confused by her answer. "And how do you obtain the oil for the lamp?"

This time she replied more readily. "It comes from my sons when they're after catching fish, but if there's not enough I buy more or use candles."

"Well, I shall write to the commissioners of Northern Lighthouses and ask that you be recompensed."

"Recompensed?" She repeated with a frown.

"Yes, indeed. Many vessels owe their safety to your light. It's not right that you should have to pay for your philanthropic actions."

"Payment? I don't want to be paid," she hissed, rising to her feet.

"Madam, I meant no offence . . . I—"

"No, but I should like you to leave now." Her eyes glittered, harsh as an eagle's.

The two men took a hurried leave. "What a pity I offended Mistress MacKenzie by suggesting payment. These Highlanders are a proud race," Henry said, as they walked down to the boat.

"She's a formidable lady, sir. She would make a terrifying admiral of the Fleet."

Henry smiled. "Well, I'm a sailor, thank goodness, not an ambassador. At least we can make her philanthropic efforts known. I shall write to Alan Stevenson at the commissioners, whatever Mistress MacKenzie might think about it." He marched to where Williams waited. The sailor hastened to steady the boat for the captain to climb aboard. When it was Tom Masters's turn his doleful face lit up in a smile.

Chapter 3

Island of Rona, Summer 1857

Janet was jolted as the cart thudded over the rough ground. It reared over an especially large rock and she was thrown against Hamish who was driving.

"Forgive me, Mistress MacKenzie," he said.

"It's not your fault but I think I'd better finish the journey on foot. You can wait here for me. I shan't be long."

He jumped down to help her dismount and ended up catching her as her legs suddenly buckled. "Old age is making me clumsy," she grumbled. As she picked her way over the stones to the shore, she admitted to herself that it wasn't only stiff bones that made her stumble but an uneasy mind as well. She knew full well that the lighthouse was sprouting ever higher from its rocky bed but she had resisted coming to see it. Everyone hailed it as a bounty and a blessing for sailors. That was true but for her it marked a loss and an ending. While it was growing skyward, imagined but unseen, she could pretend it didn't exist. This morning though as she sat with her porridge in front of her but no appetite to eat it, she felt her spirit change course and veer into the wind. She would go and look at it for herself. She stopped to catch her breath. There was Hamish still sitting on the cart. He never complained but he was old too now and would be glad of a rest. But who was that coming up behind him? Two people. The one in front was brawny and striding along as fast as if he was on a proper road rather than a rough track. Trailing behind him was a child, a frail sapling buffeted by the wind. Her heart surged up into her throat like a leaping salmon. Surely it couldn't be? She peered again, screwing up her eyes. The boy was young, maybe six or seven years of age. His head wobbled as if it were too heavy for the sloping shoulders and narrow chest to support. He staggered on uncertain legs like a newborn lamb. She could feel her own legs trembling. She waited, holding her breath, for them to come closer. As they did, she gasped with relief to see that the child was not a ghost after all, only a stranger.

Now the pair were upon her. The man touched his hat. "Good day to you, madam. Thomas Stevenson at your service."

She remained speechless, staring at the boy, resisting her desire to touch him.

"And this young rascal is my son, Louis. He's just starting to learn something of the family business." He ruffled the child's thick, dark hair that seemed much more vigorous than his slight body.

Janet tore her eyes away and opened her reluctant lips. "I'm Mistress MacKenzie from Big Harbour."

"The famous Mrs. MacKenzie!" Thomas exclaimed. "I'm delighted to meet you at last."

The boy had been wriggling under his father's hand while they were speaking. Now he piped up in a petulant voice, "I'm called Lou at home, not Louis."

His father's face showed a struggle between affection and exasperation.

"My first name's Robert, but I don't use it and I spell Louis the French way."

"Do you now?' Well, we're very accustomed to using two names in this part of the world. Iain Donald, Angus Niall or Norman Peter. It's a way of making sure we know who we're talking about when so many folk have the same surname."

Louis smiled triumphantly at his father.

"We use nicknames, too. Have you one?" Janet asked.

His father rushed to reply, "He's not been able to attend school often enough to earn one. 'The Dreamer' would suit him."

"You would be in excellent company then. That's what Joseph's brothers called him. They said it in mockery but his dreams proved very useful," Janet smiled.

"I've allowed the wee rascal to distract me from what I wanted to say about your philanthropy, Mrs. MacKenzie."

She shrugged, "That's a very big word for lighting a lamp."

"You're too modest." Seeing she wouldn't be drawn, he continued. "May I show you how our work is progressing? If you would care to walk a little this way? We've been fortunate that the weather has stayed fair."

As they got closer Janet gasped at the height of the lighthouse, reaching up like the tapering trunk of a giant tree. A heavy stone section of the tower swung suspended from a block and tackle. A gust of wind nudged it and men stood braced at the top of the thirty-foot tower, arms outstretched to guide it into position. Janet's eyes widened in amazement. She had seen a new church being built when she was a young woman still living on Skye, watched the scaffolding placed alongside the walls and the dressed stones being hoisted into place. But she had never witnessed the likes of this tower. It was both gigantic and graceful, a landlocked mast without a sail. She had often wondered how such a structure could ever keep out wind and wet. Now she knew the answer for each huge stone was trimmed so that it fitted tightly against its neighbors. How had the engineers worked out the measurements so precisely? It was a marvel beyond compare. Then she remembered a book that her teacher had showed her, filled with illustrations of the Ancient Wonders of the World.

She became aware that her mouth was hanging open in amazement and that Mr. Stevenson was watching her. Feeling foolish she squared her shoulders. "It's very fine. It put me in mind of a picture I saw of the Pyramids."

"Indeed. I don't believe anyone now alive knows quite how they were constructed." Thomas signaled to a man who had been craning his neck to watch the work.

"Let me introduce you to my foreman, Mr. Menzies. He's worked for me for more years than I can remember, as have many of the men. They travel with us from one job to the next. Do we have any Rona men with us, John?"

He sniffed. "One or two maybe. They haven't the aptitude for hard work."

Janet drew herself up to her full height. "You're very mistaken in that opinion, young man."

Thomas scowled at him. "This lady is Mrs. MacKenzie. No doubt you've heard about her ceaseless work on behalf of seafarers."

"Aye, indeed," the foreman said, looking abashed. "Of course we haven't added the light yet, the most important part. I hope you'll come to see it when it's in place."

Janet decided to be gracious and nodded at him.

"I hope that Mrs. MacKenzie will be our guest of honor when we light the beacon for the first time."

Janet surprised herself by agreeing to Thomas's offer. It's amazing how flattery overcomes doubt, she thought as they strolled away from the lighthouse.

"Stop fidgeting, Louis," the father scolded the boy who was scuffling stones with his feet. "You'll ruin your good shoes. Think of the barefoot children living here who would be grateful for a pair of stout boots." He turned to Janet. "I'm afraid his thoughts are too often away wool gathering. His mother and his nurse indulge him too much."

She saw how his father's words snuffed out the gleam in the boy's eyes, "Mr. Stevenson, I hope you will find time to visit my home while you are on Rona."

"Thank you. I should like to accept your hospitality."

"And I'm sure we can amuse you too, young man," she added, stooping down to look the child in the eye.

Later, before going to bed, she read a chapter from her Bible, its black leather cover softened through much use. Then she checked that the lamp had sufficient oil. How many more times would she light it? She thought about Louis with his handmade boots. They might be made of pliable leather but they still pinched his feet. He needed to feel the grass brush his bare soles and to dabble his white toes in the sea.

Father and son visited her a few days later. "What a pleasure to be in civilized surroundings again," Thomas Stevenson declared as he looked around her parlour. "Menzies has given us his room to use but it's cramped. So this is the lamp." He tapped its gleaming base, "I've heard that you can see this light all the way from Portree Harbour."

She nodded, swallowing her displeasure. No one else was allowed to touch or tend her lamp. She invited him to sit down. Louis meanwhile found a stool by the window and knelt on it, putting his hands on the windowsill and looking out over the wide harbor to the open sea beyond.

"Are you building other lighthouses too, Mr. Stevenson?"

"Aye, indeed, two more on Skye, at Kyleakin and Isle Oronsay. Another in the Sound of Mull. I'm spending my time traveling between them. Thomas Telford left bridges and piers across the Highlands as his memorial. With the Stevensons, it's lighthouses." He leaned forward and his heavy features lit up. "There's still plenty to do in making them more seaworthy and we need to improve the lights themselves. There'll be more than enough work to keep Louis and his cousins busy."

The boy turned around. "Look Papa at those huge rocks poking out of the sea. You can see the waves beating against them. They're monsters waiting to gobble up ships." His fluting voice hung in the air.

His father glanced at Janet but she sat motionless. Only the grasp of her curled fingers on the arm of the settle betrayed her. "That's why we need engineers to build lighthouses," he said.

"Papa, may I go outside?"

"Are you bored already?" Thomas frowned.

"Effie, my maid, can take him out if you wish, she's a sensible lass, while you have another cup of tea."

Thomas agreed to both suggestions and settled himself more comfortably in his chair. "As you'll have gathered, building lighthouses is my passion." His tide of words lapped her ears gently at first but then gathered speed and pounded strongly. "Most wee lads covet a locomotive for a birthday present, but I was so disappointed when my parents gave me a wooden engine. I was much happier with boats, even a tiny one made out of a walnut shell with a paper sail. Or I would hollow out a hull with my penknife from a piece of wood."

"And did you make a lighthouse to go with them?"

He laughed, "Of course. My father showed me the plans he had drawn for the lighthouse on the Bell Rock. I spent the whole of one winter making a model. I was so proud of it. One day I stood it on a stone in the stream, surrounded by my fleet. How the light shone out bravely. Then I was called in for my tea and rushed inside. The heat was too much for the glass. It exploded and the whole thing toppled into the water."

"You've improved the design since then," she smiled.

His face was serious. "It was a necessary lesson. The first rule is to build safely and not endanger lives. It's a heavy responsibility that Louis will need to learn. I worry that he's so flighty."

"He's only a wee scrap of a lad yet." She stood up to look out of the window. "I wonder what they're up to." She cried out and Thomas leapt to her side. Effie, little bigger than a child herself, was struggling to carry the boy back to the house. Forgetting her age Janet ran out behind Thomas.

"He's an awkward fellow, always falling over," he muttered, fear leaking into his words.

They found the child struggling for breath, his skin clammy and eyes fever bright.

"What have you done to my son?" Thomas pulled the boy from Effie's arms and cradled him.

The girl didn't understand the words but she read their meaning. *"Bha e air a dhòigh's e a 'cluich ceart gu leòr, a' lùbadh airson na corragan aige a'thumadh anns a' ghlumagh am measg nan chreagan an sin. An uair sin thuit e gu h-obann mus b'urrainn dhomh a ruigsinn. Chan eil mi a'creidsinn gun do thuislich e. Thuit e mar clach às an adhar. Dh'fheum mi na gruaidhean aige shuthadh's steal mi uisge air an aodann aige gus an do thill e chun tìr nam beò."*

She sobbed and turned to her mistress who was stroking Louis's head where it rested in the crook of his father's arm. Without taking her eyes off the child, Janet translated Effie's words.

"He was happy playing, bending down to dip his fingers in the rock pool when suddenly he fell before she could reach him. She doesn't believe he tripped. He just fell like a stone. She had to rub his cheeks and splash water on his face to bring him back to the land of the living."

"She pushed him while he was playing and knocked him over," Thomas bellowed, making the child in his arms twitch and Effie whimper.

"No, she did not. Louis fell over in a swoon before she could get to him," Janet said in a quiet voice. She mouthed to Effie to go back to the house and find blankets. "You said yourself he's inclined to fall over. We must get him into bed."

She tugged at Thomas's sleeve. He lurched after her on tottering legs, his eyes staring. Once inside he laid Louis down. Janet's fingers sifted through the black hair flopping over the boy's forehead to touch the skin beneath.

"He seems to have a fever," she said.

She watched as vexation, tenderness, and terror scudded across Thomas's face.

"He has these turns. We've taken him to so many doctors but none of them can make sense of it. He recovers after a few days in bed. I hoped he was growing out of it. That's why I brought him with me this time, against his mother's wishes. He's not well enough to travel with me now but I can't wait here for him to get better. I've so many other lighthouses to visit."

"Well, he's most welcome to remain here. We'll take care of him until you can return."

His face softened in relief. "Thank you for your kindness. My wife and I are from big families but he's our only one. He's always been delicate."

So it was agreed. For the first few days the young boy slept most of the time, sometimes so deeply as if he were unconscious, at other times shouting and throwing his limbs about. Janet and Effie took turns to watch over him and soothe him when he awoke from a nightmare. He seemed to have the same recurring dream, especially when the wind was hurling itself at the house. He would call out that a strange horseman was galloping by with his face covered by his cloak. Staring open-eyed, skewered by terror, eventually he would respond to a calming voice and fall asleep.

"What's he dreaming about? It sounds like the Devil's work to me," whispered Effie one night when she was awakened again by his howling and ran to find Janet soothing him.

"Nonsense. He's only a wee lad who's often ill enough to think that he might not last the night."

"Do you think he's having visions of some terrible disaster that's going to happen?"

"No, I do not. That's enough. Your job is to comfort him when he awakes, not to scare yourself with foolish imaginings."

Finally, the fever stopped thrashing him and he slept soundly for a night and a day. When he awoke in the evening, he had returned to himself. Janet found him sitting in bed, alert but hollow eyed. "I've got a cover like this on my bed at home, all made out of different pieces," he said as if they were resuming an interrupted conversation.

"A patchwork blanket, like this?"

"When I'm in my bed at home I play at the land of Counterpane. I have all my toys with me. I can shake the covers to make my boats sail over the blue patches or make hills for my soldiers to march up."

"Is that so?"

"I like the colors on this counterpane, wee blue patches of sea and sky and brown for the fields."

"That's very fanciful. When I look at the pieces, they remind me of the people who used to wear the clothes the patches came from."

"Who wore that piece here, the one that's the color of oatmeal?"

"Well, that's from a gansey worn by my grown-up son, Murdo, who lives in Stornoway now. He was very fond of it and wore it until it was more holes than wool. He said I knitted luck into the stitches. He always had full nets when he wore it. See the cable stitch there? That's for the ropes that keep the sailor safe."

"And what about that dark blue that looks like the deep ocean?"

She smiled, "That comes from a gown I had as a young lass, before I was married. It was a heavy cloth that rustled when I walked." She pretended to scowl. "Don't look so astounded, young man. I might seem as old as Methuselah to you now, but I was as young once as you are now."

He grinned and the dark surface of his eyes gleamed. He pointed at another square. "That piece of brown tweed?"

She hesitated, scraping at its surface with a fingernail.

The boy's face caved in. "I don't like that one. It's rough and dark like the cloak the horseman wears in my dream."

Janet shook her head. "That one belonged to a wee boy, not a man. It came from a pair of breeks my younger son wore."

"He died, didn't he, before he became a man?"

She looked directly at him, "He did die, but he's at peace with the Lord now." Seeing the haunted look on his face, she continued, "He was a happy lad. He didn't die from an illness and neither will you. Look at how much better you are now, well enough to pester me with questions. Now, have you seen this lovely scrap of red tartan?"

He nodded and she was relieved to see his face no longer looked troubled.

"It came from a skirt my daughter Catherine wore when she was your age. I only had the one daughter and she used to complain that all her dresses were dull things cut down from her brother's clothes. So for her birthday one year I made her a new skirt, even though it was an extravagance."

'Did she like it?'

"She loved it. She wore it until it was much too short for her."

"Look, it's gone dark outside. When I was ill and couldn't sleep my nurse used to lift me out of bed. She carried me to the window to see the lights in the houses across the street. I used to wonder if there were any other sick boys looking out, too. Of course I'm much too big to do that now."

"That's just as well for there aren't any lights to see here."

"The only light is the one from your big lamp in the window that shines for the sailors to see."

"It is indeed."

"Cummy used to tell me stories as well."

"Your nurse? Did she now. What sort of stories?"

"She read the Bible, a chapter at a time, all the way through and from *The Book of Martyrs* and *The Pilgrim's Progress.* Lots of psalms too."

"The Good Book must have been a comfort to you."

His face clouded and he whispered so quietly that Janet had to bend down close to hear him. "But I'm afraid in the dark that if I sleep I'll never wake up again. I would be dead then and maybe go to Hell."

Her heart ached for him. "Don't you know that children never go to Hell because God knows that they're innocent souls?"

He stared at her in wide-eyed amazement. "I never knew that."

"Well, I know that because I'm so old. Do you know anyone

as old as me?"

He shook his head.

"That proves I'm right then. Does your Mama tell you stories, too?"

His eyes dulled. "No, she isn't very strong and I mustn't trouble her or she'll get a bad head. Papa is away so much. He did try reading to me from a big book about inventors but I didn't like it. What stories do you know?"

"I know plenty. Stories about Finn McCoul and his big black dog, Bran. About the fairy folk, the seal people and the Salmon of Knowledge."

She laughed as he shook his head in wonderment. "You haven't heard those? Well, you sleep well tonight under that old quilt with all its memories and I'll see what tales I can tell you tomorrow."

Chapter 4

Island of Rona, Summer 1857

During the long summer days Louis grew taller and stronger. Janet encouraged him to play on the shore but if there were storms he stayed inside helping Effie. Kneading dough, turning the butter churn or even sweeping the floors. The simple daily routines seemed to soothe him. Every night before he went to sleep she told him a story; there were no more nightmares. She thought about the tales she had first heard as a girl. Sitting with her chin on her knees in front of the peat fire, surrounded by the rumble of adult voices. It was a long time since she had told stories to a child. Now she used the stored oil of her memories to light up his imagination.

She began with Finn McCoul. "Now Finn lived in Ireland, but he spent a lot of time traveling across the sea to Scotland. Unluckily for him he fell afoul of a Scottish giant called Benandonner who swore he would teach Finn a lesson. He built a causeway over from Scotland so that he could reach Ireland more quickly. Finn was a brave man, but he knew he couldn't beat this terrifying giant in an ordinary fight. What was he to do?"

"Papa always says that God gave us brains so that we can find answers."

"That's true. This time it was Finn's wife, Oonagh, who used her head. 'Tell your men to cut down a tall tree and make a cradle big enough for you to lie in. Meantime my women will help to make you baby clothes.' Finn shook his head in bafflement but did as she asked. Then he sent men to keep watch and warn him when the giant was approaching his castle. Not that they needed warning. They could feel the earth rocking as the giant's heavy tread came closer and his angry shouts echoed like thunder across the hills."

"What did Finn do?"

"He dressed himself up in the baby gown and bonnet and lay down in the cradle. Then Oonagh wrapped a huge shawl around him."

"He must have looked very silly," Louis giggled.

"Aye, and no doubt he had to shave off his beard or he would have looked even sillier. Finn's wife sat down with her spindle in her hand and rocked the cradle with her foot. The giant marched in, 'Where's that rascal Finn McCoul?' He roared in a voice that would chill your blood. 'He's out cutting wood but this is his young son here. Would you like to see him?' Well, the giant took one peep in the cradle and took to his heels. He didn't stop to draw breath until he reached the causeway. He charged across it. As he ran he broke it up behind him, hurling great rocks into the sea and shouting, 'If that's the size of the baby, what must his father be like?'"

Louis clapped his hands together. "Tell me more tales about Finn."

"That's enough for now. Tomorrow I'll tell you about when Finn came to Skye to stay at Dun Sgathaich, the Castle of Shadow that was built in a single night."

And so she did. "Finn was still a beardless young man. One of the heroes suggested he go to stay with Queen Sgiath who lived at the castle. She could teach him all that he needed to know about the arts of fighting."

"But how could a lady, even if she was a Queen, know about fighting?" Louis was scornful.

"Finn thought the same. He curled his lip at the notion that a mere woman would have such knowledge, but nevertheless he followed the hero's advice. He sailed across the sea in a ship whose prow was carved like a sea serpent. It writhed through the waves, its eyes scanning the horizon. When he landed, the queen challenged him to a wrestling match and with a smile of contempt he agreed. He found to his surprise that she was a nimble fighter. In the end his exhaustion made him clumsy. She was able to trip him up and pin him to the ground. After that he was ready to learn from her. So she taught him how to be a fearsome warrior, with sword and staff."

Janet could feel the rhythm of the story swing her along, spinning her like the arms of a strong partner in a reel.

"Do you remember when you made up your own story of how Finn wanted a flat space to dance on? He took his sword and swiped at *Dun Caan*. As if he were slicing a pudding, he lopped the pointed top off the mountain. Then he had plenty of room to dance." She laughed, but her voice wavered as she saw the puzzled expression on Louis's face. "No, of course you didn't. I'm just a silly *cailleach*."

Louis's eyes were deep pools as his fingers crept over the quilt. "It was that boy who said it. That's the patch from his trousers."

She nodded, fearing that if she spoke she would weep.

"Tell me some real stories. Ones from history." Louis asked her the next evening.

"I'll tell you about *The Ship Full of People*. It happened over a hundred years ago. A man called Norman MacLeod thought to himself that there were too many poor people living on Skye. So he decided to make some money by selling a cargo of human souls, instead of the usual beasts, iron or wood."

"How could he do that?"

"By seizing young men and women and bundling them onto ships bound for the American colonies."

"What happened to them when they reached America?"

"They were to be sold as slaves."

"But their families must have missed them."

"They did indeed but no one knew what had become of them. They had gone as if they had never existed. But no secret can be kept forever. One of MacLeod's ships put into a harbor in Antrim in Ireland. While it was at anchor a few of the captives escaped and raised the alarm. Some folk claimed that Sir Alexander MacDonald himself was behind the wicked deed but it was never proved."

"Was the bad man who started it sent to prison?"

"No, he ran away and hid in Ireland. But he returned to Scotland later and fought against the Prince, on the government's side.

"I heard another tale too about a Highlands gentleman traveling in Canada. He came across a maid in a house there and spoke to her. She didn't understand English. So he tried French and German but she just stared at him. Then he thought of speaking Gaelic to her. The poor lassie's face lit up. She told him how she had been gathering seaweed when she was seized and thrown onto the boat. It was a terrible thing to treat Christian souls like that. There must be a special word for such a sin against your fellow man but I don't know what it is, in English or Gaelic."

"Papa will know. He knows everything."

So Janet was the lamplighter and the flame of her stories banished the shadows for both of them.

Chapter 5

Island of Rona, Summer 1857

Tom hired the same sullen pilot to guide *The Comet* safely past the tusks of rock jutting from the mouth of Big Harbour. It was Richard Williams again who rowed him ashore. After dragging the boat onto the beach, Richard hoisted the long wooden box on his shoulder and followed Tom to Janet MacKenzie's door. Again Effie peered at them before scurrying off to alert her mistress.

"The captain isn't with you today?"

"No, Mrs. MacKenzie. He's busy on his charts. I've brought Williams the coxswain with me."

Janet nodded and surveyed Richard who was lowering his burden. Her eyes gleamed. Tom couldn't be sure whether it was curiosity or amusement. He tried on a boyish smile. "You were very firm about not wanting any recompense but I'm afraid the Lighthouse Commissioners were adamant that we deliver this to you."

"Well, open it young man."

Tom opened the lid, lifted out the contents and presented them to Janet with a bow. He was astonished to see her stern face melt into a laugh.

"Well, I feel like the Queen herself. It's a fine thing indeed, but why should I have need of it?"

"It's the most modern and best lamp available. Brighter and cleaner than any other."

"It's certainly a handsome thing." She tapped the brass base. "But I already have my own lamp and another smaller one too. I won't need them soon and certainly not a new one as well."

"True. But I have something else I trust will be more serviceable." He took a package from his jacket pocket and gave it to her.

27

She unwrapped the soft leather cover. "Now this is beautiful and there's an inscription from Captain Otter himself. How kind of him."

"A spyglass!"

Tom started at the sudden voice. He turned round to see an upturned face with large, glowing eyes and a pelt of black hair. More like a panther cub than a small boy.

Janet smiled fondly at the child. "First you must greet these gentlemen, Lieutenant Masters and Mr. Williams. This is Louis, the son of Mr. Stevenson. He's staying with us while his father is away building lighthouses."

"I've been watching your ship getting bigger as it came closer." Janet gave him the telescope and he pushed it against his eye. "Oh, it's made the ship smaller."

"Turn it the other way around," Tom bent down so that he was level with the child. "Now you can see the men on board clearly."

"I can!" Louis squealed, hopping from foot to foot.

His excitement made them all grin.

"Captain Otter is very generous. If I write him a letter, would you give it to him for me? Louis, go and ask Effie to bring us some tea."

Louis skipped off to do her bidding. "He's been ill, poor soul, but he's much recovered now. I fear he's weary of having only female company."

"Would he like to come aboard?" Tom asked.

"We'll have to make sure that he's well wrapped up."

"Can I go on the ship?" Louis erupted into the room again.

They walked across the rocky beach to the rowing boat, Louis darting between the strolling men. Richard rowed while Tom listened to Louis's chatter. He recounted the stories Janet had told him, spoke about his collection of different-colored stones and shells and told how Hamish had taken him to fish for mackerel from the rocks. Then he stared at Tom. "Did your Papa want you to join the Navy?"

"No. He was angry with me."

"You don't have to follow in your Papa's footsteps if you don't want to?"

"That's true. Don't you want to build lighthouses?"

"I want to write stories, sea adventures."

"Well I'm sure Captain Otter can tell you some tales. He's famous for them." Tom winked at Richard who grinned. "Now we're at the ship. Can you climb up the rope ladder?"

"Of course." But Louis gnawed his lip as he watched the ladder swinging against the hull. Tom clambered onto it first while Richard stood behind Louis, guiding his hands onto the rungs.

"A new midshipman, I see," Captain Otter boomed when they found him bent over his charts. "Your visit was successful?" he asked Tom.

"Yes sir, but the telescope was a greater success than the lamp. Mrs. MacKenzie asked me to give you this letter."

"Good. Well young man, would you like to inspect my ship?"

Louis explored everything. He felt the shuddering engines under his feet, climbed into a hammock to let the waves rock him and marked in some figures on the captain's chart, his tongue sticking out as he concentrated. After a piece of fish and some hard tack from the galley it was time to slither down the rope ladder and row back to the island. Before they beached the boat he had fallen asleep, his face nuzzled against Richard's arm.

Chapter 6

Island of Rona, Summer 1857

Kenneth loped over the bog cotton and springy clumps of heather. He slowed his pace as he saw a platform of rock ahead. A stocky man stood looking out to sea, his chin tilted upward. He gave no sign that he had noticed Kenneth until he was upon him, "What do you want?" he grunted.

"I was after looking for work."

"And why should I take you on?"

He felt his anger flare but doused it at once. "Because I work hard and I know about using stone."

The older man raised a questioning eyebrow.

"I've been doing building work for Mr. Rainey on Raasay."

"Well, I've my own men for the skilled jobs."

Kenneth waited, calloused hands gripping his cap in front of him.

John Menzies let out his breath in a hiss, "Well we could do with another laborer to fetch and carry, I suppose. At least you can speak the Queen's English. I'll give you a trial for a week and if you're any use I'll keep you on. Go and join the rest of them." He pointed to a small group standing by a heap of dressed stone near the shore. Beside them the tower was probing skyward. Kenneth's eyes widened in amazement at the sight of it. He had never imagined that human hands could build something so tall. He had nothing to compare it with, except the Tower of Babel whose top reached up to heaven itself. He shuddered. Surely God had punished the men who raised it for their overweening pride? But this lighthouse was not created out of vainglory. It would be a blessing for sailors. He ran to join the other men.

For the next few days, he shifted stone blocks and timber from the carts to the lighthouse. It was muscle-straining work and he had to grit his teeth with the effort. He was used to building walls around fields and repairing storm-damaged piers. But these stones were larger and needed to be nudged together to form a dovetail. Soon his back was paining him so much that he doubted he could carry on. But five days into the job things changed. He had noticed one of the carters, a dour man, too quick to beat his horse when the poor beast was doing its best. The fellow was bringing in the last load of stone from the makeshift harbor at *Loch a'Bhràighe*. In his rush he shouldered one of the other men out of the way, making him stumble and lose his grip on the stone he was supporting. Feeling it wobble, he leapt back with a shout and let the stone come crashing down. The carter didn't jump out of the way in time and a corner fell onto his toes. He screamed in agony and was led away cursing and leaning heavily on two workmates.

"It's a damned nuisance," Kenneth heard Menzies complain.

"I'm used to horses," Kenneth said. "I can take his place."

"Ah, it's you again, popping up like a bad penny. Is there anything you can't turn your hand to? Very well. I'll give you a try."

The accident seemed to be a good omen. Kenneth enjoyed working with horses and had a gift for it. He soon had the measure of the shaggy haired garron, knowing when to coax and when to be stern. His family had kept a horse on their croft in Ardelve. Papa had never named him. He was just *Each*, or "Horse." He did all the heavy work. Dragging the plough over the thin, rock-strewn soil, hauling up cartloads of seaweed from the shore and bringing the dried peats home from the moor. But how boy and beast had enjoyed the white summer nights when the sun scarcely went to bed. Kenneth would clamber up on the sweaty back, wide as the hull of a rowing boat and rub his face in the ticklish mane. Then the horse would strike out into the sea, his nose furrowing the waves. *Each* was his very own water horse but not one of the usual, wicked tricksters who lured a rider on his back so that he could drown him in deep water. Rather he was a magical horse who could swim tirelessly forever, past the Trotternish ridge of Skye, the last finger on the outstretched palm of the island. Gliding over the Minch to the outermost edge of the Western Isles through the great, empty ocean to America. So many others had made that journey but they had traveled on an everyday ship, not on an enchanted horse.

Leading the horse backward and forward from the harbor was certainly an easier job than lifting blocks of stone. This horse was nameless, too. So Kenneth christened him *Each*. "You're not as handsome or as wise as your namesake. So don't be getting any ideas." The horse snickered and twitched his ears. Two days later Menzies came up to Kenneth, tossing his wages in the air so that he had to lunge to catch the coins.

"You'll do."

That night he settled down early in the bothy, curling up in the straw before the others returned. He didn't talk much to the other men. Their swallowed Lowland accents were hard to follow. It was easier to understand the Irishmen among them. At least they spoke a sort of Gaelic. They woke him up when they trudged in later, laughing and pushing each other. They must have got hold of some drink, even though it was forbidden. Pretending to be asleep, he felt aggrieved that they hadn't asked him to join them. Still he had to save his money for more important things.

After a while the others settled down but an hour or so later Kenneth lurched awake, his heart thumping in his ears. What was that scuffling noise behind his head? Something tugging at the clothes he used as a pillow. A rat? No, he could hear a wheezing human breath. He reached back and his hands gripped an ankle. Pulling hard he made the figure stumble. Kenneth leapt to his feet and kicked the man's legs from under him, sending him sprawling. Straddling him, he grabbed a handful of matted hair, twisting his head back.

"After my money, you filthy Irish tinker?" he hissed, not

wanting to wake up the rest of them.

"No. Surely I was only after my own bed." Kenneth let him get up and shamble off. None of the humped forms around them stirred. He checked the coins were still in his jacket pocket before lying down again. How could he keep his money safe? Sleepless, he waited for daybreak.

As it was the Sabbath his time was his own. He slipped out from between the snoring, beached bodies and strode over the moor toward Big Harbour. That was where the old widow, Janet MacKenzie lived, so Jeannie had told him. He smiled as he remembered how he had come across her by chance. It wasn't long after he started working on Raasay, the island that hung like a teardrop close to Skye's eastern cheek. Hunger, both for food and for the chance of a different life, had driven him from his home. He had been glad to escape from the grim sadness in the house. His mother's haggard face and his father's gloomy silence as they stared blindly into the fire in the evenings. They had never got back on their feet again after the potato blight. Starvation prowled outside the walls of the house, howled down the chimney and rattled at the door. When the fishing season ended, he couldn't bear to go back home. He heard that the landlord on Raasay wanted men from the mainland to help on the estate. It seemed odd that there weren't enough locals to do the work. Out of the ten of them taken on that winter, eight were outsiders like himself. The two from the Home Farm were tight lipped about George Rainey, the laird, but Kenneth didn't ask any questions. Earning money to send home was what mattered.

He was amazed to see how the landscape of the estate had been tamed and made fertile. When spring came, he gazed at the froth of blossom and the soft green leaves of the apple trees in the walled garden. Even more wondrous was the twisting vine in the glasshouse, with its swelling clumps of grapes. He had heard of vines from the parables in the New Testament but he had no idea what they looked like. How he wished his mama was there to see them, too.

Kenneth picked up some English. So when visitors arrived at the Big House for shooting and fishing he was told to help. One day in May he sailed with the guests to the rocky north end of the island. They anchored in the open gape of Loch Arnish. The English gentlemen with their whinnying voices clattered ashore and Kenneth was left in charge of the boat. Once they had gone he jumped out to stretch his legs, whistling as he strolled through a small birch wood. The air was drenched with the sultry haze of bluebells. The path opened out into a stretch of pasture where some women were lifting dripping blankets out of buckets. They hung them on heather ropes strung between the trees where they flapped, landlocked sails struggling to free themselves. Girls were darting among the washing and calling to each other, gulls above the rigging. His eyes caught one lass, in particular. Her dark hair rippled in a long tail down her back as she skimmed bare footed, long limbs sprouting from an outgrown dress. She swerved, salmon sleek, past the arms stretched out to catch her. Then she hurled herself face down on the grass close to where he stood entranced at the edge of the wood. She pressed her nose into a tuft of late primroses, laughing as the petals made her sneeze.

Suddenly she frowned and looked about her as if she sensed his watching eyes. He walked up to her and introduced himself.

"Well, Kenneth MacRae from Ardelve, I'm Jeannie, the daughter of Norman MacLeod and I've lived here in Torran all my seventeen years. My family are here, apart from Granny MacKenzie who's over in Rona, right on the beach at Big Harbour. Have you heard of her?"

He shook his head.

"Well you should have. So what are you doing here?"

"I work for Mr. Rainey. I've brought up some gentlemen from the Big House." He hesitated. "I wonder, would you mind if I came to see you again when I'm not working?"

"Would I mind!"

His face fell at the contempt in her voice, "I've good prospects," he stammered.

"Aye, and there's blood on any money that comes from that devil, George Rainey. You must know how he drove the people from their homes. Old, young, sick and dying. Burned their houses down in front of them."

"I didn't know."

She stared at him, "You don't know much, do you? Don't *want* to know, you mean." She sprinted away, her long hair swinging. He started to run after her but the giggles and shrieks of the other girls stopped him.

"Would you see me if I find different work?" he shouted after her. She half turned and tossed her head before running on. Was that a shake of the head? More likely she hadn't heard his words above the mobbing of the other girls. Feeling foolish he returned to the boat. He climbed aboard and sat glumly, trailing his fingers through the water. She's just a silly, headstrong lassie, he told himself, but in the days that followed she kept shimmering through his thoughts. She had made him see how lonely he was. And he couldn't forget what she said about the laird. No wonder the local men wouldn't work for him. There was nothing for it but to find a way to earn untainted money.

So he had determined to make his way to this bleak island where the Northern Lighthouse Board had decreed that a lighthouse be built. But how to get there with no boat? He remembered once seeing a stag swimming across to Rona in the rutting season, noble head and antlers held above the waves. He had smiled at the deer's single-mindedness to reach the hinds on the far island. Now he thought, if a beast can be brave so can I. He was a strong swimmer, thanks to all those summer evenings frolicking in the water with *Each*. As a boy he had been proud of his rare skill in the water.

"Why is it most fishermen never learn to swim?" his father

had said to him one day when Kenneth came home whistling, hair dripping wet and body glowing after a dip in the sea. He shrugged. He had grown weary of Papa's dispiriting comments. "If you fall overboard swimming only prolongs your torment. Better to drown quickly than slowly."

But I would rather have a chance of life, no matter how small, Kenneth had thought but didn't bother saying. Now he looked at the powerful currents sweeping through Caol Rona, the narrows between Raasay and Rona. He could use the rocky islands as steppingstones. From *Eilean Tigh,* the northern fingertip of Raasay, he could swim in stages to *Eilean an Fhraoich* and over *to Sgeir nan Eun* before reaching *Garbh Eilean* which was linked to Rona by a causeway. He set off on a warm day and all went well at first but it was harder going than he had imagined. Struggling against the current between the two middle islands he felt his legs hardening to stone. A deadly chill was creeping up his body and numbing his heart. Was he doomed to drown slowly, just as Papa had warned? Then he remembered being astride *Each* as he plunged into the waves. The memory brought a flutter of warmth to his body as he neared *Sgeir nan Eun.* His hands scraped on the sharp rocks, slimy with seabird droppings. As he hauled himself ashore he noticed splatters of blood from a deep gash on the sole of his foot. He was too cold to feel any pain. Almost there now, no time to rest. He hurled his exhausted body into the water again. When he finally crawled ashore on Rona, he couldn't haul himself upright. He was lucky that a sharp sighted crofter was curious enough to investigate and help him to shelter. "What a tale, one worthy of the wild MacRaes," the old man said, when Kenneth bade him farewell after a night's rest. Was the *bodach* praising him or berating him?

He remembered his swim as he climbed over the moor to the Widow MacKenzie's house. How could Jeannie not be stirred by his feat? And she would surely approve of his new job? Hope made him skip along and soon he found himself looking down on Big Harbour. It was shaped like the head of a diving bird, its long beak probing the shore and its eye a clump of glistening rocks. As he dropped down to the shore he began to doubt himself again. Jeannie was so young, seven years younger than him, barely out of childhood. She would have banished him from her mind. And he hadn't given a good account of himself when they met. Maybe she was already spoken for? He couldn't delude himself that she had shown any interest in him at all. Ah, there was the house, a big one, built on the beach itself. Would the widow banish him, too?

Well, he wasn't going to waste the journey. He tapped on the front door. A young serving girl flushed as she showed him in. While he waited for the mistress of the house he peered around the front room, thinking how comfortable it was. The widow clearly wasn't poor. But what was that in the window? He fingered the brass base. A fishy smell rose from it and he realized that it must be a lamp, an enormous one, far bigger than any of the ship's lanterns he had ever seen. It would cost a fortune in oil. He supposed that Rainey owned similar lamps, but he had never been inside his house to know. What luxury to light such a lamp and restore the room to daylight. Tom was used to stinking stub ends of tallow candles.

He paced the room, kneading his cap before stuffing it into his jacket pocket. Seeing mud on his boots he spat on his fingers and wiped it away.

There was a rustle and she appeared, sombre as a minister in black. Her expression was severe as she asked him his business. She listened in silence as he told her about his family, his travels to find work and his wonderment at meeting her granddaughter.

"So you believe that Jeannie sees you as a suitor?"

He flushed as he realized how his story must sound like a romance conjured up in his imagination.

"No, not yet. But that's because I worked for Rainey. Now I have a different job, a worthwhile one. Surely she'll change her mind?" He tried to keep the desperation out of his voice.

"It's certainly a worthwhile job you're doing," she said, with a wry smile.

He smiled uncertainly, not understanding her sudden amusement. "You seem respectable and God fearing. Jeannie is strong willed, like all the women in our family." Her eyes glinted, "You'll have to strive to win her hand. Meanwhile, you may bring your wages here each week for safekeeping. I shall expect to see you at church every Sabbath."

"Thank you for your kindness." His heart plunged at the prospect of all the walking he would have to do on his one free day in the week.

She stood up and went over to the press, opening a small drawer at the top and let him drop the coins into it. Then she hustled him into the kitchen where the serving girl smiled shyly and gave him milk and bannocks.

As he was sitting eating he heard the door behind him creak open. He turned and flinched at the face that peeped round it. It was a fairy's face. Pale, bony and pointed. Long black hair. Raven's eyes. He gawped as the girl spoke, "Off with you now, Louis. I'll call you when your tea's ready."

Her tone was affectionate. The wee creature's wide mouth grinned and it waved a birdlike claw. Then the door closed and the face disappeared. The girl laughed at Kenneth's open-mouthed stare. She smiled, glancing sideways at him, "Aye, he's a strange wee lad. He's staying with Mistress MacKenzie just now. He's not a relative though but . . ."

"I have to go," he interrupted her. He stood up, wiped the crumbs from his lips and hurried through the door. He knew he was being rude but he had no time for chattering. Anyway he wanted peace to ponder all that had happened that day.

Chapter 7

Island of Rona, Summer 1857

After he left Janet stood by the window, looking out to the harbor. She ran her fingers over the cold, polished brass of the lamp while she thought about Kenneth. He seemed decent enough and she hoped that Jeannie would give him a chance. It would be her own free choice, whatever she decided. She was still very young and her parents would leave her to choose. As a girl, Janet had shuddered when she saw lively young women coupled with dried-out graybeards for the sake of having a roof over their heads. She had believed then that it was only right to marry for love. She hadn't known that love couldn't stop the rot of disappointment. If she had the gift of second sight, would she still have taken him? She had been dazzled by him but maybe if her parents had not been so vehement in their opposition, she wouldn't have held him so close. Too closely to see him clearly. She shook her head in exasperation. It was no use brooding on what was over and done with. It was the lad's name that had thrown her back into the past to her own Kenneth. This Kenneth seemed steady, a little dull even, but he had held his ground when she had questioned him. His visit had left her thoughts scuttling and scurrying, small sea creatures pried from their hiding place by an oyster catcher's beak.

Her Kenneth was an outsider too, from Lochalsh in Kintail. Well set up with his own boat, carrying meal, tools and gossip to the villages along the coast and among the islands. He provided luxuries for those who could afford them, spirits, sugar, and tea. He came into the harbor with the news of the wider world filling his sails. He threw his head back as he laughed, his tawny hair lapping around his ears and neck. He wore it longer through vanity, but it was only much later that she came to realize that.

At the time she just wanted to reach out and stroke the burnished threads. He had blown her over, gusting into her parents' staid house in Kilmuir.

"I have my suspicions about that fellow. His prices are too good to be true."

"How do you mean, Papa?"

"They're smuggled goods, if you ask me."

"But you still buy them from him, none the less."

His glare silenced her. Mama said, "You can't trust a man who's always traveling. How do you know what he's up to? Don't be led astray."

But the whiff of danger only made him more alluring. It was a warm summer and it was easy to slip away to a quiet place where they could stretch out among the sheltering trees. She was entranced with him. But the spell was broken when her parents found out that she was expecting a child. They consented to her marriage but they never forgave her. There was no softening even when she named her daughter Catherine, after her mother.

It was fortunate that Kenneth had saved enough money to get the lease on Big Harbour, but the land was poor and the rents meagre. So he carried on with the trading and the fishing. He provided for her, but after a year or two she suspected he had a wandering eye. But she smothered her doubts before they could draw breath.

This new Kenneth's visit was a surprise but not an unwelcome one. Maybe there would be a wedding soon to look forward to, a distraction from her unease about the lighthouse.

He returned each week, as agreed. He would unclench his fist so that she could pick up the coins, tied together in a twist of cloth. She would take it, carefully tip out the money into the drawer, fold the fabric and return it to his open palm, pressing it down with her hand. Once the silent ceremony was over, they never lingered in conversation. He smiled and thanked her before going to the kitchen for his *strupag*. She would hear him mumbling through a mouthful of oatcake as he talked with Effie and Louis.

One day a few weeks later she was out when he arrived. She had been walking along the shore and returned to find the door ajar. He was standing in front of the press. He'll be putting this week's wages in the drawer, she thought, surprised that he was being so presumptuous. Then she saw to her fury that he had opened the drawer below the one where his money was stored. The blue scarf she kept there was on the floor. He seemed deep in thought as he looked at the small boot in his cupped hand. She held her breath as he ran a curious finger over the cracked, bleached upper. He prodded the toecap as if it was some sort of wee beast that he was trying to poke back to life. Finally she could bear it no longer, "What do you think you're doing?"

He started and dropped the boot. He picked it up in a shaking hand and looked dumbly at her, a dark red stain blotching his neck and face.

"How dare you pick through my belongings."

He hung his head, "I'm sorry. I just wondered what the old things were doing there."

"Old! They're priceless to me. All I've got left from that terrible day."

"I meant no harm. I'll put them back."

"No! Get out of my sight." Her voice cracked. He held them out to her at arm's length and stumbled toward the door. After he left she stood still, her eyes closed. She held the boot against her breast, her hands folded over it as it were an injured chick. Sighing, she opened her eyes and took it back to drawer. She made a nest of the scarf and settled the small boot inside it.

That night she slept fitfully. She was furious with him for betraying her trust. She hated the idea of him pawing over the poor battered things.

When she eventually slept, she was trapped in a nightmare that still held her in its clammy tentacles as she awoke. In the dream she was standing on the beach in front of her house on a wild night. Sea and sky merged together, inked black with the wind-lashed rain. Her eyes strained to see a boat being thrown by the storm toward the harbor. Suddenly, a gust snatched her feet away and she was aloft, out at sea and looking down on the vessel. She could see the breakers hurling themselves at it, smashing into the hull. As they did so, the waves molded themselves into living shapes. Creatures from the sea and of the sea, blue-green and transparent. Leaping like fish they launched themselves up and into the boat and let loose a hideous wailing sound.

"The *Fir Gorm*," she cried out as she was jolted awake. The blue-gray sea creatures who climbed aboard a vessel and made the passengers copy their strange songs. They would continue until one of the terrified people stumbled in their singing. Then the furious creatures would sink the boat. In the light of day the nightmare loosened its slithering grip, but she was left stranded on the edge of the sea wondering over its meaning. Was it a warning from the past or an omen for the future? Was it about Kenneth's shame when she caught him out? Did he see her as a fearsome sea monster, one green with envy? Would he return again, next Sunday? If he wanted his money back, he would have to show his mettle and face her again. She smiled grimly to herself.

Chapter 8

Isle of Rona, October 1857

Thomas Stevenson jerked awake to find himself swaying in the saddle. The horse's steady plod and the coal black darkness had sent him to sleep. He stretched his back and shifted his legs to bring back some feeling to his muscles. Mrs. MacKenzie had sent him a letter, carried by a sea captain traveling to Edinburgh. She wrote that Louis was recovered from the fever, but she was keen that he should stay with her until November. She gave no reason for this request. Thomas though was eager to see Louis again. So he had scrawled a reply saying that he would come sooner, hoping that it would reach her in time. The men had urged him not to travel on such a dangerous night, but he had laughed at them. "*Tam O'Shanter* is only a story. I won't meet any witches." How could sensible men believe in such superstitious nonsense? He peered ahead in the darkness. It couldn't be far now.

Suddenly, the horse stopped and whinnied. Despite himself he felt his heart lurch. He could see flames slashing across the sky ahead and hear a clamour of voices. Was the widow's house on fire? He thumped his heels into the beast's sides, urging him into a reluctant canter. As he drew closer he realized that there was no emergency. The flames came from a bonfire down on the shore and the shouts were of merriment, not distress.

As he slowed the foam-flecked horse down to a walk he could see figures, running and whooping, silhouetted against the fire. As he got closer, one of them turned toward him. He gulped as he saw the horned skull with its black pits for eyes. Was the Devil himself abroad? He resisted his urge to turn and gallop away. His hand fumbled for the Bible he kept in his coat pocket. He forced himself to stay still and look more closely at the shrieking creatures who seemed unaware of his presence. They were all dressed in outlandish garb, festooned with leaves, heather, and seaweed. In their hands were turnip lanterns. They swung as they walked so that the grinning faces spouted flames. How foolish he was to be scared. It was only a group of half-witted revellers acting like pagans. He prodded the horse forward into a trot. A small figure ahead of him turned at the sound of their approach and let out a piercing scream like a hare caught in a trap. Thomas hauled on the reins. The trembling beast halted and he flung himself from the saddle.

"What on earth is going on?" He seized the figure by the shoulders. The screams were turning into violent coughing. Thomas lifted off the skull mask and started to rub the child's bent back. He looked up and both of them gasped.

"Louis! What are you doing?"

"Papa, I thought you were the bogey man on the horse." Tears coursed down his face.

Thomas bent down and dabbed his son's cheeks with a crumpled handkerchief. "Come on now, have a good blow. No wonder you were beside yourself, running around wailing like a savage." He took the boy's hand and looked toward the house.

"Is Mistress MacKenzie inside?"

"Aye, Papa but don't be angry with her."

Thomas strode to the house, towing his son behind him. He thumped on the door and the mistress of the house herself answered it. She stared at him as if he were an apparition, but then recovered herself enough to speak.

"Welcome to my home, sir. May I offer you refreshment after your journey?"

"No thank you, but I would like to speak to you privately." His voice was chilly.

"Come this way then. I believe most of our guests are still outside. So we won't be disturbed." She turned to take Louis's hand, "You come in too, *isean*, and sit down until you've stopped coughing."

"No, I don't want the boy to listen to what I have to say."

Janet raised her eyebrows but spoke calmly, "Very well. Off you go to the kitchen and find Effie," she said, smiling at Louis's anxious, upturned face.

The child shuffled out and Janet ushered Thomas into the room where the lamp still stood guard lighting the window. She settled herself in a seat. Thomas pushed the door shut before sinking down heavily on the settle.

"What's the meaning of this abomination? Is this how you corrupt my child?"

"We were celebrating Halloween as we always do. But we're all God-fearing Christians like yourself." Her voice was steady. "As for Louis, he has thrived here, both in body and soul."

"How could he thrive? Wearing a devil's mask when he should be reading the Good Book?"

"I cannot believe before God that I have caused him any harm. I took him to church when he was well enough. We said our prayers together every night and he was beginning to understand my Gaelic Bible." Her eyes gleamed fiercely. As they glared at each other in silence there was the sound of wheezing outside the door.

"Is that Louis? We'll see what he has to say for himself." Thomas rose to his feet and flung the door open. The two youngsters huddled together, white faced in the doorway.

"He ran away from me," Effie whispered in her cautious English.

"Leave us," Thomas ordered her, as he pulled Louis into the room.

The boy's dark eyes were spilling with tears as his gaze flickered between his father's frown and Janet's slight smile.

His father held him at arm's length. "What have you been doing these past weeks, apart from dressing up in heathen garb?"

"I've heard lots of stories about Finn McCoul and Bonnie

Prince Charlie. I've helped Effie and played by the shore." His voice quivered.

"You've not been to see how the lighthouse is progressing then?"

Louis hung his head and swallowed a sob, unable to speak.

"If you remember from my letter, he took some time to recover from the fever. I wanted him to gain strength and enjoy himself a little before he returned to Edinburgh."

"But his head has become stuffed with nonsense."

Thomas let go of his grip on Louis's sleeve. The boy stumbled. "Sit down before you fall down," his father sighed in exasperation. Turning to Janet he spoke through clenched teeth. "The boy certainly looks sturdier now but I'm disappointed that you pandered to his whims. He's old enough now to put away childish imaginings."

"He's not yet eight years old. Surely he has plenty of time to apply himself to a profession." Janet's tone was light, but Thomas glowered in response.

"It's almost my birthday, Papa. May I stay here for it?" the boy begged.

Thomas raised a heavy hand to silence his plea. "No. You will spend it with your family in Edinburgh. You've been away far too long."

Louis bit his lips. "I don't want to be an engineer like you. I want to write stories."

Thomas hissed.

"I remember how hard I tried to stop my older boy from getting a fishing boat. I was terrified. I pleaded and when that failed I threatened that I wouldn't speak to him anymore. To no avail. I was mistaken, of course, because it was the oil from his fish that kept the light going. We have a Gaelic proverb, '*Mas dubh, mas odhar, mas donn, is toil leis a'ghohbais a mean.*' It means, 'A nanny goat loves her kid, whether he's black, dun or brown.'"

"I've no time for riddles. I thank you for your care of Louis.

The island air has suited him. It's late now, well past his bedtime. If I may, I'll share my son's room for what remains of the night. We'll depart early tomorrow. The horse can carry us both. I wish you, good night."

Janet arose at sunrise. She had allowed herself to hope that Louis would still be with her for his eighth birthday in November. Then she could be sure that he would live to grow up. He would outlive his shadow who never reached eight years and never outgrew his brown tweed breeks. But she was determined to bid farewell to Louis. The child came and smiled shyly at her. The dark shadows under his eyes made her long to embrace him but he stayed just out of reach. He held out his bird bone hand to shake hers and his voice was a subdued cheep. "I thank you for taking care of me and hope I wasn't too much trouble."

"No trouble at all. May God bless you." She held her composure while she waved them farewell, Louis craning back from the saddle where he sat in front of his father. She stayed until she could no longer see them. Then she slipped into the boy's room and pressed her aching face to the bedclothes to catch the downy child smell of him. She felt something crinkle beneath her cheek and found a tightly folded piece of paper. She opened it to find some words written in a child's loopy, shaky script:

"This is for your boy, the one who wore the rough trousers.
Here he lies
Where he longed to be
Home is the sailor
Home from the sea."

She cradled the scrap of paper in her hands while her pent-up tears roared down the hillside, swooping across the shore until they plunged into the depths of the ocean.

Chapter 9

Island of Rona, Spring 1858

After Halloween, the weather closed in for weeks on end. No boats could safely leave or enter Rona's harbors. It was too wild and dangerous, even with the beam of the new lighthouse to guide them. Janet was imprisoned on her island both by the sea and by her grief. It was the old grief redoubled after Louis's abrupt departure. There wasn't even the consolation of tending to the light. The empty lamp squatted on the windowsill as bereft and neglected as herself. She spent hours gazing out to sea, but she no longer knew what she was looking for.

Finally, the weather turned fair and ships reappeared, like returning migratory birds. The first vessel to appear in Big Harbour was a rowing boat. Janet felt a fluttering of curiosity that prompted her to open her door and peer outside. As she picked her way among the rocks, she wondered if maybe at last she was dragging herself free from the trailing anchor that had weighed down her soul for so long. She could see two figures on the boat but couldn't make out who they were. She should have brought the spyglass the captain had given her. All she could see of the rower was his straining back and shoulders hauling on the oars against the tide. Then the passenger waved and called out. It was her granddaughter Jeannie. Janet hurried to greet them, the waves nibbling at the hem of her skirt. Jeannie leaped ashore and into her grandmother's arms while the rower busied himself beaching the boat.

"Come on, Kenneth. Come and greet Grandma. She won't bite you."

He smiled awkwardly, "How are you keeping, Mistress MacKenzie?"

"I suppose you've come to claim your money," she replied in

a gruff voice, but there was a gleam of amusement in her eyes.

"I truly regret opening that drawer in the press, especially since Jeannie told me about the shoe. I . . ." His voice guttered as Janet stared at him. "I don't know what came over me."

"It was a silly thing to do but not a hanging matter, I think," Janet replied after a pause.

Kenneth attempted a smile. Jeannie dug him in the ribs. "What else have you to say?"

His smile blossomed into a grin, "Jeannie has said that she'll marry me. She took her time though. Led me a merry dance first."

"That's as it should be," said Janet, laughing, "You had to prove yourself worthy. So you do need your money now."

"We've the promise of a croft near Mama and Papa." Jeannie squeezed her hand into Kenneth's. "We'll get married in the summer. You will come, Grandma, won't you?"

"Of course, I will. Someone has to keep an eye on this fellow from Kintail with his nosey ways." A gust of happiness set her heart fluttering free after being tightly furled for so long.

Chapter 10

Island of Rona, Spring 1858

Soon afterward, a much larger vessel appeared on the horizon, steam powered with two funnels and two masts. It waited in the outer harbor and dropped a smaller boat from its side to come ashore. The two figures in naval blue saw Janet waiting outside her door for them. Tom Masters slowed his stride to match Captain Otter's measured pace.

"Mistress MacKenzie, I trust you're in good health. We're not intruding on you, I hope?" The captain's voice boomed but his deep-set eyes darted anxiously.

"Not at all, you're most welcome, Captain Otter."

"You remember Lieutenant Masters?"

"Indeed I do. He came with you the first time and then on his own with the new lamp from the Commissioner gentlemen. I'm afraid to say that it's back in its box. I had become so used to my old one. But I make good use of this fine gift you sent me." She brandished the spyglass. "Will you come inside for some refreshment?"

"Of course, the new lamp isn't needed now," she continued when they were seated. "Should it be returned to the Commissioners?"

"Better not. I had to battle with them before they agreed to give it to you in the first place. They're renowned for being parsimonious, every penny kept a prisoner."

Tom noticed that the captain seemed much more at his ease compared to the first time they had visited. The widow too was different, less stiff in her manner.

"Have you visited the new lighthouse?" the captain asked.

"No, but I did go while it was being built. It was then that I met Mr. Thomas Stevenson and his wee boy, Louis, who stayed here for a time." Her breath came out in a sigh before she rushed on. "He never stopped talking about your ship and how he wanted to grow up to be strong and brave like the fine lieutenant. I don't know though that he'll be hardy enough for a sailor's life."

Tom smiled. "His mind was so lively but maybe his body couldn't keep pace with it."

Tom thought about the boy. He had been drawn to him as a fellow spirit. He too longed to tear up the map his father had drawn for his future. He wished the lad well. He doubted if Louis would ever be suited to an active life. But there was a will there that wouldn't be easily quenched. Tom pulled his thoughts back to the present and looked across at the widow. Mrs. MacKenzie was smiling as if laughter was bubbling up in her throat.

She caught his eye and seemed to come to a decision. "Do excuse me gentlemen. I was only thinking how my speech is much more sprightly than when you came before. When I was a lass, my father insisted I learn English. He said it was the language of the future while our native tongue belonged to the past. I did as he bade me, but living here I had no need to speak anything but Gaelic. When you came before, my tongue cleaved to the roof of my mouth when I tried to talk. Then when Louis came, he was such a fanciful wee lad, always wanting to hear stories. So I had to buff up my English words again."

"Ah, but I arrived without warning and startled you," the captain replied. After that, the conversation flowed easily enough as he spoke about his voyages to survey the Outer Isles. The new ship, *HMS Porcupine,* had nearly sunk during the terrible winter storms off St. Kilda.

"She lay helpless on her beam ends, but two local men saved her by cutting away the boats on the lee side. They got her upright again. I thank the Lord for Highland sailors, the best in the world." After an hour they rose to leave and Janet walked down the beach with them. The captain turned back before climbing into the waiting boat. "Our charts and the new lighthouses are making the sea less dangerous. But I shall never forget that before any of us arrived your lamp was saving lives."

The widow nodded, her eyes moist.

After they had gone, she stood at the window for a long time. The captain had understood. Thanks was all the reward she wanted. It was also his way of bidding her farewell. Now she must say farewell herself to the Janet who had kept the light. But what was left of her without the lamp?

She marched into the kitchen, surprising Effie who was sweeping the floor. Opening a press she rummaged inside and pulled out old cloths, a lump of soap and a jar of vinegar. Her first task was to clean the brass parts of the lamp and polish them until they glowed. Lifting the fragile glass chimney she dabbed it with a vinegar-soaked rag before swaddling it in a soft cloth to dry. When it was all back together again she stood back to survey her handiwork. Still she felt vexed.

Kenneth had brought the lamp back from one of his trips. He enjoyed displaying his wealth but to her it was bragging. The bulky thing was never suited to their house. It was a foreigner. Like the big sheep that the landlords brought in when they drove the people out.

She paced up and down in front of the window before heading to her bedroom. There she bent down to pry open the lid of an old sea chest. Groping inside it, she pulled out a length of black fabric. It released a musty scent as she shook out the folds. It was the shawl she had worn after Kenneth's death. Once the period of mourning was over, it had languished in the trunk. Now it would be draped over the lamp, the lamp that had shone out over the water for so long, but now was no longer needed.

Chapter 11

Island of Rona, Spring 1858

A week later the next visitor came, this time in a small sailing boat. She recognized the sailor at once. The sea frothed against Murdo's boots as he jumped ashore.

"I'm relieved to see you again, Mama, after that terrible winter."

"Well, I lived through it. You're the third boat to arrive. Jeannie came first with young Kenneth. Then Captain Otter with his fair young lieutenant and . . ." She paused, hands on hips and frowned at him, "Don't look at me like that. I know what you're thinking, but my mind's not failing. Of course, the captain came that first time two years ago, but he was back again this spring."

"I can see your mind is as sharp as ever," Murdo said smiling.

"And so is my tongue when needs be."

Later as they sat down he looked toward the covered lamp brooding on the window sill.

"It's strange to think I won't be bringing oil for your lamp anymore."

"Nearly twenty years I tended that light. I was still quite a young woman when I started."

They sat silent, both absorbed in their own thoughts. Then Murdo cleared his throat, "I've something to show you." He rummaged in his jacket pocket. She was alerted by the urgency in his voice, an urgency he was trying to muffle. He pulled out a folded piece of paper and handed it to her, but she barely glanced at it before giving it back.

"Don't you want to look at it properly?"

"I don't need to. The drawing of the ship tells the story. You're going to emigrate, aren't you?"

"Aye, Caristiona and I have spent days and nights talking

about it. We're both weary of the struggle to keep the family fed. Our neighbor has relatives out in Canada and their letters are full of how good it is out there. It was the building of the lighthouse that finally made us decide and . . ." he stumbled to a halt.

"The lighthouse beam shows the way to a new start. Did you think I would be upset by your news?" He nodded. "It's never too late for a fresh start. Even for a *cailleach* like me." He frowned in puzzlement. "I think I might come with you. You're looking pale, son, and your mouth's hanging open like a door that's lost its hinges. I'll fetch you a dram." She almost skipped to the press to get the bottle. "My task here is finished. There's no reason for me to stay."

She handed him the glass and he tilted it in his hand, swirling the amber fluid into a storm, "I always thought that you would never leave here. Never leave them."

She looked over his shoulder, out of the window. "I couldn't bear it that the sea held on to their bodies. How could they have peace when they had no resting place? I knew I would never see them again in this life. The light could never guide them home, but it could warm their poor wandering souls. Then after Louis left, my heart ripped open again. It was like losing your brother a second time," she gulped.

"Hamish, Mama, say his name."

"Losing . . . Hamish again. When I first saw Louis, I thought for an instant he was Hamish come back to life. The same age, frail, a mind darting like a wagtail. I thought if only Louis stayed with me until his eighth birthday, the one Hamish never reached, he would live to become a man. Somehow would live for Hamish too." She covered her face with her hands. "I know this was a madness in me and the fever has burnt itself out now."

He reached over and took one of her hands, smoothing the gnarled joints with his own roughened fingers, "Come with us to Canada. It's time to lay Hamish and Papa to rest. But . . ." he hesitated. "But before we go I want you to break your silence and tell me all that happened that day. When you sent Catherine and me away the night before. Did you have a vision?"

She gazed at his long face with its high cheekbones, so like his father's, but the cool gray eyes were her own.

"No, I had no warning. Your father only decided to sail that morning."

"He had been talking about it before though, hadn't he? We were running low on water and there was no sign of any rain coming to fill our barrels. He promised me I could sail with him to Portree. I was so jealous when he took Hamish instead. I was the one who worked hard. Jarring my arms every time the foot plough hit a rock. But no one noticed me. Hamish the favoured one could do no wrong." He dropped his gaze and flexed his fingers. "Afterward I was tormented by fears. Could my anger and envy have brought the storm?"

She remembered Murdo as he was then, a boy on the cusp of manhood. Scowling face and furtive eyes devouring the new, flighty maid as she went about her tasks. "I can see now I was too tender with your wee brother. But he was delicate. I didn't want him to go on the boat that day. He was meant to go away with you two."

"But the rascal said you told him to stay at home while we went. If you had no suspicion about what was going to happen, why did you send Catherine and me away to the Nicolsons at Dry Harbour?"

She took a long time to reply. "Your father and I fell out and there was no way we could put it right." She struggled to pull out the words. They had rooted, unspoken for so long.

"Was it about Anna?"

Janet nodded, "But even after all these years, it wouldn't be right to speak about it."

Murdo waited while she stayed silent. She was reliving that day in her mind. Hamish had begged her to go out with him for a walk. It was a jewel of a winter's day, dry and sparkling. He was on good form, no cough at all. They followed the track inland up to the pasture. Hamish skipped ahead, humming to himself. Then he stopped dead and waited for her to catch him up. "What's that, Mama?" He pointed to where the ground dipped ahead of them.

She looked too but couldn't make any sense of what she was seeing. A blur of movement, strewn clothes. A jacket and shirt. A patch of blue like scabious flowers. No, not in the winter.

"What are they doing?" Hamish asked.

The whirling fragments stopped spinning. She was looking at two figures, one lying down, limbs sprawled. The other sitting astride him, head flung back.

"Is it a game? Look, it's Anna. And there's Papa underneath. Can I go and see them?"

She couldn't speak but she clutched at his sleeve and pulled him away, back the way they had come.

"Mama, let me go, you're hurting me."

She had halted, turned him toward her and loosened her grip. "Listen to me. Go find your brother and sister. Tell them that all three of you are to go to the Nicolsons in Dry Harbour. You can say your Mama's not well."

She could see he was shaken. His mother saying he must tell a lie. He turned back but kept looking over his shoulder. She remained, rigid as a standing stone. She had always suspected that Kenneth wasn't a faithful husband. Doubts were only ghosts that shriveled in daylight but now she knew. Flaunting his sin on their doorstep. Soiling their home. How could he mock their loving acts? Once she had yearned for his touch. Her longing like the foam of the incoming waves licking her toes. The longing urged her to wade ever deeper among the frothing waves. Was this what it was like to be pulled under by a water horse? Not knowing who was the horse and who the rider? The swell rearing up, over, through her until she no longer knew if she was swimming or drowning. Then at the end flung back to shore, feeling the shingle slide away under her.

Now Kenneth climbed up the slope toward her, his mouth opening in a greeting, hoping she had seen nothing. But the lies died in his throat at the sight of her wild face. They howled and roared at each other like wild beasts. She couldn't remember the words except for one jagged stone that left a bloody scar. *"Every time I returned home to cold embers. A man needs a warm hearth. I had to go and find one elsewhere."*

Murdo's voice jolted her back to the present, "I know you won't speak ill of Papa. You said God had called him to a better place."

"Aye, we must all answer to God when our time comes."

"I'm asking too much of you. Don't say any more." He patted her hand.

She shook her head, "But I must. He's your father and it's wrong to keep the truth from you. After the fight we went home. Hamish was there. I was cross with him for disobeying me. He started to wheeze as he did whenever he was upset. So what could I do? I let him stay. It was such a lovely day, but its beauty mocked me. I paraded up and down the shore and the house, not knowing what to do with myself. In the end I lay down and I must have fallen asleep in spite of everything. I was shaken awake early by your father."

"I'm sailing over to Portree to get water. Angus MacLeod's coming with me."

"You can take Anna with you back to her mother's house."

"Aye. And Hamish is coming, too."

"I started to scream but it was no good. He carried him out to the boat and I couldn't stop him. The wee lad was white faced and I didn't want to distress him anymore. So I pretended a smile and waved them off. You asked me if I had a warning. I didn't until that moment when your father turned the prow the wrong way."

"You mean he didn't set off sun-wise?" Murdo gasped,

horror-struck. "How could he risk bringing bad fortune on them all?"

"I don't know. Was he unheeding because he was angry or was he taunting fate? I was left trembling like a beast before the knife. I couldn't move away from the window. After a while Margaret MacLeod came in. She's a cousin of your father's, of course, but a rough sort."

"Why did you let him go out today with my man?" she shouted at me. As if I could stop him. "You know what day it is?" I looked blankly at her. "You know about Kenneth's two brothers?"

"They were lost at sea years ago, weren't they?" I stammered. She was scaring me.

"Aye, both in the month of February." She came so close that flecks of spittle sprayed my face. "And both on a Tuesday. And what day of the week is it today? If anything happens to that boat, I shall curse you forever through all your generations." Janet's voice faltered.

"I hope you told the old witch to shut her mouth."

"I did. But she left me even more uneasy. All morning I kept going out to look at the sky. There was a breeze from the southwest when they left. As the morning dragged itself along, the wind quickened. I told myself your father would stay in Portree if the weather turned. At midday I sat down but my belly closed itself against any food. Surely they would sail back soon? It was a short winter's day. Two hours later there was still no sign of them. The wind was brisker now. Starting to whip up the waves, but he had found his way back through far worse. They could run ahead of the wind if they trimmed the sail.

"At last! About a mile out I saw a speck on the sea. I rubbed my eyes. I had been straining them so hard that I doubted them. But I could pick out a boat, bucking through the waves. I closed my eyes and prayed in thanks for their deliverance. When I opened them again, I saw Norman and Alistair were there standing beside me."

"I thought I saw a boat coming," Norman said, screwing up his eyes.

"Maybe your eyesight's better than mine. Are they turning into the harbor, yet?"

"Aye, I think so but I don't understand why the sail's still up. They're going too fast." He sounded puzzled rather than alarmed, but it was in that minute that I knew. After time dawdling for an eternity it began to gallop. We stared out to sea, heedless of the stinging rain. The boat turned her muzzle toward the bay, but she was a runaway horse. The mast was plunging through the swell as the boat was pounded by the waves. We could see the sail straining in the wind, tearing itself to tatters.

"Why haven't they got the sail down?" I asked.

"The tackle must have jammed. Look, you can see them trying to release it." There were two figures struggling to stand on the wallowing deck. The boat was almost on the rocks."

"Can you get a line across to them?" I cried, but I knew the answer. There was no chance at all. The boat was a hooked fish being dragged toward the rocks. I couldn't bear to watch but I couldn't look away. In my dreams, I hear them screaming but at the time the wind was shrieking too loudly to hear anything else. Then the rocks were upon them, splitting open the hull. Splinters of wood tossed into the air, but there was no sign of them. They were swallowed up as if they had never been," her voice faded. "My only consolation was that you and Catherine weren't there to see it."

Janet raised her eyes to look at Murdo, tears drenching her cheeks, "All four of them drowned, including Anna who was supposed to be staying in Portree. In my bitterness I thought how your father and Anna had been punished for their sins. But why would God have allowed the other two innocent souls to die with them? I can see now that none of them deserved that cruel death."

"So, Mama, the story has been told and the past laid to rest."

"That can never be done. But I don't need to keep the light shining for them any longer. I'm ready now to make a new life in Canada, but I have a few tasks to do first."

Chapter 12

Scorrybreac, Portree, Isle of Skye 1858

Janet clambered out of the boat that had brought her over from Rona, She stumbled as she picked her way along the stony path curving beside the inlet of the sea, past the bundled nets and tumbled lobster pots. How she wished that vanity had not stopped her from bringing a walking stick. Well, her punishment was the throbbing of those wretched veins in her leg, bulging as if they would break through the skin. She stopped to catch her breath and looked about her. The slanting winter sunshine made her shade her eyes with a hand. The tide was sliding out, exposing tawny sprawls of seaweed.

There was the cottage, right at the end. Almost toppling into the sea, its thatch more threadbare than the other houses in the row. She hobbled on again. Rounding the bend she saw a stocky, middle-aged woman, slumped down on a stool in front of the house.

"Is that you, Kirsty?"

The other woman looked up and frowned.

"It's Mistress MacKenzie from Rona." She stretched her arm out and waggled it at waist height. "You were only a wee lassie when I last saw you."

Kirsty struggled to her feet, pressing a hand into the small of her back. Her face was flushed. "That was many years ago. My mother's long been in her grave. But your last visit isn't one I would forget."

"I need to speak with you. Shall we stay outside?"

"No, you'd better come away in."

Janet MacKenzie nodded. She knew that Kirsty would be concerned about her neighbors stretching their ears to hear her business. She held her breath as she dipped her head through the

61

doorway. She could never get used to that stench of unwashed bodies and the eye-searing smoke that oozed from these houses. Inside it was much as she remembered it before. A cramped dark hovel, barely furnished. There was a rough bench and a dresser made of driftwood standing on the beaten earth. A blackened pot hung from a chain over the fireplace. In the corner she saw a sleeping baby lying on what looked like a washed-up tea crate resting on top of a pile of fusty bedclothes.

"That's my daughter's wee one." Kirsty had brought in her stool. She stood rubbing it against her apron before offering it to her guest.

Janet remembered there being a baby when she came before. And several young children peeping wide-eyed from behind their mother's skirts. They would have been Anna and Kirsty's younger brothers and sisters. Kirsty, as the oldest one still at home, had taken charge and shooed them away while Janet spoke to her mother. After Janet had told her the news, Kirsty had held her mother's swaying body and guided her to a seat. She sucked in great ragged breaths as if she were drowning. What words had she used to tell the poor woman? Janet struggled to remember. Her face on its own would have told the terrible tale before she even opened her mouth. All she could remember was the poor woman calling out her daughter's name endlessly, "Anna, Anna, my firstborn babe." Eventually, her wailing had turned into breathless coughing and the poor woman had allowed Janet and Kirsty to help her lie down. Then she turned her face to the wall. It was young Kirsty, now suddenly the eldest in the family who held out her hand for the purse Janet offered.

Aware of Kirsty staring at her, she said, "So you stayed put?"

"Aye, after Mama died of the consumption I brought them all up until they left home. Then I met Duncan and he took up the fishing. So we stayed put."

"And is your husband home now?"

"No, he's still away on the east coast boats."

Janet thought about what she had heard of Duncan. Probably an older man had seemed a safe harbor to Kirsty. But word was they never had a red penny to their name. He was a drinker. Kirsty's mottled skin and bloodshot eyes suggested that she joined him.

"You'll be wondering why I'm here." Janet smoothed down her brown dress over her lap and waited until she had Kirsty's attention. "I've come to offer you the chance of a new start."

"Oh, aye." Kirsty's expression was grim, insolent even.

"I'll pay for you and all your family," she nodded toward the snuffling baby, "to go to Canada."

"You would pay our passages there?"

Janet nodded.

"Could we not have the money instead of the tickets?"

"What would you do with the money?" Where was the woman's gratitude?

"Plenty. A new boat, somewhere decent to live. A chance for this wee one to learn a trade when he grows up." Kirsty raised her voice. The baby jolted in his sleep and mewed.

"But it would be better to give you the tickets. Then we would know that the money would not be lost." Janet spoke carefully, looking her in the eye.

Kirsty wiped her sweating face with her greasy apron. "I've no wish to go to the ends of the earth. It's always the poor who are expected to leave their homes."

"I'm going . . ."

"Aye, you'd better. I've no need of your charity." Her words were boulders, hurled down a hillside.

The baby woke up and started to wail. Kirsty hurried to pick him up. She squeezed him and her tears splattered over his startled face. Janet opened the door and walked outside, screwing her eyes against the light.

As she walked back along the path she murmured to herself, "If only you had listened, Kirsty. But you can't help someone who won't be helped." She tapped her pocket where the tickets rustled. Well, no doubt another family would welcome them. But there was something else there as well as the tickets. What was it? She lifted out the blue scarf. She had intended to give it to Kirsty. It was all that remained of her dead sister, but there had been no chance for her to hand it over.

That night Janet dreamed about the boat, as she had so many times before but this time the dream was different. She wasn't standing on the beach at Big Harbour on Rona. She was at Staffin Bay, near her childhood home on Skye. Kenneth's boat was coming in past Staffin Island. The sail was down and he was rowing while Hamish sat trailing his fingers over the side. He saw his mother watching and waved. Janet waded into the sea to meet them but no matter how hard Kenneth pulled on the oars he could make no progress. In the end, he put them down and stood up to unfurl the sail. They both smiled at her while the boat turned her face back to the open sea. She leapt like a dolphin toward a glowing light on the horizon. "They're going back to Rona," she cried out as she woke.

She knew what she must do. She opened the drawer in the press. Held the small, cracked boot in her hand. Hamish's Sunday shoes. Usually he hated wearing them, complaining that they rubbed his feet raw. But he put them on that day to sail with his papa. This boot was the only part of him that came back to the shore. She had found it spat out by the sea.

The scarf had returned weeks later, a gaudy foreigner strewn among the seaweed. Kenneth must have brought it back for Anna after his last trip away. In the old days, he used to bring Janet a present. Always tried to find something blue because she loved the color. She had nearly thrown the scarf away but it was such a forlorn scrap. Leached and frayed, flung away like Anna's young life. Now she carried both relics, cupped in her hands like fledglings, down to the beach when the tide was going out. She had a length of heather rope and a few twigs ready in her pocket. With these she turned the boot into a vessel, with the scarf as its sail. She launched the frail boat and watched it drift away.

Chapter 13

Portree, Isle of Skye, February 1861

Richard Williams was glad to be ashore. He was lucky not to suffer from seasickness, but he felt trapped if he spent too long on the ship. Not that he wasn't grateful for being part of Captain Otter's crew. A survey vessel was a better berth than an ordinary naval ship where the crew squeezed together like rats in a barrel. Still he was pleased to get away. He hated the bragging of the younger hands about what they would do with any women they met. He was even getting annoyed with poor old Willie. His chest as wheezy as his squeezebox, missing notes like dropping stitches. Willie had grown old but not wise. He would get steaming drunk with the rest of them. Richard shuddered as he remembered doing the same himself. But he wouldn't seek escape in the bottle now. It was that sort of drunkenness that led to heedless couplings. Like the one that had sparked his own life into being. Jagged words splintered his thoughts.

"You're bound for Hell, you bastard." The slash of his father's voice, the man who had taken him in.

"Overboard you go. I'll not listen to you anymore," Richard muttered to himself. He turned to look back down the hill where he could see the masts of *HMS Porcupine*, at anchor in the bay. Plenty sneered at her, saying that she looked as odd as her namesake. Doubled up with masts and funnels. Her vast engine might make the whole vessel rattle, but she could tiptoe close to the shore. A sound survey boat. Not like a skittish sailing ship. He admired both vessel and master. The captain had noticed him when he was first serving on *The Comet*. Richard had been suspicious when the captain paid him attention. No one talked to you unless they were planning to trick or hurt you.

"You can read and write? I think we can make better use of

you," Captain Otter had said.

So he made Richard a coxswain, put him in charge of one of the boats that took the soundings. He encouraged him to spend time in the airy survey room in the stern. Of course, it was the captain himself or Lieutenant Masters who recorded the figures on the charts while Richard read out the measurements for them. He knew that his fellows thought him an odd fish, but as he was under the captain's wing they let him be.

It was his first time ashore in Portree. After spending so much time surveying the wide bay from the sea, he felt that he knew the village already. But it was always strange being on land, looking into a mirror and seeing the landscape back to front. There was the apothecary tower on its rounded knoll, the plain fronted courthouse and jail below it. Farther along the shore were the turrets of Viewfield House where the captain had been entertained. Richard was heading for the inlet of the sea beneath the knoll where the fishermen's houses crouched together. *Sligneach* the place was called, "Bayfield" in English.

Plaintive wisps of fiddle music made him quicken his step. The sound must be coming from the ceilidh house, bigger than the surrounding black houses. Richard might not approve of strong drink, but he did enjoy music and dancing. He picked his way past the rowing boats drawn up on the shore and ducked through the open door.

Although it was still afternoon it was gloomy inside. Light from the flickering peat fire was hidden by the heave of bodies. He hesitated, about to turn back.

"Williams, it's you. What are you doing here?"

The voice made him jump. "Lieutenant Masters. Er . . . I wanted to hear the music. Maybe dance."

"I could join you."

Richard frowned. "I don't think that's a good idea, sir." He pointed at the artist's bag slung over Tom's shoulder. "It looks as if you were planning to do some drawing."

A group spilled out of the door, laughing and flowing toward the flat grassy area where the nets were dried. Richard turned his back on Tom's disappointed face and allowed himself to be jostled as flotsam along with them. Three fiddlers were already waiting together, the women flocked to one end of the space while the men hustled together opposite them. As the musicians struck up a reel, the men lunged forward to pick a partner.

Richard faltered, but then out of the corner of his eye he glimpsed her, hovering on the edge of the group of women. His heart somersaulted as he took in the straight, slender body. The brown hair undershot with auburn waving down past her shoulders. As he moved closer, he could see a faint cross-hatching of lines around her clear blue eyes but the smile on her wide mouth entranced him. He stood, unable to move. It reminded him of when he was the steersman on his first ship, a sailing vessel. During a gale he had been lashed to the wheel to stop the waves from sweeping him overboard. There was nothing holding him now, but he felt as if he was tied down by invisible ropes. Then she looked straight at him and he was suddenly released and found himself uncoiling toward her. Her eyes looked directly into his and a smile tilted the corners of her lips. "Màiri," she said, pointing at herself. "Richard," he replied. Her eyes scanned him again, widened in surprise and joy followed by some darker emotion, almost as if she was frightened, terrified even. She blinked and took his hand, their fingertips skimming as the dancers formed into sets for an eightsome reel. His eyes hooked onto her face as they moved through the dance. He had to clench his fists as she spun and swung with other men. He was bereft until she turned back toward him. A complete stranger, yet he felt he had always known her. Each time they met again in the dance, he tried to speak but now her eyes were downcast. It was as if she was ashamed to meet his gaze.

"I'll talk to her when the dance is over," he promised himself. The fiddlers quickened their pace and the dancers responded, whirling and weaving their steps in a frenzy.

Abruptly the music stopped. He gripped her hand and gestured back toward the ceilidh house. She nodded but as his grip slackened, she snatched her hand away and was tearing through the crowd, knocking into dancers as she hurtled past. He blundered after her, but by now they were forming new sets and unwilling to make way for him as he cannoned into them. The men snarled, their partners backed away as he kept shouting, "Where's Màiri?" Most of them looked away although a few stared hard at him first, almost as if they recognized him.

Lost and confused, he wandered back toward the group of black houses and slumped down at the corner of one of them, the rough stones jabbing his back. Had he imagined the whole thing? No, she had been flesh and blood. He had held her hand. But the way she disappeared? Like one of those seal people the captain spoke about. If they felt frightened, they would run away to find their hidden sealskins and hide for ever in the ocean. But that was nonsense. He groaned out loud.

He saw an old woman, dressed in rusty black with a faded plaid over her shoulders. She was watching him from her doorway. He sprang toward her.

"Do you know where Màiri is?"

She didn't reply but came up to him. She lifted back his sailor's cap to gaze into his eyes. As if she were blind, she brushed her fingers over his face. Standing back, she shook her head. Her eyes were dark puddles in her furrowed face. Then she slipped back inside, the door thudding behind her.

He made his way back to the ship in a daze. At least it was quiet on board with the rest of the crew ashore. He clambered into his hammock and fell into a fitful sleep. He dreamed he was in a rowing boat on the open sea, chasing a creature whose body gleamed like fish scales. He strained on the oars to reach it, and as he got closer, he could see that what had appeared to be a fin was instead a spreading tail, gold spliced with red. The creature turned its long, sleek head toward him and made a snickering sound that changed into a snarl. Its eyes rolled, splashing fire. He started awake on a scream, causing the other sailors to curse him. He knew that the only way to release himself from the nightmare was to track down the mysterious Màiri.

First, he took pains with his appearance. He threw cold water from a barrel over his shivering body. He tied back his russet hair with a piece of ribbon so that it rested neatly in the nape of his neck. With his precious razor, sharpened on a leather strop, he shaved his face until his skin tingled. Finally, he shook out his cap and arranged it on his head. He returned to the old woman's house and knocked at the door with his whole fist. She startled him by opening it at once, as if she had been standing sentry behind it. Scrutinizing him wordlessly, she stepped outside and indicated that he should follow her. They walked along the shoreline to the end of the houses and climbed up a rough track. He realized that they were going up toward the *Meall* or The Lump, to give it its odd English name. The surveying part of his mind noted how much less prominent the apothecary tower appeared from this side. From the sea it rose up like a lighthouse.

She strode along at a brisk rate for an old woman, passing a small church until she stopped in front of a whitewashed house that he realized must be the manse. After pointing out the front door, she hurried away back down the hill. Richard knocked. The door was opened by a squat middle-aged maid whose sloping shoulders slid down into a bell-shaped body. Her eyes flickered over Richard and then slithered away as she ushered him into the parlour. The minister was seated at his desk. He was as spare and somber as his room. Again that stare. He was sick of being treated like a freak in a funfair.

The minister gathered himself, saying he was Reverend MacLean, extending his hand and inviting Richard to sit down on a hard chair. He had the almost singing speech of the islands. Turning to the hovering maid, he addressed her in Gaelic. When she failed to respond at once he took her arm, making her shuffle to the door. As he shut it firmly behind her, Richard thought how the whole scene seemed like some sort of play where everyone else except him knew their part. A sick sense of shame rose like bile in his throat. As so often before in his life he felt in the wrong, being blamed yet again for some sin he didn't even know he had committed.

The minister blinked. "Mistress Nicolson brought you here at my suggestion. I'll explain why as best I can."

Richard nodded. There was no going back.

Chapter 14

Several days later. Aboard *HMS Porcupine* in Portree Harbor

It was well past midnight. Henry Otter was still sitting in his cabin, his unfocused eyes staring into the darkness outside. What a terrible day it had been. The strain of bracing himself against the gales of emotion, far harder to endure than storms at sea. He was exhausted with holding his iron hull intact and keeping his soft-shelled heart down in the hold. The men must not sniff any sign of weakness from him.

He was the fruit of a family tree heavy with its harvest of seafaring men. From his birth, it was taken for granted that he too would become a sailor. Although born in landlocked Derbyshire, as a boy he spent long summers with relatives in a Hampshire village not far from Portsmouth. He went sailing with old George, a fisherman who knew the coastal waters as intimately as a farmer knows the contours of his fields. Henry acted as his pilot, taking charge of the twelve-foot pole that the old man used when he was edging along the sandbanks. Henry learned how to cast out the lead weight on a marked line and call out the readings: "Two fathoms deep," and "By the mark seven."

When there was a shrouding mist, George gave him a lump of grease to press down into the hollow at the base of the weight. Henry lowered it into the water, making sure that the weight stuck to the seabed. After jiggling the line and letting the weight scrape along the bottom, he would haul it up again. The old fisherman would suck his teeth and prod the piece of lard to see what had stuck to it. Depending on whether it was pebbles or grains of sand, he could work out their exact position. Henry was amazed how George carried in his head a map of the hidden underwater world. But it was a secret map, trapped inside his mind. Even then, Henry thought how wonderful it would be if that knowledge could be put on a chart for all sailors to use.

When he became a midshipman, some of the old sailors commiserated with him about how the glory days were over. The beauty of a ship in full sail, the thrill of battles against the French and the bold commanders, like Lord Nelson. But the peacetime, more humdrum navy suited him. He discovered an aptitude for navigation and measurement. He enjoyed rowing offshore in a small boat with a few others, armed only with lead, line, and compass. Because he could draw, he was given the task of sketching landmarks, a stand of trees, a church tower, or the sharp angle of a cliff. Rain and squalls didn't discourage him. If the weather turned dangerous, they could pull the boat up in a deserted bay and wait for the wind to slacken. He had found a berth that suited him. Superior officers noticed his care for detail. He rose through the service until he was entrusted with this major survey of the West Highland coast and its attendant islands. As captain, he sought to give his crew a sense of pride in their labors and to encourage those like Masters and Williams who showed skill at surveying.

So Henry was far from being a battle-hardened warrior. Indeed, he had never before seen the body of a man who had died violently. He couldn't believe that one man could have poured out such an ocean of blood. The sailor who found the body noticed the legs poking out from behind the coiled ropes. Then he slipped in the sticky morass when he went to investigate. It was the poor fellow's waxy face that had most startled him. It was bleached whiter than whale bones disgorged by the sea.

Henry chafed his face. His first task in the morning would be to address the crew and try to restore their spirits. Sailors would imagine portents of disaster from any untoward happening, let alone something like this. Meanwhile, there was no prospect of sleep. He sighed and drew quill and paper in front of him.

My Dearest Jemina,

I am truly sorry to burden you with my troubles. My unwilling hand weighs me down as heavily as my heart, but I know that writing to you will afford me some relief. If I were not a rational man but superstitious like my crew, I would believe that my captaincy was cursed. You will recall poor Hugh Cramer. I secured from the Admiralty the increase in pay he was entitled to but he had little opportunity to enjoy it before he died of a swelling in the windpipe. It's nearly two years now since we buried him in the churchyard in Portree. I never dreamed that I would have to arrange another burial for one of my men in the same place or in such horrifying circumstances. My hand is slowing to a standstill but I must continue. I've been unable to make any sense of what has happened. Richard Williams, the coxswain, was a diligent young man. I know you tease me about taking the quiet young sailors under my wing, but this fellow showed exceptional promise. Although a common seaman, he had received the rudiments of an education and had an eager intelligence. Survey work suited his methodical nature. I blame myself. He was always so reliable. When he suddenly started making errors, I should have probed him rather than merely being brusque. How I regret my impatience now. When I sought him out later, he was distant and distracted. He mumbled something about how he now knew that he was as wicked as his father had always said he was. I can only surmise that as a decent young man, he was ashamed of some dalliance ashore. When I tried to reassure him, he battened down his hatches.

I resolved to try again later, but I was much too late. If only I had summoned the persistence you showed last year in helping that St. Kildan woman in her difficult labor. How amused you were by that daunting list of names they gave the poor infant. Mary Jemina Otter Porcupine Gillies, if I remember rightly.

I digress. When Williams failed to report for duty, I dispatched a hand to find him. The man returned white to the gills. Williams's still warm body was lying sprawled behind one of the funnels, with his throat cut. I feared murder but when I went to investigate I saw the open razor in his hand. When the doctor came on board, he confirmed that Williams had indeed taken his own life. "I cannot record this death as misadventure. Clearly he died by his own hand."

My imagination conjured up visions of him being buried at a crossroads with a stake through his heart. I didn't trust myself to speak. If only he had done the deed when we were at sea, we could have quietly committed his body to the deep.

"May I suggest you pay a visit to Reverend Munro at the Beal Chapel at Scorrybreac?" Dr. MacLeod suggested. "He has more of the milk of human kindness than many of his fellows."

I followed the good doctor's advice. The reverend's ruddy complexion and rough hands made him look more like a farmer than a man of God. He remained silent for some time after I had finished speaking. Although desperate to resolve matters, I thought it best not to interrupt his cogitations. I sat listening to the ticking of his clock and the howling of the wind. I could hear sheep bleating on the hillside, only ewes by the sound of it. It would be too early for lambs. February is a hard month. The promise of spring but winter hasn't yet released its grip. When he finally spoke, I started with surprise. "This man is a miscreant and a sinner. He has broken the laws of man and much worse the laws of God." My heart sank. Another heavy silence followed. "God will judge him and decide whether to have mercy on his soul." Then the minister closed his eyes and moved his lips, as if in prayer. Finally, he raised his head and his eyes snapped open. "I shall give him a Christian burial. He'll be buried outside the churchyard, by the trees."

"His shipmates will want to erect a stone for him," I said.

"That can be done," he replied.

The funeral was a grim affair. Only the minister, Lieutenant Masters and three other of the ship's company were there. Afterward, I walked along the shore, reluctant to go back on board were everyone was under a pall. I looked over the bay toward the snow-tipped Cuillin, brooding on the waste of his life. Also I feared the contagious gloom that his death had spread on board. Masters looked strained. He knew Williams better than anyone, but even he had no idea why he took his life. I assured the lieutenant that he was blameless in the matter. That's the worst part of this tragedy. We all feel a weight of guilt but only Our Father in Heaven can read the young man's soul.

As always, writing to you has cleared my head and eased my heart. I can now see a way of cheering the men's spirits. I shall tell you whether or not it is successful.

You are ever in my thoughts. May God keep you safe, dearest wife.

Henry

Chapter 15

Aboard *HMS Porcupine*, the same day

Captain Otter wasn't the only man unable to sleep that night. Lieutenant Tom Masters flung himself from side to side on his bunk. One of the officers sharing his cabin half woke and groaned. So Tom forced himself to stay still, but his mind kept heaving and thrashing so much that he wished he was on watch rather than lying there. He was badly shaken by Richard's death, especially the manner of it. Yet, it was hard to put into words what the dead sailor meant to him. Not exactly a friend but rather a kindred spirit. Richard was a similar age, maybe a little older, but there was a wide gulf between them, in rank and background. Despite this they had been drawn to each other because they both saw themselves as outsiders. Both uncomfortable with the boorish ways and coarse language that broke out like a bad smell when men were crammed close together for long periods at sea. Tom had learnt at school how to hide his unease behind an affable mask and as an officer he had more leeway to be eccentric. But the ordinary sailors sniffed out any alien scent among them straight away and attacked. Was that why Richard had killed himself? Had he been plagued by his fellows? It didn't seem likely. The men knew him to be a capable sailor and they wouldn't dare to torment him when the captain valued him so much. Also, Richard had a stoical character that could shrug off irritations. "Calm yourself down and stop rocking the boat," he would say, in his placid northern accent, if voices were raised.

Now they would all be expected to carry on as usual. Officers had to set an example. Tom knew that if he looked upset there would be asides made just within earshot. Like when he first joined the ship and had sought out Richard's company too openly.

"New officer's found someone to warm his bunk for him."

"An arse . . . whoops, a bosom pal, you mean."

Tom still cringed when he remembered how the captain had warned him to keep his distance from the coxswain, "It's bad for discipline on board if there's any suspicion of friendship between officer and seaman. Not that I'm suggesting there's anything untoward going on." He looked over Tom's shoulder as he spoke. How ignorant he had been then. The trouble was he didn't have saltwater in his veins, unlike most of the others on board. His family bred clergyman, not sailors. So when Tom decided to run away to sea, the whole idea was suffused with romance and heroism. How he had loved the story of Admiral Nelson putting his telescope to his blind eye at Copenhagen so that he could honestly declare, "I see no ships." Leaving harbor in defiance of his superiors and winning the Battle of Copenhagen.

If only he had understood then that the age of naval heroes was over. All he knew from his father was the life of a country clergyman, not much money but other advantages. A place in society, a comfortable house filled with books and the leisure to pursue your interests. As the eldest son, Tom accepted his destiny. Sent away to school he found that studying came easily to him. He looked forward to going to Oxford, followed by taking Holy Orders.

Like many men in his profession, his father had sired a large brood. Five surviving children and one who had died in infancy. During his early years Tom and Emma, his closest sibling in age, had been inseparable. "Like David and Jonathan, your souls are knitted together" their mother had said of them. They spent long afternoons in the vicarage garden, playing hide-and-seek, dabbling in the stream or building hideaways in the sprawling shrubbery. When had the bond between them started to rub and fray? He could remember Emma's tight-lipped expression, how she turned away without a wave when he left home for his first term at the age of eight. But that was the way of the world, boys leaving home and girls staying behind.

It was later when he reached fourteen that he was finally torn away from his moorings. His sister Lucy at three years of age was the youngest and Tom had imagined that his parents were now much too old to produce any more offspring. All he could think about was his burgeoning, unpredictable body. He was busy either seeking solitude to release his throbbing animal instincts or feeling exhausted by guilt for succumbing to the sin of onanism yet again.

So when he came home for the long vacation that year, he was too preoccupied to take much notice of anyone else until one morning when he was walking downstairs. He saw his mother standing in the hallway, unaware of his presence. She was holding on to the banister with one hand while she leaned backward, grimacing and rubbing the small of her back. Her unguarded face looked haggard, but it was the mound of her belly that drew his horrified attention. She looked up and he managed to croak a greeting. Her creaking smile couldn't hide the sadness in her gentle hazel eyes. His own smile was a rictus as he was swamped by the red tide sweeping up from his neck to engulf his face.

"Tom, I see you're old enough to understand that there'll be a new soul joining us in the autumn. We shall all welcome him or her. Maybe Lucy will feel a little put out at first. I fear we have all spoiled her."

No words would come to his dry lips.

"It won't affect you much. You'll be away at school when I'm brought to bed. But it'll be lovely to have a new baby with us for Christmas, won't it?" She stretched out her hand toward him.

"Of course it will," was all that he could manage to say.

"I know your father and I must seem very old to you but think of Elizabeth. What was it Zacharias said when the angel Gabriel told him that she would conceive? '*I am an old man and my wife well stricken in years."* She laughed but her eyes stayed haunted.

"You should rest more and let me help you," he said.

She touched his arm, "I shall but you must apply yourself to your studies. The headmaster wrote very highly about you."

The next day Tom chanced on Joseph, the farmer's son, in the lane. They used to play together when they were younger, but now Tom found the other boy uncouth. "Come over to the yard this afternoon and you'll see something you'll enjoy," Joseph said laughing.

"Maybe, if I've nothing else to do." He sat down to read after lunch but all he could think about was the disturbing vision of Mama's belly. He decided he would go and see Joseph after all but as he headed for the door, his father waylaid him, "Come into my study. I want to talk to you about your confirmation. Make sure you won't disgrace me in front of the bishop." He cross-examined Tom for the next hour about the Ten Commandments and the Creed. As Tom stumbled over explaining the nature of the Trinity his father removed his spectacles, tossing them down among his papers.

"Your thoughts seem to be wool gathering today, my boy. I hope you perform better than this for the masters at school or they'll think you a dull fellow. We'll try again tomorrow."

Released and resentful, Tom ran up to the farmyard, arriving breathless to find Joseph in the stable where Daisy, his father's mare was tethered, scuffling her hooves in the straw.

"You're keen not to miss anything then," Joseph grinned through snagged teeth. "Here he comes." He nodded toward his father, Jim, a wiry man holding onto a straining stallion. The beast's black coat was slathered with sweat, his eyes rolling and his nostrils wide.

"He's keen as mustard." Joseph nudged Tom in the ribs. "Just look at that." He pointed at the horse's engorged penis which throbbed as if it wanted to tear itself free from its owner.

"Get on with the job. Have you tied her back legs?" Jim

snarled at his son. The mare struggled against her bonds and danced as if the straw was on fire. Tom didn't know if it was fear or excitement that affected her as Joseph hobbled her hind legs before tugging her tail to one side. Jim pushed the stallion up behind the mare and grasped the rigid organ, guiding it until it was buried in the mare's flesh. Tom's eyes were transfixed on the mating. When it was over, Jim backed the trembling stallion away and Joseph whispered, "That's how we do it too, didn't you know? Only you don't need someone there to hold your cock. It'll find its own way."

Despite the distaste he felt at what he had witnessed, Tom could feel his own organ bulging against his breeches. Did his mother who never raised her voice in anger, shake and snort like Daisy? As for his father in the stallion's role, he refused to let his mind consider that at all.

It was a relief to return to school in the autumn and immerse himself in his studies. Sometimes though fear would ambush him. He knew from overheard conversations that childbirth was dangerous. The only birth he had seen was the arrival of Daisy's first foal, two years before. He had watched in amazement as the mare's flanks rippled and pulsed. How could the foal ever make its way out of such a narrow opening without tearing poor Daisy apart? All had ended well as the miniature hooves surfaced. Gangling front legs and a sleek head followed until finally the whole body slid out. He and Joseph had hugged each other and jigged around the stable in delight. Then, they suddenly both felt foolish and sprang apart to cuff each other around the head instead.

He was bent over his books in the library on a blustery November evening when he was interrupted by the sound of a throat clearing behind him. Irritated, he looked up to see Banks Minor's wary face. "I'm s-sorry . . ." he stammered.

Tom rolled his eyes in annoyance. "Spit it out, idiot."

"You're to go to the Headm—"

Chapter 16

Aboard *HMS Porcupine*, the same day

Tom strode across the grass, kicking up the shriveled leaves so that they flurried around him. He pushed the door of the headmaster's study open before remembering to knock. The room smelled of coal, tobacco, and dusty books. There was Mr. Bartlett sitting at his desk looking as imperious as ever. That was surely a good sign but when the headmaster rose and guided him to a chair, Tom felt his legs buckle.

"Ah, Thomas, it would be best if you read this letter I've received from your father."

Tom's hand shook as he took it. Why had the headmaster called him "Thomas"? The masters never used first names. The words skidded across the page as his eyes tried to follow them. He had to scan it several times before he could catch the meaning. "Both dead?" He croaked.

Mr. Bartlett nodded and spoke. Although Tom saw his lips moving, he couldn't hear the words. He stayed numb as he traveled home by coach to his family. He had become both deaf and dumb. He couldn't look at his father at all. His eyes skittered away. Tom believed that if he held his father's gaze, his rage would kindle a flame that would set them both alight. Trudging with bowed head across the churchyard on the day of the funeral, all he could see were the leaves turned to a sullen sludge beneath his feet.

How could it be God's will to take his dearly beloved daughter to Him? What had caused her to die struggling to bring her seventh child into the world? It was his father's will, not God's, his father's heedless lust that condemned her to death. His father who was always proclaiming how man should have dominion over the world and all the beasts within it. What a hypocrite.

How was he different from the sweating, rutting stallion?

He kept these questions boiling inside him. When he returned to school, he remained mostly silent. The only person he could speak to was his mathematics master, a retired naval captain who allowed Tom's distress to splash against him without flinching. A distant speck on the horizon drew closer until it became a plan. He would leave school and become a midshipman. Then he would never have to return to his father's hearth. Tom found to his surprise that he could stay afloat in the face of his father's angry opposition. "I'll save you the expense of the university, Father. You need to pay for a nursemaid and housekeeper now."

But his father kept up a bombardment of arguments until Tom finally said, "I cannot take Holy Orders when I doubt the existence of God. If you won't let me join as an officer, I shall go to sea as a common sailor."

In the end his father stopped roaring. He became listless, stuck in the doldrums. Tom, however, felt no compassion for him and left home without a backward glance. Long voyages created the distance from his family that he craved. His mathematical abilities meant that he found it easy to learn the skills of navigation. He sent money back to help educate his younger siblings, but he didn't visit them. Now twelve years later, he knew too well that his choice of profession hadn't lived up to his gold-braided, silver-buttoned dreams. There were few thrills and much tedium. In the early days, he had been forced to coarsen his speech and use his fists against the older men who preyed on boyish flesh. Ashore, his fastidiousness kept him away from the women of the streets. He flirted with young women of his own class but kept them at arm's length.

There were compensations, though. He enjoyed the exacting task of producing charts under the captain's benign guidance. But most of all, he relished the flux and flow of the sea, especially in these volatile Hebridean waters where a heat shimmering sky would suddenly darken into a leaden scowl.

He approved of the captain's insistence on accurate place names: *Camus Ban, Loch Eadar Da Bhaile, Eilean Tioram*. He was disappointed to find out that they were literal descriptions: "White Beach," "The Lake Between Two Villages," and "Dry Island." As a sailor, he understood the need for accuracy, but as a lover of the Romantic Poets he would have preferred some Celtic mystery. He kept a few slim volumes of poetry hidden among his belongings and he had most of their contents by heart. His favorite was Wordsworth's elegy for the unknown girl:

Whate'er the theme, the maiden sang
As if her song could have no ending;
I saw her singing at her work,
And o'er the sickle bending;-
I listened, motionless and still;
And, as I mounted up the hill,
The music in my heart I bore,
Long after it was heard no more.

Maybe he might yet find his own Highland lass? Hearing young women talking in a tongue he couldn't understand added to their mystique. Since the captain had started sending him out to check place names, he had learned a little Gaelic which he presented with his most winning smile. Sadly, those he approached would smile in return, bob a curtsey and then direct him to some dried-up old husk of a minister to translate further for him.

Since Richard's death, Tom had felt like a sail being torn from the mast in heavy seas. After the subdued service in the plain little chapel, they walked over beyond the churchyard where Richard's grave was dug ready for his coffin. Tom wondered if his friend would be lonely buried by himself or whether he would be glad of the solitude. He could feel tears escaping, not just tears for Richard but all the captive tears imprisoned since Mama's death. He was grateful for the sharp wind that watered everyone's eyes. The captain stood firm as a mast, except for a tremor in his hands as he clenched them together behind his back.

Why, why, why? was the cry carried on the wind. As the minister reached the words about dust to dust and ashes to ashes, Tom longed to clap his hands over his ears. How could warm flesh chill, decay, and disappear? For a long time, he couldn't believe that Mama was no more because he had been away when she died. When he returned home, he expected to hear her quickening step as he came through the door. This time he had seen the body. The terrible grinning slash across the throat. But no sense of why he died. What had driven Richard to such despair? Despair that made him hold the blade prickling his skin? Ramming it so that it ripped his flesh open?

Tom flinched from the sound of earth thudding on the coffin lid and turned his gaze down the slope toward the shore. There was someone standing there, watching them. Someone draped in black with the head cowled. Without stopping to think, he found himself running down the path. The figure backed away, stumbling and falling forward. The scarf slipped, revealing a flash of auburn hair and the pale oval of a woman's face. He seized her arm, "You know him? The sailor who died?"

She stared at him. He dropped his hand, shocked that he had accosted her. He gulped at her beauty. Creamy skin taut over her cheekbones, the full lips and especially the green-blue eyes, flecked with hazel. He whispered, "Why were you watching us?"

She shook her head again and then she was darting away, holding up her long skirts in one hand. Should he follow her? The other mourners were coming toward him. The moment was lost and he waited for them to reach him. The captain raised an inquiring eyebrow.

"That young woman was watching us, sir. I wondered if she knew something about poor Williams but she ran away."

"We will never find out why Williams took his own life. We must put the sorry affair behind us. Get the men busy again." Captain Otter strode on with the others following in his wake.

But lying restless in his bunk that night, Tom knew that he couldn't let things rest. The imprint of her face was everywhere he looked, shadowed on every wave, cloud, and rock. He had to see her again. He mouthed the words he knew so well.

A voice so thrilling n'er was heard,

In Spring time from the cuckoo bird,

Breaking the silence of the seas

Among the furthest Hebrides.

Chapter 17

Aboard *HMS Porcupine*, 1861

HMS Porcupine lay at anchor off Kyleakin. The sudden tides ripped through the narrow crossing to the mainland and needed careful navigation. Rather like dealing with his jittery crew, Captain Otter thought. Once the funeral was over he had been anxious to leave Portree with all its grim associations. So on the pretext of testing the engines, he had ordered full steam ahead southward. He was determined to use the new charts too, the ones that Williams had gathered soundings for. As he looked at the stiff paper, he pictured the coxswain in his small boat. Checking the line as it was hauled back aboard. When he was engrossed in a task, he would tweak his brows together and a sliver of tongue would peep from his mouth. A gush of rage swept through Henry. He wanted to screw up the charts and hurl them out to sea. How could a man who was so measured destroy himself so brutally? Instead, he went out on deck. As he strode up and down, he decided to summon the crew at once and tell them what he planned. They began with a ragged singing of, "For those in peril on the sea," accompanied by Billy's gasping squeezebox. His notes slurred and tripped over each other even more than usual. Then Henry waited for the shuffling to cease. He felt the wind ruffling across his face and watched the shards of winter sun piercing the water. He was composing himself to speak when Lieutenant Rogers sidled up. Henry checked a sigh as he leaned down to catch the words.

"Sir, there's no sign of Lieutenant Masters. He missed his watch and his belongings have gone."

Henry's right eyelid twitched. "No cause for alarm, Rogers. He's undertaking a task ashore. It must have taken longer than expected."

Rogers nodded, but there was a glint in his eye.

Why did I lie? Henry reproached himself. He smothered his doubts about Masters and spoke, "Where we are anchored today was once the scene of a great gathering. Seven hundred years ago, King Haakon of Norway brought his battle fleet of long ships here before heading south to fight the Scottish king. Haakon lost the battle of Largs. So all these western and northern islands became part of the Scottish kingdom and later part of Great Britain. The name *Kyleakin* comes from Haakon. It's also said that a Norwegian princess once owned the harbor here. It's claimed she put chains across the channel to the mainland so that boats would have to pay her a toll. Of course, it would not be possible to carry out such a feat of engineering in those distant times. It would scarcely be possible even now with our greater knowledge—"

"Yes, young Norton, I can see you kicking the fellow next to you," he roared at one of the midshipmen. The boy squirmed to avoid a cuff from the bosun standing behind him. Henry continued: "These stories remind us of how important our work is. By charting the seas we make them safer for all shipping. The sea is a treacherous ally to us all, whether we sail in naval vessels, in merchant ships, or in fishing boats. We help all those who go down to the sea and do business in the great waters. We shall never know why our shipmate Richard Williams took his own life. It's a matter he will need to lay before his Maker. What we do know is that he was a steadfast sailor who did his duty without complaint. When our survey of these islands is over, we shall leave knowing we have completed a vital and historic task. We should also pay tribute to that other great benefactor of the sailor, the Northern Lighthouse Board. Their engineers have battled against the elements to build lighthouses. We shall go to visit one of them, on the island of Rona. Those who have served for a longer time on this vessel will know how a lighthouse came to be built there. Through the courage and determination of an exceptional lady, Mrs. Kenneth MacKenzie from Big Harbour. Over twenty years ago her husband, her son, and other poor souls were drowned in sight of the shore. She turned her grief into philanthropy by obtaining oil to keep a lamp burning in her window. Many vessels owe their safety to that light. I had the honor of meeting this lady. We shall meet her again when we visit the island. First we shall bend our heads in prayer."

Steaming out on a calm sea with a brisk following wind, the ship turned north to follow the coast of Skye. It traced the line of the outstretched finger of Raasay until they reached Rona, the nail at its tip. When they came to the lighthouse, standing white against the rocks, the captain and Rogers were rowed ashore.

Last time I came over with Masters, Williams was at the oars, Henry thought. To distract himself from doleful memories, he gazed at the lighthouse. It was an odd life being a lighthouse keeper, suspended between land and water. Was a lighthouse a ship that had taken root on land? Or a tower forever wading up to its knees in the sea? He supposed that the lighthouse was like seaweed, part of both worlds. Anchored to rocks on the shore but doused by every tide.

He felt jovial as he lunched with the keepers. He even forgot about Masters's absence until he caught Rogers eyeing him. He would have to notify the Admiralty if the lieutenant failed to return tomorrow.

Back on the ship, they headed for Big Harbour. Widow MacKenzie's house looked as sturdy as before. He rapped on the door and after some scrabbling sounds inside, it creaked open.

"Dè? Cò suid?" ("What? Who's there?") Thin lips in a wizened face appeared. Then the door was slammed shut and he could hear muttering from inside. The door cracked open again, revealing another gnarled and suspicious face, but this time belonging to a woman. She eased the door partly open.

If only they had Masters and his easy manner. Henry bowed and smiled until the old woman pushed the door fully open. The old man scuttled away, cradling something in his arms. She didn't invite them inside. Instead, she partnered him in a game of mime as they struggled to understand each other. It was like a strange mating ritual by a cumbersome pair of birds. He gathered from her that Janet MacKenzie had left across the sea. These newcomers had taken over her tenancy. Finally, she conveyed to him that if he wanted more information he should speak to those of Janet's family who were living at Torran, on Raasay. Being a man who liked to follow things through Henry ordered the ship south again, past the spattering of skerries between the two islands.

He braced himself for more undignified miming but was relieved to find himself talking to Janet's granddaughter, Jeannie. She spoke English slowly but fluently while keeping an eye on a flotilla of small children cruising around her feet. She hooted at his astonished face.

"My Granny insisted that all the family learn English and I shall teach it to my children so they can make themselves understood if they travel away. Kenneth, my husband, fears that the tides of English will sweep Gaelic aside. But I agree with Granny. You need to understand strangers so that you know what they're up to."

"You think the English always mean to trick you?"

She hesitated, politeness and honesty struggling for mastery of her face. "Sometimes but not always. There's bad Scottish landlords as well as bad English ones."

"I'm a sailor, a chart maker, not a landlord. I came to see your estimable grandmother but I believe she has emigrated."

"Aye, to Canada. Did you speak to the MacKinnons, the new tenants at Big Harbour? He's a mad *bodach*. You're lucky he didn't bring out his old musket he kept from when he was fighting the French."

"Ah, I believe he did bring it out but his wife made him take it away. She was the one who negotiated peace with the enemy," he smiled.

She nodded, still wary.

"I truly regret missing your grandmother. I am saddened to see so many Highlanders leaving their native land."

"Aye. She at least could choose where to go, not like those poor souls Rainey drove out. One of them said to me, 'It'll be like death for us sailing away. We'll never meet those left behind again in this life.'

They were silent for a moment.

"Still, at least Granny can write to us."

"Will you emigrate, too?"

"No, we won't be seed blown away on the wind."

Henry went back on board with a lighter step. Jeannie had her grandmother's direct way of speaking and the same tilt of the chin. He would tell the men how, undeterred by advancing years, Mrs. MacKenzie had embarked on a new adventure. If only Masters would return quickly, they would be back on an even keel.

Chapter 18

Isle of Raasay, 1861

Jeannie stood watching the *HMS Porcupine* steam toward the open sea and raised her hand in a half-wave. She turned as she heard Kenneth running up to her and smiled, "Don't worry. They've gone. And they won't be back. Mama and Granny would be horrified that I didn't offer them a dish of tea."

"Thank goodness you didn't. They would have been here forever."

They waited until the ship was out of sight before walking arm-in-arm toward the byre, next to their house. Kenneth unlatched the door, breathing in the damp fug of cows' breath and fetid hay. There was a rustle from the far corner as a tall figure rose, looming over the backs of the beasts. He stood, brushing dirt from his trousers with a grimace of distaste. Kenneth beckoned him over.

"And here I was imagining I would be safe while the ship sailed to the mainland," he laughed.

"They weren't looking for you," Jeannie snapped. "They came to get news of my grandmother."

"Thank you for not giving me away," he said in a more contrite tone. "And for the food and clothes."

"I don't believe in helping those in charge, whether they're captains or landowners. You can come back inside the house again."

"Have you thought any more about who the young woman might be?" he asked as he gulped down soup in front of the fire. "No one on Skye would tell me anything except one woman who said she thought she had left the island."

"Well that's likely what's happened then."

"Ask him what he's planning to do now," Kenneth prompted

his wife. "If he's thinking of going south it would be safer not to head straight for Glasgow. He should go to Argyll where they won't be looking for him."

She translated. "That's sound advice. I could find work there until the hue and cry dies down."

"You can stay here until early tomorrow. Kenneth will take you over to Knoydart, on the mainland. Then you must fend for yourself."

Later that night, husband and wife lay in bed while their children slept.

"I can't help feeling sorry for him. A lost soul," said Kenneth.

Jeannie snorted. "You're too soft-hearted. No one forced him to leave his ship."

"Aye, but I can remember what it's like being on your own and pining for a girl you've fallen in love with," he said, as he squeezed her hand.

She chuckled in the darkness. "But you didn't run away like the *sasannach*. You stood up to Granny. Come on, let's get to sleep."

Kenneth stretched his legs out under the blankets. He turned toward his wife. "You think he doesn't deserve her? That's why you wouldn't tell him who the mysterious girl might be?"

She gasped.

"I always know when you're hiding something."

"Well, I do have an idea who she is. But I won't have him toying with her. Let him struggle to win her."

"You're a hard taskmaster, as you were with me."

"Well it did you no harm."

"No, having to prove myself made my reward all the sweeter." He reached his arm around her waist. "Who do you think the girl is?"

"I don't know for sure. So I'll keep it to myself." She kissed him to draw out the sting of her refusal.

"You're no Flora MacDonald helping the fugitive, are you?"

"No, but he's no prince either. Now, let's forget about the wretched man."

Chapter 19

West Highlands, 1861

Tom was a skilled navigator at sea, but on land he was fumble footed. His muscles and sinews creaked with the effort of clambering over rock, moor, and bog for hours on end. Even worse were the tangled woods that snared his legs when he couldn't see the fall of the land beneath his feet. He stayed near sea or loch side as much as possible so that he could follow the outlines he recognized from charting them earlier. Often though he was forced further inland to avoid boats or buildings on the shore. He woke shivering every morning, his hands shaking after a snatched sleep in an abandoned house or damp bothy. Still Kenneth's advice about not taking the obvious route was sound. Tom had left the ship with no plan except a wild hope of finding the magical stranger. In his fogged state of mind, he had paid a fisherman to take him over to Raasay. Too late he had realized he was in danger of arrest for jumping ship. But surely he would be safe hiding on the smaller island? The captain would expect him to aim for the mainland? When he saw the *Porcupine* dropping anchor off the north end he thought it was an apparition, a ghost ship conjured up by his terrified mind. He crashed into the woods where he had startled Kenneth who was setting rabbit traps. Tom felt less worried now about any pursuit, but his small stock of money was dribbling away in payment for food and shelter. When he stopped at isolated houses he was usually given something. The food offered was sparse, a dish of boiled potatoes, with maybe a few shellfish, coarse oatcakes or porridge with a splash of watery milk. At least it filled his belly. He asked for whisky too, *uisge beatha,* the water of life. One surly old fellow pretended not to understand and gave him a pitcher of brackish water instead.

In six days he had walked through Knoydart, along Loch Morar and Loch Shiel, and was heading down Loch Linne, avoiding the garrison town of Fort William. The last night of his wanderings had been the worst yet. The pinched-faced woman of the house where he stopped brought him a platter of shriveled, pockmarked potatoes. Two children with bare, blue-tinged feet clung to her skirt. All three of them were as scrawny as the puny hens poking around the tumbledown dwelling. Faint with hunger he wrenched the plate from her hands and crammed the food into his mouth. He spun around when he sensed a movement behind him and there were the children watching, famished eyes bulging. The younger one drooled like a hungry dog. He shouted at them until they scurried away.

He woke long before daybreak in the cold byre, in the thick smother of darkness. He stuffed his fist into his mouth to stifle a cry of terror. The damp air reeked like a midden. His groping hand rubbed the coarse hair of a cow. Relief made him whimper. He had dreamt he was back in that stable again. The stallion had approached him, snickering though swollen nostrils. He stroked the muscular neck but then suddenly the beast knocked him backward and straddled him. Breath steaming and teeth bared. Was it about to trample him or, perish the thought, mount him?

As his breathing slowed, he felt a gush of shame as he thought about the evening before. He had eaten at the expense of those starving children. What sort of savage was he turning into? What was he doing anyway, blundering through the wilderness? As the miles unraveled behind him, he berated himself for abandoning ship. He was a fugitive now, a beggar and for what? One glimpse of a vision of beauty that had made him mad with longing. A stranger whose face he recognized? A woman who held the answer to Richard's death? Those were the gusts that had driven him out from the harbor on this quest. But now he was left stranded by doubts. How could he hope to find her when he didn't even know her name? He could draw her likeness but it was so difficult trying to talk to people when he couldn't understand them. If only he had a dram to warm him up and stop the shaking. He hadn't bothered to ask that wraith of a woman last night. Or a tot of rum would do as well. Tom remembered how Richard used to stand apart when the rest of the crew waited for their daily rum ration. Tom had teased him about his refusal to take his tot. "I won't let a drop pass my lips. It turns men into devils."

Tom shrugged. He was responsible for dispensing the rum and he drank Richard's share rather than letting it go to waste. Then one day the captain gave the task of distribution to that sly Rogers instead. The loathsome fellow smirked. "The captain knows he can trust me." The events of the last few weeks had tangled themselves together in his mind. Was it before or after that business with Rogers that he received the letter? The harbormaster at Stornoway had given it to him when they anchored there. He had ripped it open with a feeling of dread.

Dearest Brother,

I'm writing to convey the sad news of Papa's death. I know that you have not seen him for many years but it's right that you should know the manner of his passing. After Mama died he was weighed down with grief and left most of his parish duties to his curate.

"Serves him right," Tom thought. The hypocrite caused her death.

He always hoped that he would see you again and make his peace with you. His quick temper hid a kind heart.

Maybe you saw his kindness, but I was always expected to live the life he had mapped out for me.

The rest of the family have missed you. I'm married now with two children and have had time to reflect on the married state. Our parents were a devoted couple, as people say about our Queen and Prince Albert. Motherhood, with its joys and risks, is a natural consequence of marriage. Childbirth is always perilous. That I'm afraid is the way of the world.

I hope I haven't offended you in writing so plainly. I trust you will reply or even better visit us when next you have leave from your duties.

I speak for all your brothers and sisters when I make this plea. Lucy in particular longs to see you. She can just remember her tall, handsome brother who swung her in his arms and made her laugh when he was home from school. She's a spirited young lady now of sixteen years and has instructed me to command your presence. She declares that if she had been born a boy she would join the Navy herself and track you down.

Your fond sister, Emma.

Remembering the letter made him groan as if his heart were being squeezed. The idea had rooted in his mind that maybe one day he would see his family again. Now in the dark byre he faced the truth and wept. How could he ever go back to see them? He was a fugitive who would face court martial and disgrace if caught. He couldn't risk it. Home was a mirage just like the beautiful woman had been. He had run away to sea and then with even less thought, run away back to land.

Chapter 20

West Highlands, 1861

Exhausted, Tom dozed and awoke with the dawn. Finding the woman of the house, he pressed most of his remaining coins into her surprised hand. He stepped out again and toward noon noticed in the distance a cluster of houses ahead on a rise of land. He walked toward them, slowing his pace as he came closer. Blind charred sockets showed where the thatch had been burnt. There were tumbled, sagging walls. The settlement looked as if it had been raided by an army and left to rot. There was no sign of life apart from the scuffling of small creatures in the rank grass sprouting through gaping doorways. He hurried on, trying to outrun the fog of desperation that swirled around the ruins. He felt as bleak and empty as the abandoned settlement, terrified that like Richard he would become entangled in the coils of despair. In his panic he hunted for signs of hope around him. The forest trees—birch, ash, and alder—were stark skeletons but they held the promise of spring sap in their marrow. He vowed that he too would hold on until the spring. If only his mind could outrun the storm to some sort of harbor. What could he remember about this landscape from the stories the captain insisted on telling them? Stories that made them want to roll their eyes and stop up their ears.

"People have lived for hundreds or thousands of years in these remote places. To you they might seem barren and insignificant, but they have been steeped in history and legend. So we must record the place names accurately." The captain spoke with religious fervour. Tom lay down in a hollow on the forest floor and closed his eyes as he tried to recollect the tales.

There was the tale about the Dog Stone below Dunollie Castle on the edge of Oban Bay. It was said that it was worn away at its base because Finn McCoul's mighty dog, Bran, had been tethered there. He had pulled and strained, dragging his leash along the rock and rubbing it away in his struggle to escape.

Then there was the Lady Rock on Mull, named after the wife of the Duart chief, the evil Lachlan Cathanach MacLean. His wife failed to produce the desired son and heir. So he planned to rid himself of her. She was rowed over to the rock and left to drown in the incoming tide. However, she was seen by a passing fishing boat, rescued and put ashore on the mainland. She made her way to her family home at Inveraray Castle. Unaware of what had happened, her cruel husband arranged her funeral service and spilled tears of pretended grief. Despite his wickedness he escaped retribution but fate caught up with him in the end. His vigilant brother-in-law, John Campbell, waited his chance and killed the chief when he visited Edinburgh, some years later.

The midshipmen enjoyed that story. Justice of the Old Testament variety was always satisfying. But Tom preferred the tale of *An Clach na Leannan* about another rock, this time on the west coast of Mull. It was named after young lovers. A hundred and fifty years earlier, a young shepherd called Iain lived on the flat land beneath the high cliffs. He was to be married to Rona, a daughter of the local blacksmith. The wedding celebrations lasted through the night at the farmhouse. With all the jollity inside, no one noticed the fuming waves and the furious storm. No one noticed either when the young couple joined hands and slipped away to their new home, a tiny house nearby, sheltered under the overhanging outcrop. The next morning the guests staggered out from the farmhouse, blinking in the light and clutching their sore heads. As they looked upward they stared in horror at what had happened, unbeknownst to them during the night. The sheltering roof of the rock had been wrenched apart by a barrage of stone that had tumbled down onto it during the fury of the storm. One huge fragment had hurtled down to crush the small dwelling and the young couple within. It was much too heavy to move so their bodies remained entombed beneath it.

"That's only a story, isn't it, sir?" one of the bolder midshipmen had piped up.

The captain had glowered at him, "Stories are not to be dismissed. They tell us important truths and as it happens this particular one is true. It occurred recently enough to leave grim evidence behind. The broken ends of the rafters can still be seen jutting out from under the rock."

Raised like arms in supplication, Tom had thought. Had Richard too met some terrible fate when he went ashore, one that crushed him before he could ask for help? But the tale had other meanings too. You must seize your chance of happiness when you can because it might be snatched away from you. The young woman he met in such odd circumstances was pointing a new, uncharted direction to him. He had raised his anchor, put away his compass, and headed out on a featureless ocean.

Chapter 21

Oban, 1861

Tom awoke with a chilled body but a clear head. He set off again, pressing on through the woods until he stopped by a stream where he squatted down and cupped his hands into the achingly cold water. He drank his fill and then watched it trickle through his fingers. Taking his pack off his shoulders, he felt a soft lump in one corner and found a squashed linen bag of oatmeal. Of course! He had forgotten that it was left over from the supply an old woman had given him a few days ago. He scooped up some more water in his hands and mixed it with the oats. Cramming the gritty paste into his mouth, he licked every crumb from his fingers.

Then he sat down with his back against a mottled birch trunk. Its branches were bare spikes grasped by gloved fingers of green lichen, a ghostly imitation of leaves. He rummaged through his pack again and took out a piece of oilskin. Inside it was a sheet of paper, as creased and crumpled as he was himself after his rough traveling. He had stuffed the paper into his pack when he fled from the ship, wondering if he might use it to write to Emma. That was out of the question now but he could put the paper to a different purpose. He rested the sheet on the pack and balanced it all on his knees. He closed his eyes to conjure up her image. It was a sculpted face with a high forehead and cheekbones, tapering to a delicate chin. Expressive lips, blue eyes flecked around the iris in woodland shades of acorn or hazelnuts. The flash of hair he had glimpsed under her scarf was a glorious reddish chestnut. He couldn't capture the colors with charcoal, but he could make a likeness to show people. He drew deftly. Holding the paper at arm's length, he was pleased that he had recovered his sure hand.

After rolling up the sheet and covering it with the oilcloth in his bag, he strode out again toward Oban. He remembered when they had surveyed the wide bay the captain said that the harbor formed almost a complete horseshoe. Tom, however, saw it as a wide mouthful that the greedy sea had bitten from the shore, spitting out a large crumb in the form of the island of Kerrera. He arrived at the village in the dark and found a reeking fishermen's shed to spend the night. Then at first light, he scouted the shore. He noticed a group of women sitting on the sea wall looking out to the water. As he came closer he could smell them. Their sailcloth aprons and fishermen's ganseys were spattered and smeared with fish scales. He had his portrait ready in his hand and strolled toward them, fixing his eyes on a bold-looking woman who seemed to be their leader. With a mixture of sign language and a few Gaelic words, he explained his mission. She took the paper in her raw beefy hands while scrutinising him from head to toe, her eyes lingering on the fork of his trousers. He could feel his face reddening and fixed his eyes on the flashing knitting needles of her companions. Their fingers were swollen and scored with cuts. He held his breath, partly in anticipation and partly to stop himself choking on the stench of putrid fish that surrounded them. They passed the picture along the row with much giggling. Eventually a younger woman spoke in hesitant English, "We don't know her. Is she your love?"

He nodded, feeling foolish.

"If she's a fisher lass she could be anywhere the herring are."

The woman he had first spoken to muttered something in Gaelic that set off hoots of laughter from the rest.

"She's saying she'll have you if you're free," the younger woman told him.

"Tell her she would be my first choice if I were." He smiled and made a sweeping bow.

One of the women shouted and pointed out to sea where several fishing boats were coming into shore. The clicking needles stopped and they were off, rolling up sleeves over brawny arms and running to the rows of wooden troughs for gutting the herring. Tom stood watching them and failed to notice the figure darting up behind him. He was lifted off his feet by a heavy grip on the back of his collar. His legs kicked from under him, he was pushed forward until he fell on his face on the shingle. He curled into a ball to protect himself.

"Leave him alone or I'll have the law on you."

Tom's attacker, a wiry fisherman, padded away. His rescuer, a tall, angular man, gripped him under his arms and hauled him upright. "Are you hurt?"

Tom froze. The first glimpse he had of his rescuer was of his polished boots and dark pressed trousers. He was certain the man was wearing a uniform. Slowly he straightened himself and breathed with relief at the sight of an ordinary dark jacket.

"No, just winded. Thank you for coming to my assistance, sir."

"The fishermen lash out if they think you're sniffing around their womenfolk. I can't imagine anyone would want to get near them in those stinking clothes. I'm Alexander Sinclair, an Aberdonian by birth. You're English by the sound of you?"

Tom took the proffered hand. "I am indeed. Tom Masters at your service."

"So what brings you here?"

"Oh . . . a family matter."

Sinclair's eyes were probing but his tone was mild. "If you don't need any further help . . . ?"

"I'm looking for work."

"Can you sail?"

"A little."

"Well, I could do with another hand aboard. A cutter's coming in soon and we're off after a consignment of illegal whisky."

"You're an excise man?"

"Aye. Maybe yon fisherman thought you were one, too." He

scrutinized Tom again.

"Of course, that would make sense." Tom smiled.

"Mmm. I've had word a boat's setting out to Tiree. Sailing the longer way, southwest around Mull to put us off the scent. Be ready in a few minutes."

Tom nodded. After Sinclair had gone he walked along to a more secluded part of the shore and waded into the sea to clean himself. When he returned the cutter was waiting, a spare thoroughbred of a vessel, rocking at anchor as if eager for the chase. Tom nodded to the five other crew members but took care to say little. A brisk wind was behind them and there was soon plenty to do, setting a course and unfurling the sails. He was relieved that some of the other sailors were topmen. He hadn't climbed rigging since his days as a midshipman. As they rounded the southern corner of Mull, he remembered how the captain had explained about St. Columba's arrival on the nearby island of Iona. He had been given his name as a joke, for he was more eagle than dove.

"Rather like Little John, sir, in the tales of Robin Hood," Tom had said.

"The very same idea," Captain Otter replied before relating how the future saint had been banished from his native Ireland for starting a quarrel that led to a fierce battle and loss of lives. "A typical Irishman!" the captain had roared.

Columba's punishment was exile. He was ordered to settle somewhere where he could no longer see his homeland. At first he stayed in Kintyre, but he found that if he climbed a hill he could still see Ireland in the distance. So he traveled onto Iona and founded his monastery there instead.

Tom felt a wrench of guilt when he remembered the captain. He was a considerate man, not a martinet or bully. The father Tom would have liked to have. He imagined the captain sitting in his cabin, rifling through recent events in his mind. To a rational man like Captain Otter, his desertion would make no sense. It didn't make much sense to Tom himself. But like Columba, Tom couldn't turn back.

They continued up the west coast, passing Ulva and other smaller islands clustered around Mull. Poking the ship's snout into every bay in case their prey had beached their boat. But there was no sign of the skiff. At last the cutter pointed northward into open water toward the island of Tiree. They all scanned the horizon but Tom was the first to see the distant sail, a feather flickering on the horizon.

"Well done, Englishman. That's the skiff. They'll make a dash for it. We can outrun them but we'll need every scrap of sail to do it," Sinclair grinned showing yellow, wolfish teeth.

So they spurred the cutter to her limit. Her sails swelled and strained against the rigging. The foaming spray at her prow bubbled like the breath of a galloping horse. Tom remembered fox hunts in the landlocked county of Warwickshire where he grew up. He had clung to the neck of his father's mare as they pounded over fields and soared over hedges. But he could also remember looking away as the spent fox cowered, waiting for the hounds to tear it to shreds. "What will happen to them?" he asked Sinclair.

"The scunners will go to prison. Hard labor is what they deserve. I need a closer look at that vessel."

Tom felt in his jacket pocket but stopped his fingers just in time as they circled the cold metal. Instead, he waited for Sinclair to take out his own telescope.

"Here, have a look." He handed the spyglass to Tom.

It was a good instrument. Tom could make out three men aboard the skiff. The chase continued with the cutter gaining ground.

"Can they escape?"

"Not now. There's nowhere to hide before Tiree itself. I doubt they could outrun us if they carry on to the Outer Isles."

The skiff turned in toward Tiree and disappeared as it sailed around the southern point of the island.

"We'll have them when they land in the bay." Sinclair snapped his spyglass shut.

The wind held while the cutter headed around the point. Tom remembered that Tiree differed from most of its Hebridean neighbors in being flat and fertile. The *machair,* strewn with wildflowers in the spring, reached down to the sandy bay. There was nowhere to hide a boat. As the shore came into sight, they gasped. Where was the skiff?

All they could see were the inhabitants about their usual tasks. A row of fishing boats was drawn up on the sand. Alongside the boats were a pile of lobster pots and two old men smoking clay pipes while they checked fishing nets for holes. Cattle were being herded through the *machair* by children who sang as they tapped the beasts' flanks with sticks. Beyond them were other figures spreading seaweed onto their potato patches.

"Where's the damned skiff? Get ashore and find out what's happening." Tom and the rest of the crew ran over to the boats while Sinclair interrogated the old men. All the vessels were glistening. They had been in the water recently. Some were speckled with sand where the cattle's feet had trampled close by.

"Have you seen a skiff, a boat, sailing past?" Sinclair asked the old men.

One stared open-mouthed while the other put his hand to his ear. "*Dè?* What?"

"Come over here, Masters. Can you understand their confounded language?"

Tom sprinted over. "*An robh bàta ann air a' mhuir?* Was there a boat on the sea?"

"*Bha. Bha torr bàtaichean iasgair a'seòladh,*" the old man shrugged.

"He says there were plenty of fishing boats out at sea," Tom told Sinclair.

"Ask him if they saw a boat sailing past the point."

The old man tilted his head to listen to Tom's stumbling question, "*An do sheòl bàta seachad air an rubha?* Did a boat sail around the point?"

The *bodach* removed his pipe from his mouth and spat a sticky black globule on the sand before shaking his head.

"He's lying. They'll be heading for the Outer Isles after all. Get back on board," Sinclair ordered.

The crew scampered toward the cutter. As Tom turned to follow, the old man grabbed his sleeve and started talking to him but his speech was too rapid to follow. The fisherman smiled and patted Tom's arm. So off they set again. Sinclair ordered the crew to continue even if it meant sailing through the night. They would follow the coast of the Outer Isles from the south northward, scrutinizing every harbor on their way. The wind still favored them but Sinclair's temper worsened as they found no trace of their quarry in Barra or the Uists. He stopped pacing up and down the deck to confront Tom. "Tell me again what that old fool said to you."

"Nothing, except for that last speech I couldn't follow."

"There's something fishy here. When we get to Stornoway, I'll hand you over to the authorities. We'll get to the bottom of it." He turned to bellow at the bosun, "Make sure he's watched all the time."

Tom clenched his fists but stayed quiet. He was terrified of being arrested but inwardly rejoicing at the thought of the people of Tiree toasting each other with the illicit whisky. What a clever plan it was to hide in plain view what you wanted to keep secret. The boats had all looked the same, all soaked in seawater. The sand had been churned up by the cattle so that no marks showed where the whisky-laden skiff had been hauled ashore. Where had they hidden the drink? Among the nets he suspected. They had worked very fast but they hadn't allowed for Tom's keen eyesight. When he walked along the line of boats, he had noticed the letters *EA* painted on the side of one of them. He remembered squinting down the telescope earlier and reading the skiff's name, *Eala*, or "Swan." He hadn't understood the old man's words but he had heard the plea to keep their secret safe, as had Sinclair.

Chapter 22

Stornoway, 1861

Without intending to, Tom dozed fitfully during the hours he waited, sitting propped up against a mast and watched over by a succession of crew members. Each time he awoke it was with a start. How was he going to escape? His only chance would be when they neared land, perhaps while the crew was busy mooring the ship. He tried to remember the chart of Stornoway Harbor. Like Big Harbour on Rona, it had a lurking dragon at its entrance. Here were the rocks known as the Beasts of Holm. The lighthouse had been built at Arnish, ten years ago. It was a white, iron tower, bitterly cold the keepers complained. Alan Stevenson, Thomas's brother and fellow engineer, had made an ingenious reflecting beacon on the nearby rock shelf. It projected the beam across so that even the local fishermen swore that the light shone from the lighthouse itself.

Sinclair and the crew ignored Tom as they approached Stornoway. They knew an early escape would be too dangerous, even for a strong swimmer. I'll have to stay alert and seize my chances when we've entered the harbor, he thought. Highlanders hate the excise men. So maybe they'll help me escape.

As the crew coaxed the cutter into the neck of the inner harbour, the youngest hand came and stood over Tom. He was a slight fellow, still in his teens, rather insulting to post him as a guard. But then maybe that could work to his advantage?

Stornoway was a busy port. The flow of water was clotted by fishing boats, so many of them that they formed floating islands. The cutter had to pick her way between them, lifting her skirts like a lady in a muddy farmyard. Tom's jailer leaned over the side to gawp. Tom took his chance, crashing into the lad so he overbalanced. Leaping over the side and praying that the water below him was deep enough to break his fall. It was! But he was choking and stunned by the impact. He surfaced and headed toward the shore. His flailing arms reached the side of a small boat. He spluttered, "It's the excise men," and the astonished rower hauled him aboard. Tom flopped, coughing while the sailor rowed them toward the shore, scurrying between the larger vessels.

Angry roars came from the cutter. Her size impeded her, a man on stilts struggling through a crowded street. The rower reached a flock of small boats moored together close to the shore. He gestured to Tom to jump. Grinning while Tom waved his thanks and clambered aboard the first boat. Leaping from one wobbling vessel to the next, he used them as steppingstones until he was able to wade ashore.

Not safe yet. Glancing behind he saw the cutter's launch lowered already. Where was he going to hide? There were the usual harbor buildings with their clutter of carts, heaped-up barrels and men unloading cargo. Nowhere there. Farther over, he spotted the gutting tables. There were the fisher girls, their quicksilver fingers darting among the fish. He ducked behind the buildings and using the barrels as cover crept up to the women, finger to lips. One of them looked up, a greasy curl sneaking out from her kerchief. Barely stopping her work she jostled him over toward a huge trough that stank worse than anything he had ever smelled in his life. Shuddering and holding his breath, he lowered himself into the oozing mound of fish entrails. A hand pressed him down and scooped more of the foul mess over his back.

Time stood still while he lay engulfed in the slime. *What would my shipmates think if they could see me here?* He smiled to himself, then immediately closed his mouth as a rotting fin slithered against his lips. He had always been so particular over his dress, vain almost. Now he was only fit to be a hermit. But he was safe, at least for the moment.

Finally fingers, bloated with strips of bandages, tapped him on the shoulder and strong arms pulled him to his feet. His legs buckled and he was propped against a barrel. The girls laughed, holding their aprons up to their faces. He joined in the joke, lifting his sleeve to his nose and reeling back from the stench. There were two girls. The stocky one with the escaping curl introduced herself as Beathag and her slender, pale friend as Peigi. He saw with relief that the sky was darkening as they urged him to follow them. He tottered along behind their brisk steps through narrow streets behind the harbor. Soon they left behind the shops, businesses, and blacksmith's forge and walked along a pitted track toward a group of black houses. They took him to a well at the back. Beathag kept a lookout while Peigi started to pour bucket after bucket of icy water over him until he begged her to stop. Close up, he saw that beneath the grime she had the soft skin of a young woman. Shyly she stretched out her hand. "*S e lochlannach a th'annad,*" she whispered as she touched his dripping pale hair.

He smiled at being called a Viking and wished that he had a Norseman's ferocity. Then he could have tackled the crew of the cutter, laying about him with a war axe. That would have been better than lying among putrid fish.

She mimed that he should take off his soaking clothes. He removed jacket, gansey and vest but kept a tight hold on his trousers. Later, as he warmed up by the fire, she handed him a bowl of porridge. He wondered if the foul smell from the fish trough would destroy his appetite but to his surprise he felt his mouth watering.

"Manna from Heaven," he said.

The fisher girls gathered around him, smiling encouragement as if he was an orphan calf they were trying to rear. Tom decided it would be a good moment to bring out his drawing. His pack had been doused in seawater and smeared with fish innards but the paper had survived inside its oilskin wrapping. They scrutinized the drawing but then shook their heads.

Beathag explained to him how the group of girls stayed together in the house for the fishing season. He could sleep in the outhouse. They had found him some clean trousers and drawers. There was much giggling from her companions as she handed them over. She would speak tomorrow to the fishermen about a passage back to the mainland for him. It wouldn't be difficult. The story of the fair young Englishman who helped the folk on Tiree to fool the excise men had sped across the sea before him. He made a nest with some old blankets on the earth floor of the outhouse and fell into an instant sleep.

Awakening the next morning his heart plunged with fear until he recognized his surroundings. Feeling more cheerful than he had for days, he rushed outside bare-chested and sluiced himself at the well. His hair and beard still seemed greasy. So he found his razor inside the pack, rust splattered but intact. He shivered as he examined it, running his fingers along the side of the blade. He felt a pang of grief for Richard, slicing his neck open like the fisher girls split open the fish. Tom knew he could never do that. He would only use the razor for its intended purpose. He felt cleaner after his shave and hoped that a change in his appearance would make it harder for him to be recognized.

A rumbling stomach drove him into the house. He wondered about asking Beathag if she would cut his hair but the house was empty. He had no idea of the time. Had they already gone to their work? Surely they would have told him before leaving? His heart thudded as he wondered if they had betrayed him. Had they been kind so that they could lure him into a trap? He peered out of the small, bleary window but all was quiet. Tearing around the single room he sent stools flying. He kicked the black pot hanging over the fire so that it listed and spewed out porridge. After swearing and stamping through the ashes he noticed the press in the corner. He flung the doors wide. Crouching down to cram oatmeal and pieces of smoked fish into his pack.

Chapter 23

Argyll, 1861

The door scraped open and Tom swung round, fists up. There in front of him stood Beathag, Peigi and the others, staring. Red-faced he lowered his arms. Beathag shook her head and held out the Bible she had clutched in her hand.

Now that his heart had stopped banging in his ears, he saw that they were all dressed in clean, sombre black. Several of them had Bibles cradled in their raw fingers. He could barely recognize them out of their rank work clothes. Before they were anonymous but now they had become shapely young women. Only their ravaged hands betrayed them. He felt contrite at doubting them. He had condemned them as being coarse and loud mouthed, felt a secret relief when they didn't recognize the portrait. He had loathed the idea that his Celtic princess might be reduced to becoming a fish gutter. Yet, despite doing foul, tedious work, they took such pains to spruce themselves up to attend church.

He stammered an apology. They smiled and nodded, but they were subdued for the rest of the day. He didn't know whether it was because he had offended them or if this was their usual Sunday demeanour. At the break of day the next morning, Beathag stuffed his pack with provisions. She just smiled when he turned out his pockets to show their emptiness. She led him along narrow tracks to a quiet inlet away from the town. Two men waited by a skiff very like the one that had eluded the cutter. He owed these poor women so much. He felt in his pack and took out his telescope, the one that he used to keep in his uniform jacket. His father had given it to him when he left to become a midshipman. His last link with home. Damp had dulled the brass and streaked it green but it was still valuable. He pressed it into her reluctant hand and ran to help launch the boat.

The fishermen sailed first to Tiree. "Before they run dry," one of them said.

There was a cheering crowd to greet them and a forest of arms to pull the boat up onto the smooth golden sands. Tom was feted like a hero. All the men wanted to pump his hand or slap him on the back. The children pulled at his jacket or tweaked his fingers. The women were more circumspect, giving him sidelong glances from lowered eyes. In the evening, a fiddler appeared and everyone danced on the springy *machair*. Now the young women became bolder and held onto his hand as they spun with him in the reels.

Disentangling himself he sought refuge with the men drinking the smuggled whisky.

"*Seo an duine bàn,* Here's the fair man," called out Alasdair, the old man who had been sitting on the lobster pots. The whisky was raw and Tom had lost the habit of taking strong drink. His legs crumpled under him and he remembered nothing more until he woke up on a sweet-smelling, heather-filled mattress. He groaned as daylight dazzled his eyes. Alasdair came to see him, accompanied by a man wearing a starched collar and tie. Tom leapt to his feet but Alasdair's smile reassured him.

The stranger was a neatly made man with smoothed down hair. He explained that he was the schoolmaster, Alan MacMillan. He had come to translate for Alasdair. "He says you were somewhat, er . . . intoxicated last night."

Tom laughed. "I wasn't alone in that."

"No indeed, but Alasdair was worried about what you said when you were with drink. You spoke about deserting your ship, a serious matter."

Tom groaned and rubbed his eyes.

"He says that no one here would dream of betraying you, but you must guard your tongue. Whatever you've done the people here think highly of you and want to be of service. Alasdair has a son who works at Tainuilt, not far from Oban. There's a big ironworks near there at Bonawe. It employs hundreds of men. He believes you would be safe enough there."

"I know Tainuilt, 'the house by the stream.' I remember the Cap . . . no matter. I suppose it's all men working there? I'm still looking for that lassie." Alasdair gleaned enough of his words to break into a wheezy laugh while MacLean cleared his throat.

"You're fortunate to have a chance to redeem yourself. I would advise you to stay sober and work hard."

Tom blushed with a mixture of annoyance and embarrassment. Alasdair patted him on the shoulder and winked.

His new friends from Tiree delivered him to the quay at Bonawe. A row of carts were being loaded with iron ore disgorged from a steamship. Tom ambled after them when they set off inland. He didn't want to risk seeking work on a boat again but what else could he do? Sailors laughed about landlubbers who turned green in a storm but they were the ones out of their element on land. He had spent all his adult life at sea and knew nothing about iron smelting. There had to be a furnace, of course, but what else? He felt as dumbfounded as he did when he first arrived at boarding school, standing alone among jostling crowds of boys who knew their way around. He would have to look nonchalant and watch the others until he knew what to do. As the carts lumbered along, he could see a sullen fog above the trees ahead. Soon there were more carts coming up behind, piled high with charcoal. Horses whinnied, men shouted, and hammers thudded. They passed by houses, a solid stone terrace alongside makeshift wooden cabins. Then he could see the furnace itself, stretching over forty feet into the sky, a hulking landlocked lighthouse, spewing out smoke instead of light. There was the wheel turning with a gentle slap of water. Nearby was a collection of stone buildings. He supposed they would be used for storing the fuel that was shoveled into the furnace's gaping mouth. The first man to catch Tom's eye was a figure clad in business black with a clutch of papers in his hand. He stopped when Tom intercepted him.

"I'm looking for a position. I've a fair hand and I was quick at arithmetic at school." He thickened his voice, trying to appear both humble and keen.

"Hmm. I've enough clerks already."

"I can turn my hands to most things. I used to work with horses."

The other man looked doubtful.

"John Robinson at your service," Tom said with his most winning smile. He had decided to use his grandfather's Christian name and his mother's maiden name, hoping that their familiarity would make them stick more readily to his tongue.

"I'm William Brown. I look after the business side of things for Mr. Armstrong while he's down in Furness."

"And you're from there yourself? It makes a pleasant change to hear an English voice, especially a North Country one."

Brown didn't reply at first. He seemed to be puzzled by a stranger with a gentleman's manners who wanted a laborer's job.

"We use local men for the fetching and carrying. Hmm, well we are losing the Campbells, father and son. They're off on an emigrant ship. Very well. I'll give you a week's trial."

Tom's face lit up.

"Six days a week, loading the carts. Half-day on Saturdays. It's hard labor."

Tom brushed the warning aside but he soon found out the truth of Brown's words. He would have said that he had endured long hours as a naval officer with the endless round of watches. But there were plenty of slack times while the ship steamed on her way and he could sit quietly at the chart table. His body had hardened with all the tramping through rough countryside, but even that hadn't prepared him for what he faced now, loading iron ore and limestone from the quay and charcoal from the woods, carrying hay to the horses and sweeping out their stables. He set to the work willingly and Brown kept him on after the first week.

Tom moved easily among the other workers, always with a cheerful word for everyone but giving away little about himself. He was a garden robin, hopping close with head cocked but backing away from an outstretched hand. Weeks sped by in a routine of work and sleep. He didn't risk going into Tainuilt for a drink. He spent what little free time he had sketching in the woods, wishing that he had the paints to reveal the hues and textures there. The bronze green of the beech branches, the pungent cushioned yellow of the lichens and the musty, deep brown, crumbling forest floor beneath. An oak tree wrecked in a storm lay with most of its roots writhing in the air and its moss-furred trunk flat on the ground. Its outstretched branches pleaded for life, a few limp leaves still clinging to its fingers, a felled green giant slowly dying. After discovering the fallen tree, he avoided that part of the forest.

The charcoal burners lived in the forest, wary as deer. Eventually they crept close enough to watch him. He drew portraits for them but they wouldn't accept them.

Sometimes he went sea fishing with Ewan MacKay, a man of few words in either Gaelic or English. They would catch mackerel and string them over a fire on the shore. Tom felt some peace as they baked potatoes in the embers and sat juggling them from hand to hand while they cooled. Mostly he lived in the moment like the horses he tended. He let hard physical labor numb his mind but as spring and summer stretched into the slow decay of autumn he woke early in his bothy with a sense of clammy dread.

What would become of him? Would he have to wander through his life with a secret past and no future? Soon it would be a year since he deserted and for what? A will o' the wisp glimpse of a girl he would never see again. Like the departing swallows she had disappeared into endless sky.

Mostly, though, he wouldn't let himself think. Just concentrate on leading Hector he scolded himself one misty morning as his breath mingled in the sharp air with the horse's. What was the matter with the beast today? Usually placid he had become skittish, prancing on his huge feathered feet. He seemed to be infecting the horses behind with his unease, for they too were snorting and tossing their heads.

In exasperation, Tom raised his whip. As he did so, he felt his arm tremble and his body sway. Using all his strength, he hauled on the reins to stop Hector and turn the beast's head around. The carter behind him swore as he had to pull his own horse to a halt. By then, Tom had leapt down from the cart, knife in hand and slashed through the traces, slapping Hector on the rump to make him run back. He was cutting through the harness of the horse behind when the ground shuddered beneath them. The sky exploded in spouting flames, spitting out rocks like molten hailstones. A searing ash fell on them. Tom hunched low to avoid the barrage and leapt to seize the reins of a bucking horse farther back in the line. Then something heavy thudded into his back, thrusting him forward. He was tossed into the air before being pitched into a thundering blackness.

Chapter 24

Argyll, 1861

"Captain Otter, you've found me. I'm so sorry for all the trouble I caused you." Through his tears Tom could make out the burly figure with the bristling beard.

"Not guilty, young man. I'm Matthew Armstrong and I've never commanded a ship in my life."

Tom gripped the edge of the sheet and closed his eyes. A groan escaped from someone else's throat. When his eyes popped open again, the bearded face was still there although it shifted and shimmered as if in a heat haze.

"Lie back. There's nothing to fret about. You're in a snug bed, not on a ship."

He closed his eyes, heard another groan and squinted through half-closed lids. No, it couldn't be the captain. The voice was wrong and surely his beard was grayer than the captain's.

It was all too much to endure. Terrible dreams, or were they memories, swirled around in his head. Images of being pinned down and suffocated. He had to get up. As he kicked his legs against the bedclothes a scream sliced through the air. This time he knew it was his own voice.

A heavy hand pressed down on him. "Keep still. You had a nasty break. The doctor put you under to reset it. You were delirious for days."

Tom shook his head and crawled back down into tunnels of sleep again. Next time he awoke, the bearded man was there again but solid this time, not a mirage.

"You're back in the land of the living at last,' he said, holding a glass of water to Tom's cracked lips. 'Can you remember what happened?"

Tom shook his head gingerly. His neck seemed too weak to

support it.

"It's two weeks since the furnace blew up."

Two weeks, how have I lost two weeks of my life? Tom wondered.

"We don't know how or why it happened. The smelters all knew their business back to front and inside out. We can't ask them for every last man died in the explosion. Boiled like lobsters. Their flesh melted like candle grease. But your quick thinking saved more men from dying. You turned the carts back. Do you remember doing that?"

"Hector, what about him? Is he safe?" Tom jerked himself up into a sitting position, grimacing with pain. Armstrong looked blank. "Hector, my horse. He sensed what was happening and warned me. Is he safe?"

"What? Oh, all the beasts survived. It was only the poor men in the furnace who died." He snatched a ragged breath and said more gently, "but you're still in a state from that bang on your head. A flying piece of metal. Then in all that mayhem one of the carts ran over your leg."

Tom fell back on his pillow, exhausted. Warm tears trickled down his cheeks. "Too many men dying horribly." But it wasn't the smelters of Bonawe who were at the forefront of his mind.

"So many, and Andrew among them. He shouldn't even have been there. But he wanted to know all about the business." He blew into his handkerchief.

"Andrew?"

"My son. He'd come up from Furness to learn about smelting. Forgive me, I didn't come to burden you with my sorrows but to thank you."

For a moment they were both silent. Armstrong roused himself. "Now what about you? You must have relatives who want to hear from you."

Tom felt the shaming moisture oozing down his cheeks again. "There's no hurry. You're still in pain." They both stayed silent, each marooned in his own grief.

The next day when Tom heard Armstrong's tread on the stairs, he had his answer ready. "Thank you, sir, but I haven't any family who need to be told."

"You're alone in the world?" Tom stayed silent. "Or you've drifted away from them?"

Tom could have lied or refused to answer. But the wish to confess to this kind, fatherly figure swept over him in a neap tide that he couldn't resist, drifting as he was without rudder or mast. He longed to be towed into a dry dock, safe from the storms at sea. Over the next few days, Armstrong coaxed the whole story from him. It was like tipping an unstoppered pitcher upside down. At first, the flow was sluggish through the narrow neck, but once it speeded up it wouldn't cease. All of it splashed out. The pain of his mother's death, his rage toward his father, his disappointment with life in the Navy, the shock of Richard's death, the obsession with the mysterious girl, and the shame of his desertion. Once it was all hurled overboard, he felt himself floating lighter in the water.

"I shall go away and think," was all Armstrong said at the end.

Tom let hope trickle into his mind.

The tread on the stairs was brisker the next day. Armstrong smiled as he perched on the edge of his seat.

"You can't carry on with this half-life, always looking over your shoulder. Even if by some miracle you were to find this girl and she wanted you, how would you get by? You couldn't bear to live in some hovel." He raised his hand, as Tom opened his mouth in protest. "No, hear me out. And you have to keep off the bottle. Some men can manage it but in your case it's a bad master."

He laughed at Tom's scowling face. "Lecture over. I don't want you to waste your life. I lost my son and there's nothing I can do for him anymore. I've decided to repair the furnace and sell the whole business. I'll get a better price for it that way and the men here will keep their jobs."

His voice was businesslike but his expression bleak. "Money's no good to me now. My hopes are sunk but I can get you afloat if you'll let me."

Chapter 25

Liverpool, 1862

Where was she?

Tom sat in a window seat, smoothing the expensive cloth of his new suit over his knees. No sign of her at the hotel entrance. He forced himself to sit still. He didn't want to draw attention from the other people drinking afternoon tea. Families, couples, groups of middle-aged ladies but no sign of a woman on her own. Had he made a mistake over the time or the place?

Ah! There was a woman at the doorway now. No, that couldn't be her, too matronly surely, too dowdy. Then she looked in his direction and her eyes crinkled in a smile. It was her. He was on his feet, hiding his shock in a broad grin.

She must see a change in him, too. Both of them were youngsters when he had left home. Still he thought with satisfaction that the differences in him were an improvement. He had stayed slender but hard work had broadened his shoulders and bronzed his face so that it made a striking contrast to his pale hair. He knew that women slid their eyes over him with approval.

"Emma, at last." He reached his arms out and then let them hang, as she stood still in front of him. He gestured for them to sit down and caught the eye of a waiter. After ordering afternoon tea, there was a bristling silence while they stared at each other.

"Well, here you are, back from the dead. I was astonished to receive your letter." Her tone was clipped.

"I'm so glad you could come up to see me."

He had forgotten how direct her gaze was, her dark brown eyes fixed on his face.

"You didn't say in your letter, but I already knew what you had done." Her words sank like a stone into a deep well.

"When you didn't answer my letter after Papa died, I feared

some terrible accident had befallen you."

He hung his head.

"So I made enquiries and—"

His head shot up, eyes flashing, "Not at the Admiralty?"

"No, I was circumspect, through an acquaintance I could trust. He was mortified to be the bearer of bad news about your . . . disappearance. Captain Otter was reprimanded for the loss of two of his crew. You didn't know?"

He shook his head.

"How could you, to . . . to John? You've brought shame and disgrace on yourself and your family."

He didn't reply at first. He had hoped for more compassion from this sister who had looked up to him when they were children. He stared at her clenched face and thought that it wasn't only her appearance that had changed. So had her character and he felt he didn't know her at all. "I'll try to explain."

He told her how the manner of Richard's death had left him floundering and rudderless.

She listened until he lurched to a halt. "I can see your shipmate's death upset you greatly, but I don't understand why it made you desert."

He squeezed his hands together. "Well, I haven't told you the whole story. Here's the missing piece." He took the stained portrait out of his pocket. "This has survived everything. I believe it's an omen."

She traced the outline of the face with a finger, as he told her about the fateful meeting. "You do understand now?"

She said nothing at first. Then abruptly she ripped the paper from his grasp. He lunged for it, but she wrenched it away and held it on her lap under the table.

"Understand what?" she kept her voice low, as she spat the words out. "Are you some lovesick boy? You've ruined your life and tainted us all for some young woman you glimpsed once? You've not changed at all. You're still as selfish as you always were. And now you appear again, dragging a broken wing and expect sympathy for trouble you brought on your own head." She jumped to her feet, nimble in spite of her plumpness and thrusting back her chair, rushed out the door.

The buzz of conversation around them faltered as heads turned at the noise before the voices resumed talking in loud, bright tones. He glanced around him, furious at her for drawing attention to him. Throwing some change onto the table, he strode out, trying to look composed. He scanned the busy street in both directions. He had to get the portrait back. Although he could draw another likeness, this picture was a talisman. A superstitious part of his mind was terrified at the idea of losing the drawing he had kept safe through all the hazards he had endured. Would losing it mean he had also lost all chance of finding the girl? Sweat drenched the back of his fine new jacket. Emma had no right to snatch the paper away and lecture him about his actions. A new fear gripped him. Maybe she would be spiteful enough to report his presence in Liverpool to the Admiralty?

Ah, there she was ahead on the right, dodging around the strolling shoppers. He followed her, never taking his eyes off her bustling figure. With his longer strides, he soon caught up with her. As he drew level he ducked down to whisper, "Please wait."

She kept hurrying on, "Why should I? I've traveled all this way at some personal inconvenience. I didn't dare risk tell anyone I was coming and you've not even had the decency to ask me how I am."

"You're my only link to my old life. I don't want to lose you again after we've just met."

By now she had slowed to a halt. "We can't go back to that hotel. They'll all be talking about what a hoyden I was."

"Or what a cad I was for upsetting a respectable lady. Look, we're heading toward the water. What about a ferry trip over the river?"

"Very well. I don't get much chance to see the sea, unlike you."

Tom was wary of being aboard any sort of boat. He felt as if he still wore a sort of naval manner that other sailors could recognize. His restless eyes swept over the passengers as they boarded. Emma watched him but said nothing. Once they were settled he smiled, but her face stayed strained.

"Your fawning worked on Mama but it won't on me. You have no idea how lucky you were. The oldest and the favorite of both parents."

He opened his mouth but closed it again when she glowered at him. "You had the best schooling our parents could afford. I would have died for that. 'It would be wasted on a girl,' was all I ever heard."

"That wasn't my fault, and it wasn't easy being sent away."

She snorted. "Do you remember when I pleaded with you to teach me some Latin? You promised you would on the next holidays, but instead you spent all your time with the horses down at the farm."

He didn't want to anger Emma by arguing with her. "We did have some happier times together, didn't we? When we were younger? Do you remember Bosun? He used to be like a nursemaid, watching us while we played. Barking if we strayed too far." They were sitting opposite each other on the deck and he risked touching her hand.

"I remember when he shook his head, he soaked everything with a fountain of dribble. I know you're trying to win me over. You always thought you could charm your way out of trouble. You even got Papa to agree to your going to sea although it broke his heart."

"And a sorry mess I made of that."

"You've not told me the whole story. How are you able to afford your passage? Are you expecting me to give you money?" she asked, a hostile glint in her eyes.

He winced at her words, but told her about the accident at Bonawe.

"This Mr. Armstrong, I don't understand why he has been so generous to you. He would hardly have known you."

So Tom told her about how Hector had warned him about the explosion.

"But it wasn't the horse that saved the other carters, was it? It was you," she said, her expression becoming much warmer.

Tom shrugged. "Enough of me. Tell me about your life."

"Frederick is a good husband and we have two children, Thomas and Sophia."

"You named your son after me, despite everything."

"I hope it doesn't bring him bad luck. They're a blessing, but Fred is so busy with his doctor's practice that he doesn't see much of them."

"And you, are you happy?"

"I love my family dearly but . . ."

"It's not enough? You always had so much vigour."

"Not a quality that's valued in a married woman."

"Could you perhaps assist Fred with his work?"

She sighed. "That wouldn't be considered respectable."

"I daresay if you had been given my chances in life, you wouldn't have squandered them."

"No, I wouldn't. But the world is run by men and women are confined to the corners."

"What will you do now that all this is closed to you?" She pointed at the Mersey, full with shipping of all kinds.

"I thought you'd heard enough about me."

She cuffed him with the crumpled piece of paper.

"Well, as Mr. Armstrong has been my saviour in paying for my passage to Canada, I can make a fresh start over there." His smile couldn't hide the sadness in his eyes. "But I shall never be able to return home or see you again."

"You've no choice. But you can write to me and tell me about your new pioneering life. I believe there is a postal service over there?"

"Now that you've possibly forgiven me, can I have my drawing back?"

She put her head on one side as if deciding whether to agree and smoothed out the crumpled paper, "I didn't know you were such a good artist."

"Thank you. Neither did I. Painting wasn't encouraged at school, but all naval officers have to learn how to draw as an aid to navigation. I discovered a taste for it and had plenty of practice once I was on the survey ship." He stuffed the scuffed paper into a pocket. "While I was at Bonawe, I made a little money penning portraits for the men who worked there. I thought I could do the same for passengers on the ship and maybe find work as an artist in Canada."

"Hmm. Sounds rather harebrained to me."

He frowned in annoyance while she groped at the collar of her blouse until she had unclasped the silver chain around her neck. "What about this instead?" She opened the locket and put it in his hand. He gazed at the small photograph of two solemn-faced children.

"My nephew and niece? It doesn't look as if either of them are fair like me. But they're fine-looking children."

"No. They're both dark haired like their father. It's not the children themselves I want you to consider, but what they represent."

"You mean family life? You think I should take a wife? How can I?"

"The look of horror on your face is hardly flattering to my sex. Of course, you're in no position to get married. I'm thinking about your choice of profession. I wanted to show you how the artist is being replaced by the photographer. This is the future."

"Oh, and who was the eminent photographer who took this portrait?"

"Me. A suitable pastime for a respectable married woman, do you think?"

He peered more closely. "It must be difficult getting your subjects to sit still. And carrying all that heavy equipment . . ."

"Too much for a mere woman?"

"Obviously not. Do you concentrate on portraits or compose landscapes, as well?"

"Landscapes, still life, botanical studies. I especially enjoy taking close-up pictures of flowers and leaves. Effects of light and shade, too. I develop the photographs myself." The words spilled out.

"I can see how photographs would be useful for sailors, too. They wouldn't replace charts though." His face clouded. "All that's over now for me."

"But you've a second chance. When are you sailing?"

"Tomorrow. Will you come and wave me farewell?"

"No, I must return home today."

"You haven't told Fred you were coming here, have you?"

"You're not the only one who has to keep secrets, but unlike me you're in command of your own life. Write to me."

By unspoken agreement they steered conversation back to shallow waters. "If you had your camera here, you could have taken my photograph," Tom said.

"Or even better, some views of the city and the waterfront."

"But I'm a wanted man now. The only photograph of me is likely to be a likeness by the police."

After returning on the ferry, they lingered by the water before walking to the railway station. Tom bent to embrace her, his hands resting on her tightly corseted waist. He pushed some sovereigns into her resisting hand.

"No, I insist. Mr. Armstrong gave me much more than I need. Buy yourself a pretty gown . . . no, a piece of camera equipment." He ducked as she swatted him with her free hand and they both laughed.

Chapter 26

At Sea, April 1862

Tom waved farewell to Emma as she boarded her train, but there was no one on the quayside to watch him depart on the *Ocean Monarch* two days later. The shipping companies advertised fast steamships for the Atlantic crossing, but he had chosen to sail. Was that what John Robinson, a shipping clerk, would do? Probably not. A sensible young man would prefer a modern, safer ship, despite his limited means. So why had he chosen the old-fashioned way? After all, he had spent most of his naval service on steam vessels. But to cut himself adrift from his old way of life, he needed to separate slowly, strand by strand. It would also delay his arrival in Canada. He had spoken breezily to Emma about his plans but seeing her again had left him buffeted by doubts and regrets.

This ship looked too shabby to live up to her name. She was more like a queen in faded exile, and very different from the sturdy old *Porcupine*. Would she sink and turn into a monarch of the deep? Shivering, he turned up his collar and surveyed the other passengers waiting to board. Most of them were in family groups, especially those with steerage tickets who stood together in drab huddles. He felt relieved to see that there were a few better dressed people waiting too, mainly young men. He let the surge of bodies push him up the gangplank. His cabin was on the deck above steerage. The three young men already there were dressed in clean, well-used clothes. They greeted him affably in Irish accents and Tom was polite but sparse in his replies. John Robinson was a wary, anonymous man.

There was no one to wave a handkerchief to him. He stayed inside as the ship departed, but once they were under way he went on the upper deck, carrying his painting materials and wearing a broad-brimmed hat. Drawing would pass the time and provide him with a disguise, even if, as Emma claimed, artists would soon be out of date. He wedged himself against the side of the ship near the prow and sketched the grubby tug that was pulling them out of the Mersey to the open sea. After adding the tall port buildings, he stowed his paper away in a canvas bag and paced the deck. How strange it was not to hear the constant thrum of engines beneath his feet. This ship made a cacophony of sounds as the wind prodded her, timbers grinding and grumbling, ropes scraping and chafing, and sails straining and slapping. The smells were different, too, from the *Porcupine*. No reek of coal and oil to mask the scent of salt-encrusted timbers. He could detect a farmyard stink, coming from a pen where goats, pigs, and poultry were shuffling and grunting. There were voices too, swooping from the top deck and the decks below, shouted orders, the hum of women talking, and the crying of babies.

After an hour or so, most of the passengers had gone below. Now he could inspect the vessel. Using his pocketknife, he poked the wood as far down as he could reach over the side. The timbers seemed sound enough and the caulking was stuffed in tightly. He hoped the planking lower down was as good. This ship wasn't as tidy as a naval vessel would be. Coils of rope were roughly bundled rather than neatly stashed. The crew seemed sparser and sloppier than he was used to. And that scrum of passengers in steerage would be difficult to control if the ship hit bad weather.

I must stop questioning everything, he told himself. I'm not a sailor now. This ship had survived many voyages up to now. The captain wants to dock safely in Canada and even if the deckhands were ruffians, it didn't mean that they didn't know their business. He squinted upward and was pleased to see the lookout in position. On his first ship, a relic from Nelson's time, an old hand had told him, "It's quiet up in the crow's nest. Even in a fog you know when you're near land. You can hear the surf breaking on the shore and smell the earth."

The *Ocean Monarch* made fast progress, the wind whisking her toward Ireland and beyond into the Atlantic. The steerage passengers lined up on their section of the deck each day to fill their jugs with water and get their ration of oatmeal and salt beef. The women took it in turns to cook on small fires set in sandboxes, chattering as they worked. The wealthier travelers like Tom had their food prepared by the ship's cooks to eat inside, but he preferred to take his plate out on the deck. The children from steerage would peer through the gate separating them from the better-off passengers. His unsettled mood, the musty food, and especially the hungry eyes made his stomach clench. He took to handing most of his meals through the gate, trying to select different begging hands each day.

Over the next week the wind became stronger, making the ship buck and lunge through the swell. Most people on board, including the young Irish fellows, became sick. Tom had never been troubled by seasickness. He remained alert while the others sagged on their bunks, groaning and heaving, not caring if they lived or died. He felt safer, like being the only sober man among drunks. Richard never drank and once Tom had asked him, "What's it like being the odd man out when you're ashore?"

Richard gave one of his rare smiles. "I'm free as a bird."

That's where we're different, Tom thought sadly. I'm a seabird that needs to nest close to the colony. I've had to learn how to be solitary. One night he remained late on deck, sitting propped up against a mast. It was too dark to see much, but he had no wish to go back to a cabin full of moaning bodies and pails of vomit. He welcomed the wind that spurred on the ship and closing his eyes he let his body sway with the motion. Suddenly, he stiffened as his ears detected the soft padding of bare feet, followed by a murmur of voices.

"Come on. I bet he's in here. Have a look."

Tom peered into the gloom and made out two figures. One of

them was a short, bowlegged man he knew was a deckhand. His companion, taller and heavier, was unfamiliar. Possibly he was a ship's cook who rarely left the galley. The smaller one clambered over the side to reach the ship's boat suspended there. He jumped down, grunting as he lifted the heavy tarpaulin cover and then snickered as he peered inside. There was a bleat of alarm and scuffling feet. The big man shuffled up and helped his companion haul out a small, struggling form. They dropped their catch on the deck. The small sailor kicked it with his gnarled foot. They were too preoccupied to notice Tom tiptoeing up behind them. He cannoned into the bigger man, catching him off balance so that he tripped forward and cracked his head against the ship's timbers. As his friend turned, Tom grabbed the back of his shirt and lifted him off his feet,

"You thought you'd have some fun, did you?"

Out of the corner of his eye, Tom saw the felled man lumbering to his feet and booted him in the shins.

"Get belowdecks. I'm a naval officer, so don't try any tricks."

The bigger man staggered away, cradling his head. Tom shoved the smaller man hard in the back to make him follow. He watched over their prey as the two men scuttled away. The scrawny sailor half turned, "Want it all for yourself?"

Tom stood beside the creature. What to do now? He'd done the one thing he'd vowed not to, given himself away. A filthy paw groped from under the pile of rags and tugged at his trouser leg. Tom skittered back. The thing lifted its head. A monkey face with staring eyes and snarling mouth. Was it some kind of ape? Tom recoiled, gasping at the smell that arose from it. Its face looked cowed yet knowing.

This is the last thing I need or want, Tom thought. "Who are you? What's your name?" The creature got to its feet and stood upright. It was human after all. He couldn't abandon it. It sidled closer and clasped his leg again. What should he do? Take it back to the cabin for the night and hope the others are too sick to notice? He turned and it followed him, almost standing on Tom's heels as he went back.

Thank goodness the others were asleep. Tom mimed to it to take off the dirty plaid round its shoulders. He threw down a blanket and pointed to the floor beside his bunk. He knew it was a child. Its height suggested about ten years of age. Boy or girl? The hair was long. That meant a girl, but the torn trousers indicated a boy. Whatever it was, it was jumping with vermin. The best plan would be to get up early, hose it down so that it didn't smell so foul and then take it down to the steerage deck. Maybe some family would adopt it. One more mouth wouldn't make much difference to a big family and Tom would pay them. There would be no need for the captain to know. The officers took no interest in the passengers anyway, especially the poor ones. Feeling easier in his mind, Tom drifted off to sleep.

He escaped to a dream where he was swimming in a tropical sea among a shoal of vividly colored fish that brushed against his legs and nibbled him with soft gums. They didn't feel cold and slimy to the touch but warm and supple. As he watched, they were transformed into creatures like mermaids with slender limbs and streaming hair. His heart surged with joy as one of them turned toward him and smiled. He recognized the flame-colored hair and creamy skin of the mysterious girl, but as he reached out toward her, she flashed away. He followed and she glanced over her shoulder, half smiling. As she did so her face changed. It rippled as a wave swirled across it, shifting her features so that the brow deepened, the jaw became firmer and the mouth widened. She had transformed herself into Richard. Tom threw his head back and laughed with joy as he recognized his friend.

The laugh turned into a stifled cry as Tom jolted awake. He could feel a feathery touch on his leg. That was what had woken him. The sensation inched up to his groin. He slammed his hand down, squeezing until he could feel birdlike bones grinding together.

"What do you think you're doing?" he hissed, pulling the whimpering boy from under the blanket and throwing him on the floor. The boy huddled there with tears oozing down his cheeks, leaving clean rivulets on his grimy face.

"I'm not going to hurt you, but do not touch me. Do you understand?"

The child dipped his head and they both went back to bed. Tom felt too anxious to sleep again and once it was light he shook the child awake and took it up on deck. He found some canvas spread out by the crew to catch rainwater. Miming to the creature that it should strip, Tom scooped some of the water into a pail and sluiced it down. It shrieked and raised its arms. It was a boy, then. For the first time Tom felt pity for the stowaway with his puny, goose-pimpled limbs and closed face.

"Who are you?"

But the lad looked away, slack jawed. Probably simple minded and abandoned by his family. His pale skin, black hair, and blue eyes suggested Celt rather than Saxon. Irish maybe, but the plaid he had been wrapped in looked Scottish. Tom handed him a blanket from the cabin to dry himself and sighed as he remembered the fisher girls in Stornoway, and their rough kindness in swilling away the fish guts that clung to him when he hid from the excise men. He gripped the boy's shivering hand as they climbed down through the decks to reach the steerage accommodation. As they descended, the air grew stifling and fetid until they were in the stinking, slopping bowels of the ship. The stench of vomit, bloody flux and rancid bodies forced Tom to pinch his lips together to stop himself from gagging. Captain Otter had told him about the coffin ships he had seen leaving Ireland at the time of the famine, years before. Starving, dead, and dying all heaped in together and bodies, weighted down with stones, slipped overboard every night. The emigrants had suffered more than the slaves snatched from Africa and transported in chains to the New World. Slaves were worth keeping alive for the price they would fetch. Poor Irish people had no value. Surely conditions had improved now the famine was over? It was hard to believe they had.

Tom strained to see anything as no natural light trickled down here. As his eyes adjusted to the darkness, he saw that the space was crammed with people lying on pine boards, stacked from floor to ceiling. They were laid out like corpses but corpses that groaned, spluttered, and sobbed. The child gasped and pulled back, but Tom tightened his grip. He noticed someone sitting upright and looking over at them.

"Does anyone know this boy?" Tom shouted.

The figure staggered toward him and Tom steeled himself not to run away.

"For the love of God, sir, are you a doctor? There's people here dying of the fever."

Tom hesitated, his grip slackened on the boy, and the child wrenched himself free.

Chapter 27

The Voyage Continues, 1862

"I'll get help," Tom shouted over his shoulder, as he tore after the boy.

He noticed that the ship had slowed. The wind must have dropped. A sailor was always suspicious of a sudden calm. He soon caught up with the boy, lunging forward to seize his leg as the child scrambled up the ladder to the next deck.

"You should be grateful I saved your skin you wretch," he spat. "Now I can't even get rid of you."

It was no use seeking medical help. In his experience ship's doctors were failures in their profession on land, often drunkards as well, and what could they do anyway if fever had broken out? It was best if the sufferers stayed isolated. He would just have to keep the child with him for now.

When he returned to his cabin, the three Irish lads were there, pale but no longer green.

"Listen, you chaps. This stowaway here was hiding in a boat and I came on two of the crew ill-treating him. I thought he could stay here for the time being."

"He stinks to high heavens. Sure we paid more for this cabin, so we could get away from riffraff," the tallest one said, with a hostile stare.

"Why's the Englishman so kind-hearted? What's in it for him?" His friend sneered.

"I know it's inconvenient, but I could see my way to recompensing you. . . ? They nodded.

Tom went back to his routine of spending as much time as possible out on deck, despite the chill in the air. The boy hovered, silent and watchful. After three days of stillness, the wind changed to the northwest, blowing against the ship rather than with her. All Tom's instincts made him uneasy. He remembered the story of how the wind had uncoiled itself from a calm sea, swelling into a tempest, and slamming Mr. MacKenzie's boat onto the rocks. That was a small vessel in a narrow sea, but a large ship on a wide ocean faced the same peril.

Sure enough, during that night a violent storm swooped down on them. Tom awoke to feel the ship caught in the jaws of the waves. She was hurled from side to side and tossed into the air before plunging downward again. Out of breath, she wallowed, her decks swamped before shaking herself upright again. How long could the ship survive that sort of thrashing? In the cabin, the oil lamp on the ceiling was flinging itself from side to side. All their bags and boxes were skating across the floor. The Irishmen clung to their bunks in terror while the boy sat on the floor, head flung back and howling. Tom knew that he couldn't endure being trapped helpless belowdecks. He shrugged on his jacket and found the bag he had tied to the leg of his bunk the night before. Taking out his boots he rammed his feet into them and was busy tying a length of rope from the bag around his waist when he realized that the biggest Irishman had gripped his arm.

"Where are you going?"

"Outside to help. Stay here until the storm's over."

He prised the man's fingers from his sleeve. Then he was running to the ladder, scrambling to reach the top deck before the crew battened down the hatches. Stopping at the top of the final rungs he untied his rope, knotting one end to the hatch cover. He looked about him and gasped. The ship's prow was rearing up, cresting a wall of waves while on all sides the sea rose sheer, molten mountain peaks topped with white foam. He saw a sodden figure in front of him on the tilting deck, crouching low and trying to outrun the waves before they smashed down and swept him overboard. Tom crawled forward clinging onto his rope. His feet were swept from under him, but he was able to seize the man by his legs and pull him back to the hatch cover. As they lay there winded, Tom could hear sounds beneath him as if the ship herself was howling. It was the voices of the passengers, a chorus of praying, screaming, hymn singing, cursing, and wailing. Mixed in with the human cries was the bellowing and trampling of the terrified animals trapped on deck. As he watched the pen splintered apart, destroyed by the storm outside and the flailing hooves within. The deck was swooping and heaving. Everything movable had already been swept over the side and now the goats and pigs were flung off their feet and hurled overboard as they scrabbled desperately to regain their footing. Tom winced at their distress but hoped that they would at least drown quickly. The hens seemed doomed to a longer period of suffering. He could hear them squawking as the wind tossed them into bumbling flight before pitching them into the waves. He looked away as he waited for the ship to right herself before nodding to the sailor. Together they wriggled along the deck, gripping the rope. The helmsman was strapped to the wheel, straining to keep the ship on course in the towering seas. When they reached the main mast, Tom's companion tied himself to it and joined some other sailors who were battling to haul on the ropes and secure the sails. Tom inched his way along the deck and found some of the crew clinging to a hatchway. They looked like stewards or cooks rather than deckhands, their faces dazed. Tom bullied and cajoled them so that they joined in the struggle to pull in the sails and stop them being torn to shreds.

Once the masts were stripped winter bare all they could do was wait and ride out the storm. Most of the men went belowdecks for grog and soup, but Tom slipped away to his cabin. He laughed as he saw the three men and the boy crushed together on one bunk, their faces a tableau of despair.

"The worst's over now. We'll live," he told them, tugging off his soaking clothes and wrapping himself in a blanket as they stared at him, blankly.

He was right too. The next day the storm slipped away as suddenly as it had emerged. Tom's exuberance disappeared, too. He felt weighted down by all the dangers and near disasters he had faced during the last year. He never wanted to be at sea again.

Everyone on board seemed subdued. The steerage passengers came back out, blinking and wandering in aimless circles, like prisoners allowed out for exercise. Even the boys and girls stood, arms hanging limply, unwilling to play.

It was as if a pall of foreboding hung over the ship and two weeks later as they finally neared Newfoundland, a real pall descended as if their dread had taken on a physical form. They awoke to a deathly silence, to find the ship groping her way in a smothering fog. When it lifted, it revealed an ocean grazed by drifting mountains. The passengers came back to life, exclaiming like excited children at the icebergs that rose high as cathedrals with sheer walls, glistening towers, and swooping buttresses. Tom thought that they resembled an over-exposed image in one of Emma's photographs. They were hills that had been bleached and looked ghostlike but they used their glittering bulk to stalk ships. Rocks were moored to the seabed. They could be marked on charts and avoided but these floating predators dragged their huge, hidden foundations through the water and bore down on a helpless ship, waiting to ram her hull and tear her open below the waterline. They were so tantalizingly close now to land, to the Cabot Strait that separated Newfoundland and Nova Scotia. The ship breathed in and tucked in her skirts as she edged past the icebergs.

Then in the night, the wind rose and the marauding ice pack slunk away. The coastline shook itself free of the fog and they could see ahead the Magdalene Islands flung like loose change in the Gulf of St. Lawrence. The masts were canopied in full sail once more. Relieved at being so close to the end of the voyage, Tom felt composed enough to start a letter to his sister.

Dear Emma,

After a difficult, stormy journey we should soon be anchoring at Sydney on Cape Breton. The journey has been wearisome and I'm eager to be on dry land once more. We've just passed through some icebergs. They towered above the ship like ghostly mountains. I've sketched them, although it's hard to do justice to their scale and grandeur. Would a photograph do better? I doubt it could convey the size and perspective of the scene. You'll be pleased to hear that before leaving Liverpool I purchased a Rouch Universal camera. Have you seen one? The bellows are tapered so that it will fold almost flat for traveling. Years of living in cramped quarters has made me value devices that don't take up much room. I can see myself riding out in the Canadian wilderness, an intrepid itinerant photographer.

He hesitated, wondering how much more to tell her about the events of the journey.

I helped the crew secure the sails in the worst of the storm as I felt it was my duty to offer assistance. I also took pity on a young stowaway who was being ill-treated by some of the crew. I shall try and find a family to take him in—

A booming voice sounded behind him, making Tom's hand shake and splatter ink across the paper, "You're the one who helped us during the storm."

Tom turned and scrambled to his feet,

"Well, you needed all the help you could get."

He put down his papers and stuffed his trembling hands inside his coat pockets.

"Hmm. You've been to sea. An officer? You know how to handle men." The lean, straight-backed man continued, in a West Country burr, his deep-set gray eyes assessing Tom. "Peter Searle, captain of this vessel." He extended a hand.

"Well, that was all a long time ago. I'm off to start a new life now . . . er, John Robinson's the name," Tom said smiling, but he could hear the strain in his voice.

"I'm in your debt, sir, and if I can repay you in any way. . .?"

"That won't be necessary." The captain continued to stare at him before turning his attention to the boy who was sitting hunched up close by, his head bowed as usual.

Tom spoke, "Ah, but there is something. I found this boy stowing away in one of the ship's boats. I fed him and cleaned him up, but I've not been able to find out anything about him. He seems to have lost his tongue, but I suspect he might be a Scot, a Highlander. Someone in steerage could maybe adopt him? If I pay them a small consideration?"

The captain's lip curled, as he looked at the boy.

"I'll see."

Tom remained on deck with the boy despite the cold. It was safer than being trapped inside his cabin if there were any awkward questions. The child started to shiver and after a while leaned against Tom's side and dozed. If only this infernal journey was over.

After a time Captain Searle returned, accompanied by an elderly minister, a man of spare build but with a lush beard that frothed over his shirt. The captain introduced him as the Reverend MacLaren. Barely acknowledging Tom's greeting, the minister stared at the boy who flushed and looked away.

"Yes, it's Iain MacLean," he pronounced.

"He has a family aboard the ship?" Tom asked sharply, as the silence lengthened.

"No."

"Is there anyone who would be willing to adopt the boy?" asked the captain, stiff faced.

"No," the minister replied, before clamping his lips together.

Tom could endure it no longer,

"Why on earth not? He's biddable enough and I'll give them some money for his keep."

"Bad blood," the Reverend MacKay intoned.

Tom looked at Iain who hung his head, too miserable to wipe away the tears flowing down his cheeks and dripping from his chin. Captain Searle turned to the minister.

"Well, sir, we need to decide what to do with the lad, but first you must tell us what you know about him."

"Very well. My flock is from the Isle of Skye. We couldn't survive any more bad harvests and the landlord wouldn't allow us land to build a church. I prayed for God's guidance and advised the people to leave for Cape Breton." Again he waited.

"And what about Iain's family?" Tom asked, through gritted teeth.

"They were no part of my congregation," the minister declared, his lips pursed. "His mother had no husband and . . . led an immoral life. Shortly before we left, we were led to believe that the woman's brother who lived with her and the boy was guilty of unnatural . . . er, practices," he stumbled to a halt.

"With other men?" Searle asked.

The minister looked aghast and shook his head.

"Incest, then?" Tom asked.

Reverend MacKay swallowed and nodded. "The rest of the villagers went to burn their house down but the landlord stopped them. Gave the man some money to go away I believe. We thought the boy had disappeared with his mother, but he must have secreted himself on the ship when we left."

The other two men looked grim but said nothing.

"Now you understand why no one will take him in," the minister continued. "He's tainted with their sin. There must be an orphanage somewhere?"

"He's only a child. How can he be blamed for his family's sins?" Tom struggled to keep his voice steady.

"The sins of the fathers are passed down from generation to generation." Tom ignored him, taking the boy by his shoulders and looked directly in his eyes.

"Do you want to go with me, Iain?" he asked.

"He won't understand you. He's only got Gaelic."

"He knows well enough whether people are kind or cruel," Tom said, smiling at Iain.

This time the boy looked up, scanning each face in turn. Finally, he fixed his gaze on Tom and nodded. The Reverend and the captain both looked relieved, but Tom felt pounded by waves of anger, fear, and pity. As if he needed the burden of another life, another outcast.

The minister scurried off and the captain turned to Tom.

"We'll soon arrive at Sydney. That's where we throw out the ballast."

Smiling at Tom's puzzled expression, he added, "the steerage passengers, especially those damned Scots. The ship will smell sweeter once they've gone. Then the short cut up the Strait of Canso to the St. Lawrence."

Tom strode back to his cabin, Iain stumbling at his heels. When he stopped suddenly, Iain thudded into him but Tom barely noticed. Should he change his plans? He had booked his passage to Quebec where he could melt away among the throng of travelers, but dare he stay aboard for so long? That felt dangerous now that he had drawn unwelcome attention to himself, first during the storm and now over the business of the boy. There would be nowhere to hide if the captain got suspicious. Yet it would be risky going ashore to an island full of Scots where he would be conspicuous as a stranger. But he knew that he couldn't bear staying on this vessel any longer. And there was still a flicker of hope that he might yet find the mysterious girl among her countrymen in Cape Breton.

Chapter 28

Landfall, May 1862

The next day they moored at Sydney. The bobbing fishing boats in the harbor reminded Tom of the Scottish ports he had visited. Here, though, the buildings were made of wood rather than stone. He could see timber yards and new buildings being constructed. There was a throbbing life here. It seemed like a place that could swallow up newcomers and not care about where they came from. Tom approached the sailor who was securing the gangplank and asked him to fetch his trunk.

"Can't do that, sir. You need to speak to the captain first."

"Why?"

"Quarantine, sir. All those that get off the boat have to wait in sheds on the quay. Get looked over for the fever."

No chance of melting away, after all.

"It's usually only steerage passengers who leave here," Captain Searle said, looking hard at Tom. "But you and the boy haven't been with them. The ship's doctor can look at you and give you a pass."

So Tom was forced to stay on deck, fighting the urge to run while the steerage passengers disembarked. The children scurried ahead, their parents staggering behind them. Weighted down with bundles, their haggard faces were limp with relief to be ashore. They were scooped up by waiting officials and herded away. The doctor arrived. Tom noticed the drops of sweat on the man's brow as he peered into his mouth. After doing the same to Iain he pronounced them both to be healthy. Yet another wait while his trunk was brought up from the hold.

"Have a jar or two for us."

Tom turned to see the tall Irishman who had shared his cabin. He laughed but didn't stop to talk because there at last was his trunk, on the back of a sailor clattering down the gangplank. Anxious about his new camera getting jolted, Tom hurried after him. As he did so he felt a sudden tug on his arm. Iain was pulling him back. "What the devil . . ." But then he saw that the boy's face had turned deathly white. As the sailor lowered the trunk to the ground, Tom groaned. It was the deckhand he had caught pulling Iain out of the lifeboat.

"Stay still."

He braced himself and pushed the lad behind him as the sailor turned to look. Surely the ruffian wouldn't dare to cause any trouble with all these witnesses about? But the crowd was melting away like damp snowflakes. The sailor grinned, exposing rotting stumps of teeth,

"We're quits now, ain't we? You held on to me legs in the storm."

"So I did. I didn't stop at the time to see your face."

The man threw his head back and cackled with laughter. Well. That's one enemy less to worry about. Maybe that's a good omen for my new life in Canada, Tom thought as he shouldered the trunk. His task now was to find some sort of lodging. He paced along the main street of clapboard houses with Iain trailing behind him.

"Try Widow MacKenzie," he was told by a passerby. Surely it couldn't be the same person? Tom squeezed through the door of a small shop stuffed full with barrels of dried goods, heaped-up tools and sacks of seed. The owner bustled in as the doorbell jangled. It wasn't her of course, but a short, round woman with busy eyes. Her voice was different too. Just a few tatters left of a Scottish accent. Tom breathed again.

"Aye, I've a small room upstairs that would do you and the lad. There's my husband's old workshop you could have too, if you give it a lick of paint. You'd take your meals with us, all included."

Tom nodded. It would do for the time being. He gave the

smaller bags to Iain and heaved his trunk up the ladder to the first floor. Mrs. MacKenzie hovered in the doorway of the clean but bare bedroom until he said he needed to rest. Even then he had to almost push her out. The evening meal was a big bowl of fish stew. He and Iain fell on it, famished after their weeks of mouldering oatcakes and salted meat.

"Here's my family. Eliza's just had her twentieth birthday. Helen's my youngest," Mrs. MacKenzie presented them as if they were part of the menu. "And Rab, of course, my firstborn. I've had to be both mother and father to them since their papa died," she sniffed. "I never expected life would be so hard in a new country. Still the girls will have an easier time of it when they get married."

Her eyes stopped their constant flickering and fixed on Tom's face. Eliza simpered while her sister blushed and their brother grunted. Oh dear, she's as bad as Mrs. Bennett, determined to marry them off, Tom thought. Both of them are penny plain too, with their broad hips and moon faces, younger versions of their mother. Rab though was a sturdy lad, with a firm jaw. Maybe he took after his father. Tom envied Iain whose youth and lack of English meant that he could concentrate on eating his way through the tasty food without having to talk. Tom meanwhile faced a fusillade of questions at that meal and every time afterward when he ventured downstairs.

"I hear tell that you saved the lives of everyone on board," she announced the next morning at breakfast, nodding in excitement so that her double chin jiggled.

"That's not true at all," Tom replied, keeping his voice light.

She tapped the side of her nose. "Surely you know you can't keep any secrets here, just like back home. I heard you were a hero." She surveyed his long frame, sitting stiff and uneasy. "A brave sailor, they said."

Tom munched on his bacon while he ransacked his memory for the stories the captain used to tell about his early life. If only

I had listened to his ramblings, he thought. I need to borrow them now.

"No, not a proper sailor although I was raised near the sea. I learned about boats from an old fisherman when I was a boy. But I never went to sea to earn my living. I was a shipping clerk in Liverpool."

She kept nodding but her smile slipped a little. "What will you do in Canada?"

"Buy a farm but that's not all. I've brought something very novel with me. I'll show you."

They waited until he came back with a wooden box. Mother and daughters gawped at him while he unstrapped it.

"Have you seen one of these before? I brought it across the Atlantic, the finest camera I could buy. Photography is all the rage now."

They all ooed and ahhed in a satisfactory way.

"I'm sure your camera is very fashionable but I'd prefer a proper portrait. Would you draw a likeness of me?" Eliza pouted.

Tom smiled tightly, thinking that she was barely worth the effort of a photograph, let alone a portrait. He would prefer to paint Rab's rugged features.

"I would be honored to do so, but my first task is to buy some land," he said.

"Aye. You'll need to be settled before the winter," said Mrs. MacKenzie. "You've never seen a Canadian winter? It's colder than you would ever believe."

"Iain can give me a hand. And maybe you would like to earn some money helping me?" Tom asked Rab.

The young man shrugged. "There's not much left now. All the good land's been taken. If folk sell up, it's to people they know."

Was that a hint of malice in his eyes? Tom squared his shoulders. "We'll have to see what we can find."

So he hired a horse, swung Iain up onto the saddle in front of him and set off to explore the countryside. He asked advice from everyone they met and found to his surprise that the boy was very useful. Now that he was clean and well fed, the urchin had become a handsome lad with delicate features and wistful eyes. He charmed people, especially middle-aged women. His hesitant English only increased his appeal. So he smoothed the way for Tom, translating the Gaelic spoken by people outside the town and making Tom seem less of an outsider. But after two weeks of riding out in ever wider circles, they had found no land for sale. One evening, sweating, saddle sore and scourged by mosquitoes they were riding along the northern shore of Bras d'Or Lake, near the settlement of Wagamatcook. Dispirited they stumbled off the horse's back and set about making a camp on the shore.

"I'm sure our luck will turn," Tom said, trying to cheer himself up as well as Iain. "Look at this lovely sea loch here and the hills on the other shore. Not so different from home."

"I don't like those dark woods behind us." Iain pointed at the ranks of birch, maple, and larch. "Who knows what beasts are hiding there?"

When they rose the next day, Tom affected a heartiness he didn't feel as he heated up some porridge on the still glowing campfire. "Well at least no bears came to eat us in the night. There is another living creature though. Isn't that a man I can see coming this way, with a fishing rod?" Tom greeted the stranger as he drew closer and with Iain's help asked his usual questions about farms for sale. To his astonishment Mr. MacLelland gave a wary nod of his head, shouldered his rod, and led them to his farm. Iain talked to him with more excitement than he had ever shown before. Tom couldn't follow much of their quick-fire Gaelic; so he concentrated on inspecting the farm. Most of it was pasture with healthy looking beasts and hay meadows. A patch of the original forest remained alongside a fast-flowing stream and there was an orchard of apple trees and sugar maples. Seventy acres altogether, with a solid one and a half story house of squared logs. After their tour Mr. MacLelland, a hardy-looking man in his sixties tapped Tom on the chest. "I'm willing to sell to you," he said, in careful English. Both men turned to Iain for him to translate in detail.

"Why has he agreed to sell to a stranger?"

The boy's face was solemn. "I told him you're a good man, a hero for saving the ship and a saint for adopting me." He paused and grinned. "That's only a wee bit of the reason. His parents are from Skye, like mine, and he would prefer his farm went to a *sgitheanach* and a *sasannach* rather than some odd fellow from Lewis or Barra. His second cousin would like to buy it, but he's a miser and a drunkard who won't offer a fair price."

"Ah, I see. And what would Mr. MacLelland call a fair price?"

"The cousin offered £150, but it's worth £200."

"Hmm." Tom suspected he was being tricked. £200 was a great deal of money and it would use up most of what Mr. Armstrong had given him to start his new life. But what choice did he have? He had to escape from living with the MacKenzies even if he still rented a studio from them. The farm would mean he and Iain wouldn't starve. The boy was more animated than he had ever seen him, his eyes pleading for Tom to agree. But then he was a Gael, rooted to the land. This land might be in another country, but Iain wanted to burrow down deep into its red soil.

"£200 it is," he said, shaking Mr. MacLelland's hand.

Chapter 29

Cape Breton Island, Summer 1862

So Tom left his photographic equipment in Sydney and became a farmer. The rush was on to get everything ready before the winter set in. Hay to be cut, potatoes lifted, oats and apples harvested. Rab came to help with cutting down trees and preparing logs. Tom drew quick sketches of him, trying to capture his supple strength as he wielded an axe or poured a pitcher of water over himself to cool down.

"Waste of time," Rab growled when Tom showed them to him. "Go draw the girls."

At this time of year neighbors helped each other with getting harvests in, repairing roofs or lending a horse. Tom went to local farms to help with Iain to translate although Tom's understanding of the Gaelic language was improving. The farmers were hospitable and courteous, if a little reserved. So after a dram or two had been drunk in the evening, he took out the crumpled drawing he still kept in his pocket. They humored him as he passed it round, turning it this way and that, with a scratch of the head. Then came the teasing.

"She's a redhead, you say? Well that makes her a rare beast among hundreds of others."

"You don't know her name? Or if she left home at all? She could be in Australia, hopping along with the kangaroos."

"Or a grumpy wifey with a clutch of children."

He noticed how Iain cringed each time the paper appeared and Tom himself began to feel foolish. So after a few weeks, he stowed the drawing away in a cupboard.

Then one sunny evening when he was out on the lake and watching the sun dip behind the sentinel trees it came to him that he was enjoying life more than he had for years. One of his greatest pleasures was paddling this old birch bark canoe Mr. MacLelland had left behind. After a few tumbles into the water, Tom had learnt how to steer while balancing on his knees. He had thought he had lost his interest in boats of all kinds but the canoe, like a coracle, was light enough to be carried on head and shoulders. Agile as a salmon in the water and so easy to maintain. Any damage could be repaired with a piece of rolled-up bark from a paper birch tree made watertight with twine from spruce roots and a splash of resin. The first time he watched someone do such a repair he thought how the bark could also be used as a parchment and wondered if the local Indians had ever used the material for drawing maps. Probably they had no need to do so, for like Highlanders they would store every feature of their surroundings in their minds. Every contour of the land, each rock and tree would be familiar, tattooed in their memories.

He had heard accounts of the native tribes of the Americas with their outlandish dress and fierce habits but never seen any of them. A faint memory arose from his childhood of visiting a fair at the Abbey Fields in Kenilworth although surely not with his father who disapproved of such places. There were tall, glossy skinned Zulus and some paler tribesmen with intricate patterns on their faces although he couldn't say where they came from. They had an exotic air but were shrunken in captivity, caged lions with drooping heads.

The memory aroused his curiosity about the native people of Cape Breton. He asked the neighbors who responded with varying degrees of incredulity.

"Savages," said Simon MacDonald, as he paused in filling his pipe with tobacco. "There's a few still hanging on up in the hills. An idle lot with no idea about farming." He spat into the fire.

Simon's aged mother had been dozing in her chair but suddenly she opened her eyes wide. "They're no savages. Papists maybe, but that was the fault of the French missionaries. When I came here as a wee girl, we would have died in the first winter if the Indians hadn't helped us. They brought us game. Showed us how to make snowshoes. Mi'kmaqs they're called, Macs like us. You know they call their shoes moccasins? That's from *mo chasan*, 'my feet'."

Her son snorted and spat into the fire again, making the flames hiss.

There was only one drawback to his new existence: the MacKenzie girls. They invited themselves for a visit, their cart brimming with hampers and their mouths spilling gossip. Tom was pleased to see Betsy the mare, with her soft snickering mouth and rounded belly, but the same features on the young women were not so appealing. How he wished he could quiet their chatter with the gift of an apple for them to chomp on.

The greatest surprise was the change that came over Iain during the summer. Once scrawny and timid, he had turned into a different boy. As if the stolen child had returned to replace the sickly changeling. Stunted before, he sprouted skyward now he was rooted in more fertile soil. Strong and athletic, it was clear that he was older than Tom had thought, fourteen years at least and rapidly becoming a man. He had become fluent in English and with Tom's help soon learnt to read and write. The lad was useful, too. He could set snares to trap squirrel and possum for the pot, catch trout and chub from the river, as well as plant oats and potatoes. Outdoor work had calmed and strengthened Tom, too. He awoke each morning, relishing the day ahead. He was still at a loss though when it came to fending off Eliza and Helen. He tried staying taciturn when they came, but that only served to pique their interest in the moody, mysterious Englishman.

Although he was bone weary, Tom couldn't always sleep well in the midsummer nights that scarcely darkened. One night he woke abruptly, feeling uneasy. He lit a lamp and took down the rifle from the wall before walking to the door and listening hard. Was there something outside? A bear, crazed with the need to load its stomach before hibernating? Hearing nothing more he tiptoed over to Iain's bed to see if he was awake. All was silent, too silent. There were no sounds of breathing. Tom swept the beam of light over the bedclothes and saw that the bed was empty. Heart pounding in his ears, Tom searched the rest of the cabin. Ian's coat and boots were gone too. Had he run away? But why? He had seemed happy enough. Murky fears darkened Tom's mind as he got ready to go into Sydney. If only he had a horse, but he had been unwilling to buy a beast with his shrinking savings. He debated whether to take the gun but then put it back. If things turned nasty, he would have to bluff his way through. The partial light made the forest threatening. The ranks of red spruce brooded, the strange furrows on their grayish pink trunks so different from any European tree. There were rustlings and scrapings beneath the thickets of maple and dogwood on the shore as he paddled along the lake. Foreboding drove him onward, through the woods, past the humped shapes of cabins and barns toward the sleeping town. There was no sign of wakefulness except for a few wavering lights gleaming down at the harbor. One after another he pushed open the doors of the drinking dens and scanned the faces within. Some shouted at him, others squinted blearily or slumped dead eyed but there was no Iain among them. Tom's desperation was in full flight now. Had the boy been lured onto one of the boats? If so, he would never be seen again except as a bloated corpse snagged in a fishing net.

He stopped in the empty alleyway, trying to slow his breathing. As he did so, he heard a murmuring. He stumbled toward the noise that seemed to be coming from inside a timber shack near the shore, even more ramshackle than the other ones. There was a sliver of light beneath the door. He nudged it open. Inside was a group of people, of both sexes and all ages, swaying together as they hummed. Above them soared the strains of a pure tenor voice. Tom gasped and pushed his way into the crowd. There in the center, standing on a stool, was Iain singing, his eyes half-closed in concentration.

"What are you doing?"

Iain's voice faltered and the bemused audience gaped at Tom. He seized the boy by the arm, dragging him outside.

"How dare you run away? When I think of all I've done for you."

"How could I ever forget? The big man taking in the stinking beggar boy."

"Have you gone back to selling your body? Old habits die h—"

Tom's words were throttled, as tough fingers crushed his neck. It took all his strength to pry them off. They stood glaring at each other, Tom rubbing his neck and Iain groping in his jacket pocket. He held out a fistful of coins.

"Aye, I earned money right enough. For singing, singing to homesick people. Some of them came over with us. You wouldn't know them. Far beneath you." He trickled the coins through his fingers, letting them drop to the ground. "That's for my keep." He turned on his heel.

"You've more than earned your keep. Come back home."

Iain stopped and Tom waited. Finally, the boy nodded and they trudged back home together. For a long time neither said a word, until Iain blurted out, "You talk about me running away but it's you who's hiding secrets. What are you running away from?"

Tom was silent, thinking how the two of them had become fellow travelers, much against his will. What was Iain to him now? An adopted son? The nearest he had to any sort of family. Someone who deserved the truth. So as they walked he told the boy his story in a simple way, not wanting to load him with too much adult cargo. He explained how grief over his mother's death had made him go to sea and how he was drawn to survey work. He skimmed over the details of Richard's suicide, but he was honest about why he jumped ship, lingering over his later adventures to entertain the boy. Iain listened without interrupting and stayed silent when Tom had finished.

"What are you thinking?"

"Well, I'm glad to hear you've not done anything really terrible, like killing someone." Then he added, with an edge of anxiety in his voice," Will you be safe here?"

"I'm sure I will be," Tom replied with more confidence than he felt. "But we must always guard our tongues."

"Especially with the Ugly Sisters"

"Now that's no way to talk about the Misses MacKenzie." Tom tried to sound stern, but his laughter bubbled through.

"You don't want anything to do with ladies?"

"No, that's not true. It's only ill-favored ones I avoid. I would dearly love to see the girl whose picture I keep."

Iain shivered, "She sounds like a fairy woman or a vision from another world."

"No. Flesh and blood."

"But she's gone for good. You need to find someone else. Then the MacKenzies would leave you alone."

"If only it was so easy."

Once they were back inside the cabin, Tom took off his coat. As he hung it up he heard a crackling in the pocket. Reaching inside he found the letter he had been composing on the ship and had never finished. Pricked by guilt he resolved to finish it after he had slept. The next morning he smoothed it out and started to write.

My apologies, Emma.

So much has happened since I began this letter. I put it away in my pocket and have just discovered it. In the end I adopted the boy Iain, with a bad grace, I fear. He has since proved his worth in helping me clear the ground I bought and stopping me from becoming too lonely. At first, I lodged with a widow lady. Unfortunately, she's extremely inquisitive and sees me as a good prospect for one of her daughters. That of course is impossible because any marriage would risk revealing my true identity. Not that either daughter tempts me. Iain says I must find another lady to woo so that the MacKenzie sisters and their mother will leave me in peace but how can I do that? It would be dishonorable to mislead another lady when I'm in no position to marry anyone.

Tom sighed, wondering what to write next. Then he banged the table with his fist and started to scribble at great speed.

Inspiration has suddenly come to me. I trust that you won't be offended by how I word the envelope, but I do believe it will do the trick.

He rushed to complete the letter and put it in an envelope, whistling as he did so.

Two days later, Betsy came trotting up to the cabin and for once Tom was pleased to see Eliza and Helen. "I've a plan to suggest," he said smiling. They gurgled and giggled as he proposed returning in the cart with them to the town so that he could take the long-promised photograph.

"Not wearing these old things," wailed Eliza, scowling at her checked cotton dress. "I must put on my hooped crinoline and best gown."

"Don't worry. I've business in town. I'll take you home first to change into your finery."

He delivered the twittering girls to their mother whose eyes glinted as they told her about the proposed photograph. Then he walked back along the main street until he came to the hut near the quay that acted as shipping office and post office.

"Good day, Miss Munroe," he said to the thin, sharp-eyed woman enthroned behind the counter. He knew her as a friend and confidante of Mrs. MacKenzie. "I would like to send this letter to England. It's very important."

She took it from him, fingering it as she put it on the scales. Tom watched her pore over the address, mouthing "The Grange," before reading aloud, "Royal Leamington Spa, England," and lingering over the name of the recipient, "Miss Emma Wilson."

"It's going to someone very dear to me." Miss Munroe stared at him, her lips parted and pale eyebrows raised so high that they almost scuttled into her hairline. "A young lady?"

He drew nearer the counter and nodded. "A very particular young lady. My betrothed."

Miss Munroe gasped.

"To my great sorrow she has had to remain at home with her mother who's an invalid."

"But she will be sailing to join you?"

"In due course, but I don't know when."

"Well . . . may I offer you my felicitations."

After paying the stunned Miss Munroe for the stamps, he sauntered back to the MacKenzie house.

"Oh, my goodness gracious, you should have given us more time to prepare ourselves," trilled Eliza, who had changed into her best gown, a lemon shade that didn't suit her ruddy complexion. Never mind, Tom thought, the color won't matter in a photograph. Helen was dressed in pale blue, her bodice pulled tightly across her bolstered bosom. He guided them to a bench beneath a maple tree in the garden where they fidgeted, arranging their bulky skirts. Finally he settled them and explained the importance of complete stillness. They stretched their mouths into wide smiles that drooped before the four minute exposure was over. Still, he couldn't care at all what the result was like because he had secured his escape. He packed up his equipment and made his farewells as quickly as possible, declining the offer of tea. As he emerged onto the street, he nearly bumped into Miss Munroe who was striding up to the MacKenzies' door. Excitement and disapproval battled on her face as she nodded to him.

Chapter 30

Cape Breton Island, Winter 1862

Once the farm and its buildings were readied for the winter, Tom turned his attention to the two rooms he had rented from Mrs. MacKenzie. One was to be a studio for customers and the back room would be used for developing photographs. Iain scrubbed walls, floors, and ceilings. Tom watched the boy's muscles flexing and stretching beneath his rolled-up shirt sleeves. Once he had finished, Tom told him to clean everything a second time, despite his grumbles.

"Everything must be shipshape. Any specks of dust will find their way into the camera. Then we'll have black spots on the plate ruining the picture."

Iain made a face but did as he was asked. Tom was keen to set up his business before winter tightened its grip. He scrubbed the windows facing the street, rubbing the smeary surface with crunched-up newspaper soaked in vinegar until the glass gleamed. One side was to display his artistic skills with framed watercolors of forests, farms, and coastline. Above them, he mounted a row of painted miniatures based on sketches of passengers from the ship. His Scottish landscapes had all been stored away even though they might well appeal to immigrants who wanted a memento of home. After all, John Robinson the shipping clerk from Liverpool wouldn't have the means or leisure for painting expeditions so far from home. When Tom had leafed through his earlier work, his heart lurched when he saw her. Creased but still glowing, her features in tune, tawny curls drifting from under her scarf. What secret lay behind those limpid, wide-spaced eyes? What should he do with the picture? He wondered whether to recreate it as a miniature and display it with the others. Maybe one day she would suddenly appear and recognize herself in the window? He didn't want to banish her to a dusty drawer after carrying her in his pocket over so many miles, but how could he live in peace if she was there, her gaze following his every movement? He stroked her features before hiding her away among the other rejected sketches, dried and pressed relics from his earlier life.

The other window was to be the modern one, devoted to photography. Here were to be pictures of local homes and workplaces, cabins, farmhouses, and fishing boats. The sort of scenes immigrants might want to send to families back home as a record of their newfound prosperity. Mostly though he displayed portraits. He had asked people to pose for him, fishermen with faces as roughened as the bark of spruce trees, youngsters shining with hope and vitality, and babies with joyous smiles. He winced as he looked at his studies of the ungainly Misses MacKenzie. He had better include them or he would risk offending the family even more. What plain and unprepossessing young women they were! Technically though it was an excellent photograph, sharply delineated and well composed with the maple tree spreading its canopy behind them. Finally he added photographs of Iain that he thought showed an artistic sensibility. He had achieved a blurred effect that added pathos without sentimentality. Emma had told him how popular such studies of street urchins were in England.

Iain was now busy in the workroom dusting down the props they had collected for portrait studies. He had already carried some of them through into the studio. A spindle-legged chair, an occasional table, an elaborate vase in the Chinese style. All items that gave an illusion of civilized comfort to the rough reality of living on the edge of a wilderness. Tom stood back to survey his work. He could hear Iain's feet shuffling behind him as he manhandled a second load from the workshop. A shout, followed by a crash, made Tom jump.

"What on earth?" He turned to see a cracked picture frame

and pottery fragments strewn around the boy's feet.

"Those things cost me money I can ill afford," he snapped but Iain took no notice. He pointed at the pictures of himself.

"You can't put those up."

"I can do whatever I think right." Tom was angry, but he glimpsed something fugitive behind Iain's fury, like the shadow of a deer hiding among the trees. So he drew a deep breath, "What's wrong?"

"They shame me. I look like a wretch, a stray dog."

"I wanted to show how you've changed from a ragged waif to how you are now. Strong, on the cusp of manhood."

"Do you think I want folk to pity me?"

"But they won't. They're inspiring."

"You don't know what it's like to be despised."

Tom patted him on the shoulder. "I'll take them down. Get a broom for the rubbish."

Iain did as he asked while Tom removed the prints, disappointed as they were his best work so far. For a moment he found himself hankering after naval life where men held their tongues, obeyed orders, and kept unruly feelings stowed away.

When he opened for business the next day, Tom was heartened by the interest shown in the small town. Plenty of people trooped into his studio, exclaiming at the displays, especially the photographs and wanting to know how the camera worked. Unfortunately, their interest didn't extend to spending much money.

Autumn, or fall as they kept reminding him to call it, had roared in with its chilly breath. Tom realized that traveling each day from the farm would be dangerous once there were heavy falls of snow. It would be best if he stayed at the studio while Iain looked after the farm, feeding himself from their stores and any game he could catch. Their neighbors had warned them about how cabin fever could drive a man demented, but Iain was sensible enough to manage.

At least by the coast the snow was cleared enough so that he could venture out if he stuffed himself into so many layers of garments that he moved like a stiff-legged marionette. One December morning he felt restless and went out for a walk along the shore, beyond the wooden warehouses and shacks, along to where the small boats were dragged up on dry land for their winter hibernation. He trudged along feeling dispirited. Everything was a dingy iron gray. The sullen sea where ice was forming a slush on the surface, the snow heavy sky voided of color, and the grubby heaps of cleared snow beside buildings. Hearing running feet behind him he turned to see David, the lad from the shipping office, with a parcel under his arm.

"It's just arrived from England and I thought you'd want it at once."

Tom thanked him and grasping the heavy package to his chest, hurried back to the studio. He was sure that everyone in the street would be peering through their windows and speculating about what he was carrying. It was exciting to receive such a weighty parcel. It must be from Emma, his only link to the outside world. He hurried back to his workroom. Inside the box there was something bulky protected by a layer of sacking but he turned his attention first to the envelope lying on top.

Dear Brother,
October, 1862
I was greatly relieved to receive your letter and to know that you arrived safely. I understand your reason for addressing me as an unmarried woman but I was also vexed. What would have happened if Fred had seen it first? He doesn't know that I met you in Liverpool and it would have been very awkward to have to explain my secrecy. Fortunately he is away from home so often tending to his patients that he would be unlikely to intercept the postman before me and he is too preoccupied to be curious about my activities. Nevertheless, I thought it prudent to give him some infor-

mation about you as deceits are often uncovered later. I explained that you had left the Navy, suggesting without actually lying, that you had departed of your own accord. He was distracted as he was preparing to leave to attend a confinement.

"I wish him good luck in the colonies," he said, snapping his bag closed.

"He addressed the letter to Miss Emma Wilson to give the impression that he has a fiancé in England. I believe that he's being plagued by the unwelcome intentions of two young ladies and wanted to discourage them."

Fred seemed not to be listening but then he surprised me by looking up sharply.

"Well, I understand his motive but I disapprove of falsehoods. How will he extricate himself when the young lady fails to appear?"

That's a very good question, I thought but not one I can answer.

Turning to the more congenial subject of photography I hope you will be pleased with the contents of this parcel. At first I thought I would merely recommend the equipment to you and suggest that if you couldn't obtain it locally you could send to America for it. The Americans are at the forefront of photographic developments. However, I then wondered if the terrible civil war there might disrupt communications with Canada.

After you left I was worried that the advice I gave you about photography was not as helpful as it could have been. I'm an amateur who can please myself and experiment with whatever artistic fancy I choose. You need to earn your living. A few weeks ago, when I was doing some shopping in Leamington Spa, I noticed a new photographic studio had opened. Curiosity drove me inside and I spoke at length with Mr. Ellis the proprietor, under the pretext that I wanted to have some family portraits taken. He showed me examples of very fine portraits, the size of a visiting card, the modern version of the painted miniature, you could say. They were available at a modest cost. I was amazed and asked what sort of camera he used. With a flourish he produced a carte de visite camera with four small lenses. An ingenious sliding mechanism enables you to take eight photographs at once on a single wet plate. These can all be the same pose or you can cover and uncover different lenses to produce a variety of studies. Then they can be cut up and pasted on individual mounts. They became popular in France first and are all the rage here now. I had to smile sweetly while he gave me a lengthy exposition on the principles of photography, delivered at a slow pace suitable for a young child, or a lady. However, this was a small price to pay for acquiring such useful knowledge about this particular camera. I hope that it will bring you good fortune.

With my fondest wishes,

Emma

After reading the letter Tom couldn't wait to excavate the camera. Its four lenses in their brass surrounds gleamed inside their wooden casing like portholes looking out to a new horizon. Tom had no difficulty in kindling interest among his neighbors. The next day there was a gaggle waiting and stamping their feet outside the door before he opened. By the third day, he had an array of portraits in his window, with a list of prices. He topped them with a sign declaring that these miniature portraits were the height of fashion in London, Edinburgh, and Perth. He chose not to mention their popularity in Paris in case Presbyterian sensibilities considered that information too racy.

Emma was right about the appeal of these small, affordable photographs. They sold well and come the spring thaw more people would arrive from the countryside. I can afford a horse now, he thought, and if I get a mule too for the equipment I could even set myself up as an itinerant photographer, traveling to the more distant communities. That idea cheered him. It wasn't so different from his surveying days when Captain Otter would send him out from the *Porcupine* to Highland villages to find out the names of the bays, hills, and beaches.

Chapter 31

Cape Breton Island, Spring 1863

Spring arrived in a late flurry during May and Tom was in a buoyant mood as he rode on a hired beast toward the farm after several weeks away. He would buy his own horse. Better still, get Iain to choose the animal. It would be a reward for the lad after the long winter months that had been every bit as severe as Mrs. MacKenzie had warned him. Everything here was on a grander scale than in the Highlands, the cold more bone numbing and the storms more brutal but it was the marauding sea ice that most surprised him. After Christmas, the thickening slush had grown into great ice pans along the shores before breaking free and then melding together into platforms. Sea currents pushed these out but they returned in frozen billows that ground against the shore. Tom found himself whistling, a sea shanty of all things, but who was to hear him? Everything looked in good order as he passed through the curtain of woodland around the farm. The house itself appeared sound although the elements had turned the wood dark gray. It's my own landlocked vessel, he thought, glowing with the pleasure of ownership. The last of the snow was swept away from the door and smoke was curling up from the chimney. He shouted out a greeting as he loosened the latch and stepped inside. There was no answer but then he was half expecting Iain to be busy outside. No, he could hear running footsteps and there was the boy himself, tucking his shirt into his trousers, his fair skin reddening and his dark hair sticking up in stooks. He seemed dazed and surly, like a bear roused early from his winter den.

"It's good to be back. I'd forgotten how beautiful it's out here in the woods. I've spent too much time indoors, taking endless portraits."

"I'll make us tea." Iain stumbled toward the fireplace and unhooked the pot from its chain.

What was the matter with the boy? He was usually so neat in his movements. Tom wondered as he took off his coat and hung it on a hook by the door. Of course he was growing fast and that made a lad clumsy. As Tom lowered himself onto a stool he heard the sound, a sneeze, a stifled one but definitely a sneeze. He froze as he tried to locate it. It was coming from behind the partition that separated the kitchen from the sleeping quarters. Iain stiffened and banged the pot down on the earth floor. He turned to Tom with a strange expression on his face, a mixture of guilt, defiance, and triumph. He darted behind the partition and re-emerged, followed by a slender young girl. Tom nearly fell off his stool as he stared open-mouthed at a sculpted brown face with a strong nose and dark eyes, framed by black ropes of plaited hair. All three figures stood motionless as if in a tableau. Tom recovered first and cleared his throat.

"Are you going to introduce me to your friend?" he croaked, aware of how ridiculous he sounded.

"They called her Effie but she's got a Mi'kmaq name, too."

The girl stood impassive beside him. Iain shuffled sideways and pulled her close. Here was this youth, this urchin he had adopted, turned into a man. Tom clenched his fists so hard that his nails bit into his palms.

"You'd better explain," he said eventually, looking from one to the other. He felt disgust as he looked at the girl. He had seen young Indian women like her skulking among the shacks down on the shore, but he was horrified to find one of them inside his own house. He remembered feeling sickened by the prostitutes, swarming cockroaches who spilled out from the shadows toward their ship when it arrived in port. They sullied everything they touched, scuttling away when an officer appeared but creeping back again, an unstoppable plague of vermin. How he hated the idea of Iain, this wholesome boy, this young David, being tainted by such a woman. Still, knowing the lad's quick flares of anger, he forced himself to stay silent.

"I went crazy on my own," Iain said, sticking out his lower lip. "I had to get out of this valley, to see what was inland." He shrugged, "A couple of weeks ago, I reached one of the old trading huts where the Indians used to bring in furs to sell. It looked empty and I turned back but then I heard voices from inside."

"A drinking den, no doubt."

Iain glowered. "They invited me in to the fire and gave me venison stew. The sweat had turned to ice in my hair and eyebrows. It was grand to thaw out and swallow that tasty food. I went back a few times, for the company. Then one day I found Spring Thaw. That's her proper name, put into English." He smiled at the girl, squeezing her brown twigs of fingers in his own pale, broad hands. "This time it was different. Two men had come in, strangers looking for a fight. I slipped out and was just strapping my snowshoes on when I heard a scuffle behind me. They were kicking Spring Thaw. She fell out of the door. Blood all over her face and dripping down into the snow. They went back in and slammed the door shut. She lay there as if she was dead."

Tom stared at the girl. She stared back and then opened her mouth. Tom was astonished to hear her speak English clearly, in a quiet but insistent voice.

"I fainted and when I woke up Iain was wiping away the blood." She gulped, and went on. "I know what you're thinking. I'm not one of those women who sell their bodies to white men."

"Or let them force her," Iain added. "She drew a knife on those two."

"Tell me who you are then." For so long Tom had hunted for a mysterious girl who had scarcely seemed real. His gorge rose as he faced this flesh-and-blood woman who had appeared from nowhere. A completely different girl, a dark negative image of the one he had lost. Completely wrong.

She kept looking at him. Tom shivered. It was as if she were reading his thoughts.

"My people lived here when the white men first came. Like biting insects, forcing us back into the hills. I was born at the time of the thaw when we went down to the shore to fish. One year, when I was very young, men with dogs attacked us in the night. We fled but I couldn't keep up and was captured."

Iain squeezed her hand but she took no notice, fixing her dark eyes on Tom's face.

"I was taken to an orphanage, not here but on another island."

"Prince Edward Island, I think," Iain said.

Her voice grew fierce. "They tried to beat the Indian out of me but once I was old enough I ran away. Came back here to find my family again."

"But she couldn't. You're safe here though."

"And how old are you now?" Tom asked.

"About fifteen summers, I think."

"She doesn't know exactly, just like me." Iain nudged her, so that she giggled. "She can stay with us, can't she?"

"It's not a matter for jesting. Is she here as a guest? A servant? Or another adopted child for me to raise? You're not a full-grown man yet, but you've lain with this young woman. Am I right?"

"She's my friend." Iain's face was on fire.

"A friend who shares your bed? I can understand why you rescued her, but I can't have this kind of thing going on under my roof."

"Why not? Lots of men live with native women."

"Back in the old days unmarried men took a country wife. People frown on that now."

"You only care about what people think."

"Because I have to. I can't draw attention to myself. You know that. What if she has a child?" Tom gestured at Spring Thaw, without looking at her.

Iain seemed to shrink in on himself, but Spring Thaw let go of his hand and moved closer to Tom.

"I can work hard. I learnt the ways of hunting from my people and the orphanage taught me white women's work."

Tom forced himself to turn to her as she stood in front of him. Barefoot and wearing one of Iain's shirts that billowed over her slight frame, she stood tall and looked him in the eye.

"I'm sure you would. But it's not so simple. Leave me while I think what to do."

Iain looked thunderous. They went away to put on outdoor clothes, leaving Tom to nurse his cup of tea. Whatever decision he made would create ripples of attention from their neighbors. If he told Iain that the girl would have to leave, Tom knew that the headstrong young man would likely go with her. He couldn't manage the farm without him and besides, he was used to his presence. Forbidding them to share a bed wouldn't work now that the boy had discovered the pleasures of her body. If he tired of her when she became pregnant, he might want to send her away, like a country wife in the old days. But this girl had no family to take her back. Tom knew he could never agree to her being discarded. He was no churchgoer, but he still held to Christian principles. He sighed in exasperation. Was he doomed to be forever battered by storms? Each time he battened down to ride the winds, another tempest would rear up. He used to chafe at the doldrums of life when he was at sea, but how he longed for some tedium now. Was there no safe harbor anywhere?

Chapter 32

Cape Breton Island, Spring 1863

Tom downed his tea, wishing that he had some rum to add to it. Then he banged the cup down and stomped outside. No sign of the young people, thank goodness. He tramped over the fields, the reddish soil shrugging off its snow blanket. He saw that Iain had built a shed and stacked the tools inside. The sugar maple trees had been readied. Iain had bored holes in their trunks, secured the wooden spouts and hung the buckets from them to collect the precious sap. There would soon be so much work to do for the new season, and if he bought a horse they could do so much more, but who was the "we" to be?

His first impulse had been to throw out the lad and his Indian whore. He didn't believe for a moment Iain's tale of her defending her honor. The boy was gullible. Tom shook his head to dislodge the black swarming torment in his mind. Why was it that he was so plagued by images of the two of them together? Images that erupted in his mind of the lad's arched back and taut buttocks as he mounted that little slut. Clenching his eyes shut, Tom held his breath until his heart stopped thudding. He bent down at one of the maples to breathe in the sweet woody smell and remembered the terrified boy who had stowed away in the lifeboat. How many broken children there must be in the world, uprooted and tossed aside? Richard Williams had been one of those children, abandoned by his mother and then ill-treated by the man who took him in. Did he despair and kill himself because he was unloved? Spring Thaw too had suffered. But Tom sensed that she was supple like the birch bark he used to mend his canoe. She could bend without splitting.

By the time he returned to the cabin an hour later, Tom had made up his mind.

He told them to draw up their stools in front of the fire. There was a new one there too he noticed. Iain must have made it during the winter. Tom slid his hand over its planed surface.

"I've decided you two will marry." He held up a silencing hand as Iain opened his mouth. "You're of an age to marry with my consent. You can cut down more trees and use the wood to build your own cabin. You'll still be my apprentice in the studio and if you work hard I'll pay you a man's wages."

Spring Thaw's eyes darted between them. Iain sat with his chin resting on his fist. Then he thrust out his arm. "I'll shake your hand on that."

"Good. The first thing we must do is to arrange your wedding. We had best speak to the minister in Sydney and hope he's not too fierce a Calvinist," Tom said, with a thin smile. Iain nodded glumly.

"And afterward we'll go and buy a horse and cart, or buggy, I should say." Tom laughed as Iain's face lit up.

"And we'll need a sleigh for the winter. I could make it."

Dread hunched down in Tom's stomach as they neared the manse in Sydney the next day. The last time he had visited a church had been at Richard's funeral when he had vowed never to enter a place of worship again. He hated the thought of his friend being treated like a leper, banished outside the churchyard wall.

Tom made sure that the young people were scrubbed and neat before they set out. Iain wore a new worsted jacket that strained across his shoulders and the girl was in a serviceable dark green dress although she refused to wear shoes.

"I've never seen any of you in my church before," said the Reverend Fraser as they sat opposite him on hard chairs. The air in his study was as cold as his voice. "Is the Indian with child?"

Tom flashed a warning glance at Iain. "The young woman is not with child and if she were it would surely be to Iain's credit that he intends to marry her."

The minister grunted, "It's all very irregular."

Iain spoke up, "How is that, sir? I'm young but old enough to know my own mind. I remember an old elder from the church back home. He said, 'God didn't give sheep horns so that they could wound the lambs.'"

A red mottling crept up the minister's neck. After a silence, his lips unsealed themselves enough to squeeze out an agreement to marry the couple. Tom felt proud of Iain's dignified courage. Heads turned, eyes swiveled and tongues clattered as the three of them walked into the church next Sunday to hear the banns read. Tom nodded to faces he recognized and ushered his charges into a pew near the back. How sturdy and open-faced Iain was. The soft contours of his face had melted away to reveal the prominent cheekbones and strong jaw beneath. The girl was modest and neat in her movements, showing no fear in what must be an ordeal for her.

After a sermon that wallowed slack-sailed with no following wind of inspiration, the minister announced that he had banns to declare. Tom smiled encouragement at Iain, but to his amazement the names announced were those of Stephen Miller and Eliza MacKenzie. The minister's voice boomed but then slurred when he came to Iain and Spring Thaw's turn. Tom craned his neck to see Eliza's fiancé, but too many Sunday hats blocked his view. Tom took no more notice of the words of the service. They were waves slapping and slurping against the hull of a boat. His companions sat rigid. At the end he motioned to them to stay seated while the congregation filed out. They had been gawped at; now it was their turn to gawp. Tom was overjoyed to see that Stephen Miller was short, stout and nearly twenty years older than his intended bride. He had round startled eyes, drooping moustaches, and no visible neck. Mrs. MacKenzie flashed her large yellow teeth and introduced her prospective son-in-law. Tom was politeness itself; only his sparkling eyes betrayed him. As he followed his charges through the churchyard, Tom could hear Mrs. MacKenzie talking loudly to another matron, "What a disgrace! Native or half-breed, would you say?"

Tom kept marching, eyes forward until they reached the buggy. Once they were trotting through the countryside he flung his head back and laughed. "He looked like a sad walrus stuffed into a suit." They all whooped until their sides ached. Maple, the new dappled pony, caught their mood and broke into a canter.

Chapter 33

Cape Breton Island, Summer 1863

"You can't go on your own," Spring Thaw said, "You don't know the land."

"Why not? I tramped through Scotland well enough."

Tom planned to travel to Lake Ainslee and the branches of the Margaree River as a traveling photographer. There were French and Irish settlers there as well as Scots, all with money to spend after netting the migratory salmon and gaspereau fish swimming upriver to their spawning grounds.

In the month since the wedding, Spring Thaw had lost any pretense of being docile. She had first shown her stubborn nature over the wedding arrangements. Refusing to wear a proper wedding dress she had insisted on a doeskin tunic, leggings, and moccasins. True, the garments were finely crafted, more supple than any suede leather that Tom had ever seen. The tunic was fringed and decorated with beads and porcupine quills. Her heavy black hair, glossy with oil and entwined with more beads, hung in a single thick plait down to the embossed leather belt that encircled her narrow waist. Standing among their neighbors she was an exotic, migratory bird blown off course and roosting among farmyard hens. Certainly she and Iain made a handsome couple, walking up the aisle with a gravity beyond their years. Tom sensed that this mongrel marriage might succeed.

After their wedding, they spent a few nights camping in the forests before returning and building a cabin for themselves. He saw how Spring Thaw could apply herself to any task, both women's and men's work. She could trap all sorts of game, bird, animal, and fish. She dragged heavy logs from a rope stretched taut across her forehead all day, barely pausing for a rest. Then he would find her in the evening, squatting cross-legged and sewing a shirt embellished with porcupine quills. It was only in farming matters that she was ignorant but she learned quickly. One evening while Tom watched her jabbing a sharpened bone needle through the sole of a moccasin he asked her, "Where did you learn these things?"

She looked up, eyebrows raised in surprise. Tom didn't usually speak to her directly. She took her time replying,

"My mother wanted me to learn the old ways. She said that a true Mi'kmaq can live off the forest without having to beg from the traders." Spring Thaw paused, her dark eyes unfocused, "Then just before the time for me to choose my woman's name, I was dragged away to the orphanage where they tried to beat the savage out of me." She spat the last words out.

"And did you choose your name?"

"I spent a day and a night in the woods waiting for an answer from my spirit creature. When I awoke I knew my name. The Spring Thaw is when I was born, a time of hunger but of hope, too. Anyway, I couldn't be called 'Dimpled Cheeks' for the rest of my life, could I?"

They both laughed.

"What spirit creature did you choose?" asked Tom.

"I won't tell it to white faces who could use it against me, only Iain."

"I wouldn't do that."

"But you are doubly white, in your skin and your hair. How can I trust you?"

"Well, I would imagine that your spirit would be a bird." It would seem that she doubted him as much as he doubted her.

Now here she was speaking bluntly again. Was it disrespect or a native habit of speaking the naked truth, rather than swaddling it in layers of good manners?

He decided to make light of it and said, "If I were a bird I could fly over to Prince Edward Island, too."

He laughed, but she frowned and said, "If you go to *Abahquit* you should take a proper sea canoe. Have you ever been in one?"

"No, but I can handle any sort of boat, including a canoe. What does the name *Abahquit* mean?" The old itch of asking about place names still needed scratching.

"It means 'The island alongside the shore.' My people went there for the summer fishing since the beginning of time."

"I only intend to travel along the rivers this time."

"But you don't know the safe currents in the rivers, let alone the sea. You need a guide."

"Do you have someone in mind?"

"I do. Will you meet him?"

Curious despite himself, Tom agreed.

Two days later, he was standing outside smoking his pipe in the early morning and enjoying the blueing of the sky when he felt a grip on his shoulder. He spun around to see a small, lean figure. The man grinned, strong white teeth gleaming in his sunburnt face. The tendons stood proud from his wiry arms as he folded them across his bare chest.

"Who are you?"

"Silent Owl. My sister told me to come."

Tom recognized the dark, deep-set eyes with their uncompromising gaze.

"Well, you were silent creeping up on me. But I thought that Spring Thaw had lost all her family?"

"She found us again when she came to the Split Lake with her man."

"Bras d'Or Lake? She never said anything about meeting you."

"There was no need to say anything until now. I've brought my canoe for us to try out."

"If you wish, but I can handle a canoe."

Silent Owl nodded and led the way, loping down to where the river flowed shallow but fast, toward the lake. He pointed to his canoe stretched out on the bank. It was bigger than the one Tom was used to, a slender snake with a crescent-shaped prow and stern curved like a ram's horn. At the front, a delicate pattern of geometric diamonds was pricked out in porcupine quills dyed black and green. After handing Tom a paddle, he pushed the vessel into the water and leapt into it. Tom's first task was to climb aboard the slithering vessel. Red with exasperation he floundered in the water. Finally, he flopped headfirst into the stern and started paddling. His fumbling efforts made the canoe spin and take in water. Silent Owl leant his body over to the other side and feathered the water with his own paddle to right them. Tom sat back on his heels and watched Silent Owl's deft movements. As Tom copied them they sped along, the canoe skimming and darting like a swallow over the water. After several miles, Silent Owl swung the boat around and they returned upstream back up the river, Tom gritting his teeth against the throbbing in his arms and shoulders. He jumped out and hauled the canoe ashore when they reached their starting point. His breath was rasping while Silent Owl was unaffected, apart from a sheen of sweat on his back and chest.

"Now we carry the canoe up to the cabin," he told Tom. They ran up the slope holding it aloft. By the time they reached home, Tom's legs were buckling. Spring Thaw stood waiting for them. Her brother spoke to her in their own language while Tom lowered the boat to the ground and tried to stop the tremor in his arms.

"My brother says you'll do if you practice some more. He'll take you on the trip."

Tom could only stand open-mouthed. He had thought that he was the one doing the choosing.

Chapter 34

Journey Across Cape Breton Island, Summer 1863

Tom and Silent Owl set out, carrying as few provisions as possible to save space for the heavy camera equipment. Tom felt naked traveling without a chart. Silent Owl packed a rifle, knife, and axe each, as well as beaver skins to sleep in and a stack of iron tools that they could trade with if they met any Mi'kmaq.

"The white men did bring some useful things over with them," he said.

Tom added oatmeal and smoked fish. Silent Owl smiled but made no comment. Spring Thaw was insistent that they take no spirits with them. "It's poison." Tom though was tired of being told what to do and hid a flask of whisky inside an oatmeal sack.

They set off in the early morning, paddling across Bras d'Or, past the basking islands where rocks lay on the shores, sleek and mottled like sealskin. The wind frisked and creased the deep blue waters. The meadows were a lush green with darker swathes of forest behind. Both water and land reminded Tom of the Hebrides but these colors were more vivid, like a child's painting. A blue heron flew over them. It too was bigger and brighter than its sober-suited British cousin. Silent Owl pointed to it and grinned. He must see it as a good omen for our journey, thought Tom. How he wished that his camera could reproduce those colors. His life had for too long been shaded in drab tones. It was time for some bright pigments.

Tom had no more time for thinking. Both the paddling and the portage were exhausting. His body had never been so tested before. As his muscles hardened he felt a kind of peace in contemplating his own insignificance. He was only one speck of life among the teeming forms of nature. Silent Owl was well named. His footfall was like an owl's muffled flight. His hunting skills kept them supplied with hare, squirrel, and waterfowl. They feasted on salmon and oysters. He spoke little but his body was eloquent as he slipped through the woods, as much part of the natural world as the raccoon or the deer. Like them he stopped often to cock his head or sniff the air. One time, he waited near a clearing and showed Tom how some of the leaves on the bushes were glistening. He bent closer and grinned at Tom. "A buck has just gone through."

Tom could understand that his companion could recognize the animal through the scent of its urine but surely not its sex too?

"How do you know it's not a doe?"

"Surely you know that the buck makes water in a high spray and the doe only on the ground."

Using spear or bow and arrow for hunting he kept the rifles for defence against strangers. His patience was endless. Another time, crouching for hours behind a large birch he mimicked the mating cry of a female turkey and eventually lured three males into his snares. He untied them and examined the birds before letting the largest two fly away.

"Why did you only keep the smallest?" Tom asked.

Silent Owl looked at him with pity. "The strongest ones will father more chicks and keep his kind alive for later hunters."

When they approached farms near Cheticamp at the western point of Lake Ainslee village, Tom was cautious. He knew that this was an area where the farms belonged to French-speaking Arcadians, a people he wasn't familiar with. The first time he told Silent Owl to wait at the edge of the settlement in case the local people set their dogs on him. Tom soon found though that he was welcomed. It would be much the same whether the settlers spoke English, Gaelic, or French. A child would spot them first and follow at a distance before skittering closer to peer at the equipment on the back of the horse.

"What've you got there, mister?"

"Never seen a magic box before? One that takes pictures?" Tom would reply.

Then the boy would rush ahead, shouting to everyone he could see and banging on doors. The adults appeared, excited too but more restrained. The men strolled over, nodding in a knowledgeable way as if it was a new plough they were examining. The women rounded up their wriggling offspring to wipe their faces and smooth down their hair. Meanwhile, Silent Owl was largely ignored as he unpacked the equipment, except for a few sidelong glances. This is how a pedlar would have been greeted in the old days, Tom thought, as someone exotic, a little suspect but welcomed for his trinkets and ribbons.

One day though they had a different reception. They met a farmer and his small son well before they reached the village.

"What do you want?" the man asked, in a voice with a hint of an Irish accent as he stared at Silent Owl. Tom pointed out the camera while the boy tugged at his father's sleeve. "Look at the Indian. Will he dress up in war paint?"

Silent Owl scowled, making the child hide behind his father's legs. Afterward he disappeared, leaving Tom to prepare the camera on his own. It took some time to shepherd the large family into position in front of their cabin. Tom hoped that Silent Owl hadn't gone for good.

Then a startling figure strode toward them out of the woods. His long hair was oiled and smoothed over his shoulders. Red, ochre and black stripes splashed his cheeks, forehead and body. Everyone turned to gape just as Tom was taking his photograph. He tossed back the curtain from his shoulders, furious that he would have to start all over again. Now the children were clamouring to appear with Silent Owl. Once those pictures were finished their mother straightened their collars for the family group photograph. Afterward Tom moved into the darkness of a barn to develop his pictures while Silent Owl stood outside, leaning on the door frame with his bronzed arms folded. His muscles squeezed the dark tattoo of his namesake bird so that it flapped its outstretched wings across his glistening bare chest. The small boy who had first greeted them now sidled up. Groping in his trouser pocket he brought out a tarnished mirror and held it up to Silent Owl's face. He recoiled in horror, covering his eyes and then peeping between his fingers before jumping back again. The child screamed with laughter. One of the men heard and came over, holding out a pocket watch. Silent Owl listened to it ticking with his mouth agape, turned it over and bit it. Scratching his head he held it out at arm's length, head cocked, before returning it. A crowd was gathered now to watch him. He started to dance in a circle, leaping and spinning in the air while he roared out a song. By the time Tom had developed the pictures, Silent Owl had collected a fistful of coins thrown at him by his audience.

When they returned to the woods that evening Tom said, "Well, we both earned good money there."

He watched his companion closely to see how he would react. Did he feel humiliated by his treatment? Silent Owl stared at Tom before roaring with laughter.

"The white faces are easier to trick than the turkey cocks," he said.

"You would do that again? It would be even better with a headdress."

Silent Owl's face stiffened. "Only a chief can wear one and I would never be chosen."

He turned his attention to the trout they were grilling. After eating they were ready to curl up in the beaver skins for the night. Tom rolled up his jacket to make a pillow and felt the hard edge of the forgotten flask. They should celebrate. He gulped some whisky down and handed the flask to Silent Owl. He coughed after the first swallow, wiped his eyes with the back of his hand and then drank steadily, his Adam's apple bobbing. Tom settled down, feeling his head swaying. It was so long since he had taken any spirits. Silent Owl started crooning in a falsetto voice. The singing soon turned to snoring. Tom smiled and fell asleep.

Chapter 35

Journey Across Cape Breton Island, Summer 1863

Tom's eyes snapped open in the darkness. He could feel his heart fluttering against his ribs. Some noise must have awoken him, something different from the usual creeping and rustling night sounds. It was close by, a murmuring in his ear, followed by a grip on his shoulder. He jerked his body into a sitting position and saw the gleam of Silent Owl's teeth in front of him.

"What's the matter?" His tongue stumbled in his parched mouth.

Silent Owl grinned and pressed Tom's chest to make him lie down again. There was a shuffling as he lay down too, grasping him with sinewy hands. Tom stiffened and struggled to get up. The hands loosened and started to gentle him by stroking up and down his back. Tom's head, still befuddled from whisky, was unable to command his heavy limbs to move. He stretched and sighed as the agile hands ranged the length of his body, over his rump and down his legs. He couldn't stop himself from rocking on waves of pleasure. Then he clenched, anticipating pain as he felt pressure from behind him. Silent Owl held back, waiting as he sensed the resistance.

Suddenly Tom remembered the cave, the cave that he and Richard had found. They were hugging the coastline and taking soundings, somewhere on the western side of the island of Harris. Tom knew that they had to take the boat inside the cave to check its dimensions, but he was terrified of the darkness within.

"Let the oars go. The tide'll carry us in," Richard whispered. Tom agreed, trembling.

Once inside, he gasped in surprise as the cave opened out into a chamber with a vaulted ceiling, like the nave of a church. So now he let his body open and accept, letting it be filled. He felt whole, complete, no longer alone.

They lay entwined and Silent Owl soon fell asleep. Tom looked at the darkness surrounding them, vast and star-speckled. A half-forgotten phrase brushed past his thoughts. "Under a wide and starry sky." Where did that come from? Wordsworth? For so long he had kept that book of poetry, but he must have left it behind on the *Porcupine*. As he floated into sleep he suddenly remembered a lisping voice saying those words. Louis, the solemn boy, looking out through the window. Louis who wanted to be a writer, not an engineer.

In the morning he wondered for an instant if he had dreamed about what had happened, but there was Silent Owl gazing at him. They both grinned. Tom's heart unfurled and billowed, breasting the waves. There was no undertow of guilt or regret. He knew now that he could be at one with another person, without harming him.

They were the only people in the world, the first inhabitants of the wilderness as they sped along in the seal-sleek canoe, stalked game, or lay down wrapped together in beaver skins. When they approached a village Tom would act the master, displaying his captive warrior as a photographer's prop, charging extra for Silent Owl's inclusion in the picture. Then in the evenings, Tom would take out his paints and try to capture the flight of the spirit behind the hooded eyes.

"You had a good hunting trip," Spring Thaw said, when they returned. "I knew you would."

Her eyes gleamed and Tom could only nod. Silent Owl slipped away the next day without warning. Tom kept his joy and his loss to himself as if his feelings were a monstrous being, a Minotaur hidden out of sight in a labyrinth. He tried to resume his life. He had delayed writing to Emma because he didn't know what he could tell her. But the thought of her generous present shamed him into taking up his pen.

Dearest Sister,

I won't begin with my usual apology although I have been tardy in replying. I know you are very busy tending to your family's needs. I can understand better now what that is like as my own family is growing. Iain has married and although he is young, I believe that he will make a success of matrimony. My daughter-in-law is a wise young woman. No doubt you will be surprised to hear that she is called Spring Thaw and is an Indian, a Mi'kmaq. She was sent to an orphanage and given Effie as a name. She refused to answer to it despite being punished. Eventually she ran away, met Iain and a fondness grew between them.

In the early days here, some of the settlers married Indian women. Now we are more civilized, the practice is frowned on. I used to share that view but Spring Thaw has opened my eyes. She exemplifies the best in both native and British mores. In some ways they are not so different. Certainly she and Iain have a similar attachment to the land. Both are frugal and industrious but like to sing, dance, and make merry once work is finished. I have wondered about how it is that they are so in tune with each other. Maybe it is because they both come from races who have been maligned by we English.

Our family will soon welcome a new member as Spring Thaw expects an arrival early next year. She has gone to live with her own family until after the birth. "I can't stay in this house of men," is what she said. Although Iain misses her he understood her decision. "Women at home always go back to their mothers for the first baby," he said.

I have recently returned from a journey across the island as an itinerant photographer. I was accompanied by Silent Owl, my daughter-in-law's brother who is a fine guide. For the first time since Richard's death, I have a friend whom I would trust with my life.

For a moment Tom stopped writing. *If only I could tell her what he means to me,* he thought. *I cannot believe there is anything wrong in our affection for each other. He makes me a happier and a better man than I would be without him. Indian society, as far as I can tell, would not condemn us but Christian society would brand us sinners.* He picked up his pen again with a sigh.

As well as taking all those photographs on my journey, I painted a portrait of my companion. Much as I enjoy using a camera I don't believe it can match a picture. It isn't only the absence of color in the photograph but because it can only capture the subject's expression for that one instant and then freeze it in time. The artist, however, has more leisure to convey the subtle play of changing emotions in his subject's face. So he reaches further into his soul. Maybe you would consider that opinion fanciful and argue that the camera is a more dispassionate observer whereas the artist imposes his own impressions on his subject.

I was amazed when I painted Silent Owl in his native war dress. He changed from a well-proportioned but unremarkable young man into a figure of such dignity and authority.

Do you remember many years ago when our parents took us to a circus in the Abbey Fields in Kenilworth and we saw the lion tamer with his beasts? How mangy and thin those lions looked. Not at all the king of the beasts. We diminish both animals and men when we force them out of their natural setting.

And I remember how angry Father was when I wept at the sight of the poor lions. "Don't be a ninny. Dry your eyes."

All this traveling in the wilderness seems to have turned me into a philosopher. Or is it age and family responsibilities that have made me serious? Tell me about your family. What of your photographic experiments?

Your affectionate brother,

Tom

"What are you doing?" The voice at his shoulder jolted him.

"Daydreaming. I've just written to Emma."

"The farm's so empty, isn't it?" Iain said. "We're like two old *bodachs* rattling around the house. When I was back home on Skye, there used to be lots of old bachelors, men who lived alone. Some couldn't afford to marry. Others just preferred it."

He patted Tom's shoulder and walked away. Tom blinked the moisture from his eyes, thinking how strange it was that his grown son had spoken to him in the words of a kind father.

Chapter 36

Newfoundland, 1864

The cabin fever seemed worse that winter. Tom pined like a prisoner with a life sentence whether he stayed on the farm or worked in his studio. Sometimes he would shudder, thinking of how he would be locked up for desertion if he were ever captured. Finally, the tumbled ice that had piled up in the bay began to shift and slink away out to sea while on Bras d'Or Lake it shrank, thinned, and broke into floating islands. The thaw meant warmer days, muddy roads, and the return of Spring Thaw. She was accompanied by her brother and cradled in her arms was the new tiny stranger, a boy named Owlet. Like his namesake he had round, startled eyes. Both parents doted on him, his mother carrying him everywhere strapped to her body while Iain darted to and fro like a bird feeding his chick. The baby never cried because he was consoled the instant his face started to crease with distress. Tom tutted at such spoiling until Iain drew him aside. "Both Indians and Highlanders know that you can't give a baby too much love."

Tom was in no mood to argue. He and Silent Owl were planning their next expedition.

"Your hunting trip, only you catch pictures instead of game," Spring Thaw said.

"We'll go to the summer hunting grounds on Cold Island," said Silent Owl. "And you will trust me to find my way there even though I've no pieces of paper."

'Newfoundland, the oldest settlement of all,' Tom replied.

'Not new to us. Our people went there every year, long before any of your white tribe arrived. You didn't need nets or spears to catch fish. You scooped your hand over the side of the canoe and picked up handfuls of them."

"I trust you, but why don't you draw a map for me?"

Tom explained to him about scale, distance, and geographical features by drawing a map of the farm and its surroundings. "Your turn now."

Tom gave him a sheet of paper and some charcoal. After frowning at the empty paper, Silent Owl drew a ridge of soaring peaks cut through by a deep fjord. Then he sketched a herd of caribou and above them an eagle on the wing. There was no sense of scale but the spare, expressive lines made Tom gasp with envy. Silent Owl finished with a group of wigwams.

"That's our destination? You've an artist's eye but it's not a map. It doesn't show me how to get there."

"All that's in here." Silent Owl tapped his head. He hurled the charcoal away and crumpled up the paper. "That's good for war paint. Nothing else." Tom was left smoothing out the creases and wondering at the skill of a man who had never had a drawing lesson in his life.

They had to cross the Cabot Strait in a large sea canoe. Six others joined them as crew. At first, the newcomers stared at Tom when they thought he wasn't looking and one of them reached out to touch his hair, wondering at the strange white cloud. After that they settled down to paddling. Once they made landfall the others headed off for the northern peninsula, a raised finger pointing toward the coast of Labrador. They would hunt for caribou in the mountains that Silent Owl had drawn. Meanwhile, Tom and Silent Owl would travel to the fishing villages of the eastern coast before heading north to join them.

The landscape was different from Cape Breton. There was no imagining here that you could be in the Highlands. It was harsher, colder, more barren and bleached. The clammy skies sagged with sea fog and the winds still blew a winter breath in June.

As before they were welcomed as a diversion in the remote villages. Children skipped after Tom as if he was the Pied Piper, full of questions and wanting to carry his camera. Their cries would bring out their mothers and one of the women would invite him to sit in front of the fire with a dish of tea. The man of the house would often saunter in and offer a dram. Tom always refused. "You don't want a blurred photograph."

Meanwhile, his wife was trussing up the children in their Sunday clothes. Once Tom had been invited into one house, the neighbors would not want to be outdone and he could work his way down the whole row of houses. After the formal pictures were taken, he would suggest that they might want to be pictured with a savage, making sure that the children overheard.

Afterward Tom liked to wander along the shore to take less formal studies of people in their work clothes. The men in their fishermen's jerseys agreed but the women were reluctant to be photographed wearing rough aprons with their sleeves rolled up and their feet sturdily booted. They reminded him of the generous fisher lasses in Stornoway who had been so particular about their Sabbath dress.

Tom and Silent Owl made their way along the eastern seaboard, letting their pack horse plod along at his own pace through villages perched like an afterthought on the ancient rocky surface. The wooden houses were all built in the same way, bunched together, mostly single storied with only the church standing taller. So when they approached the small settlement near Notre Dame Bay, Tom noticed at once the two-storied house, head and shoulders above the rest and separated from its neighbors by a stone wall. They must be richer than the others, he thought and decided to try there first. He walked up to the doorstep, camera case perched on his shoulder. While he waited for an answer, he peered into the lighted window. He was staring at the ornate lamp there when the door was opened. The figure in the doorway seized his arm and pulled him inside on tottering legs. The door into the front room was ajar and she pushed him inside.

"Here's a stranger come," she announced before disappearing. "I'm a traveling photographer." Tom's voice cracked. They all turned to look at him, open-mouthed children, bearded men with ruddy faces and women with wary smiles. None of these he recognized, except the woman who sat, straight-backed and hawk-eyed in the midst of them. A queen surrounded by her court. He knew her face although the flesh of her skull was scraped back further to the bone.

"I remember you from across the sea. You've changed occupations, I see." Her voice was as strong as he remembered. "I heard about the terrible things that befell Captain Otter's ship."

Tom wanted to flee but his feet were anchored to the floor. What did she know? Would she betray him?

"We've all made a fresh start. Would you like me to photograph your family?"

She surveyed him and then seemed to make up her mind. "Very well. Take them outside at the front of the house. Off you all go and make yourselves ready." Tom Masters and Janet MacKenzie were left alone. "We still live by fishing. I had visions of us becoming farmers, but my son Murdo has saltwater in his veins. So I still light the lamp to guide him home safely."

Tom took a deep breath. "I've been given a second chance and I haven't wasted it." He held out his arm to help her as she rose to her feet, wincing a little. She nodded, her expression unreadable.

Once he had shuffled everyone in place outside in the watery sunshine, Tom looked around, puzzled. "There's someone missing? The lady who came to the door?"

There were some indrawn breaths before Janet spoke. "Take your picture. She can join us later."

The auburn-haired woman appeared for the last picture. She joined the end of the line, chin up and face flushed. Tom had to tell Murdo to shunt along to give her room. Side by side they looked so alike although she was younger. Brother and sister surely? She reminded him of someone. So who was she?

When he had finished Janet came up to him, holding out his payment. "Go to the kitchen for something to eat."

Tom didn't know whether he felt affronted or amused. Traveling photographers must be a lower form of life than naval officers who stayed in the parlour for their refreshment.

Chapter 37

Newfoundland, 1864

He sat down at the kitchen table, watching as she poured him out a cup of tea, this stranger who was so familiar to him. Her knuckles were clenched white and she kept her gaze averted.

"Please sit down for a moment." She edged herself into the chair opposite him. "I saw you in the doorway and thought for a moment that . . . but I was wrong."

"I know who you must be."

"Please tell me who you are. I could see at once that you're one of the MacKenzies."

She laughed, a scratchy sound. "Not one they admit to. Poor Mistress MacKenzie, torn between her Christian duty and her sense of shame. I'm the dirty family secret, the bastard child." Tom flinched. "Not hers of course. His, her husband's. Not a moral man. A woman in every port."

"I don't even know your name."

"Màiri." Tom waited, but she said no more.

"How did Mistress MacKenzie learn of your existence?"

Again the grating laugh before she replied, "She didn't for many years. He was away a lot and could keep his misdeeds secret. He did at least provide for my mother but that all ended when he was drowned."

"So how did you come to meet her?"

"By chance, on the ship. I dropped my bag coming aboard and a man stopped to help me. My brother, Murdo. We looked at each other and he nearly dropped the bag again. Our father passed his features on to both of us. He was said to be a handsome man." She looked hard at Tom. "I'm not speaking out of vanity. Beauty is a curse. Men pursue beauty. They only care about the face, not the woman herself."

Tom looked down, thinking how he was guilty of that obsession too.

"I couldn't endure staying on Skye any longer. I wanted a new life but I was too scared to fly far. I took Mistress MacKenzie's offer to stay as their servant."

"And do they treat you well?"

"Aye, except when strangers like you interfere."

She sat with her eyes closed while Tom drank his tea and willed himself to stay quiet. After what seemed an eternity her eyes snapped open and probed his face again,

"I'll tell you about what happened to your friend that day."

And she did as the wind swooped and the gulls wailed outside.

"There isn't a day when I don't wake up with wet cheeks for that life lost, twice over," she finished. "It's God's judgement on me."

"I'm in no position to judge."

"What will you do now?"

He took out the creased drawing from the pocket of his jacket. "You must tell me what you know about her."

She avoided his gaze, her hands scrabbling together in her lap. "But you've found another love now." It was a statement, not a question.

"Yes, I have but I won't give up hope of finding her."

He wanted to shake her but instead he sat rigid. Finally she whispered, "I can tell you who she is, but I've no idea where she is."

She told him, the words wrenched from her throat. Tom stumbled to his feet and mumbled his farewells. He left her hunched over the table, her body heaving with unshed tears.

"You look like a man who's hunted all day and not caught anything to eat," Silent Owl said, when they set off again.

That night Tom lay sleepless, his thoughts writhing. While he sought her, he thought he was following a lighthouse beam, but all the time it was a wrecker's lantern to lure him onto the rocks.

He had a more urgent worry. He was convinced that Mistress MacKenzie knew about his desertion. She had given no sign that she would betray him, but she might change her mind. If she did he would have to escape before he was arrested. First though he must protect his family. Iain was still inexperienced. Many people disapproved of him taking a native wife and wouldn't help him as they would one of their own. Even if Janet MacKenzie kept quiet, he might not be so lucky another time if someone else recognized him. He wished there was someone he could confide in. He had shunned making friends because he didn't dare trust anyone. Maybe he could ask Emma's advice? But did she understand his predicament? Her last letter suggested not. He remembered the gist of her words:

I plucked up my courage and went to a meeting of a photographic society. When they recovered from their shock at the sight of me they didn't know how to speak to me. They seemed amazed that I could carry a camera, let alone take any photographs. What was it Dr. Johnson said about hearing a woman preach and it being like seeing a dog balancing on its hind legs? It wasn't done well but he was surprised it was done at all. Fred raises no objection to my hobby. He finds it mildly amusing but it's hard to persevere when you feel patronized. I would love to be free to travel as you are and to be paid for my efforts.

She couldn't see beyond her comfortable world to understand the danger of exposure he lived with all the time. Well, she made her choice when she became a doctor's wife. He could travel but he was as cursed as if he were aboard the *Flying Dutchman*. Never able to settle in port. Condemned to be always looking over his shoulder.

Chapter 38

Back to Cape Breton Island, 1864

The next morning Tom made up his mind.

"We must go home at once to make sure everything is safe there."

"What about the summer hunt?" Silent Owl asked.

"That will have to wait until next year."

"You don't believe in my map."

"It's nothing to do with your damned map. It's about the old lady deciding to report me and soldiers arriving on my doorstep."

"You'll miss the caribou chase. We head the animals over the cliff face."

Tom grimaced.

"We do it to eat. Not like you white men, killing for fun. We respect the spirits of the beasts and slit the throats of the wounded ones."

Tom shut his eyes to squeeze out the image of Richard with his slashed neck, gaping like a blood-filled smile.

"You go. I'll return on my own."

"You can't manage the sea canoe on your own."

"I'll get some help."

He turned away to load up the packhorse. Then he plodded eastward without a backward glance. How could he expect a native to understand why he was so worried?

He was exhausted after three hours of trudging over hills, covered with rocks that poked out of the ground like petrified tree stumps. As he looked around for somewhere to rest, a feather of breath stroked his ear. There was Silent Owl behind him.

"You can't expect the wolf to eat leaves."

"Is that some sort of native riddle? It makes no sense."

"Every creature has its own nature and you can't change it. You're trying to run away from yours."

"Nonsense. I just need to get home. Are you coming?"

Silent Owl nodded. They barely spoke while they journeyed, first on foot and then by sea. Tom recruited a scratch crew, mainly half-breeds. Silent Owl looked down his nose at them. Never much of a talker he seemed unperturbed by Tom's silence. They parted once they had landed at Sydney. Silent Owl was heading down to Lake Ainslee to wait until the rest of his band returned from Newfoundland. Tom handed him a heavy bag of coins.

"Here's your share. Will I see you in the spring?"

Silent Owl grinned and swung the bag above his head in a wide arc before tying it to his belt. "Before then. Spring Thaw will show you the way."

That promise anchored Tom during the next weeks although he yawed every time there was a knock on the door or reports of a stranger. He kept his concerns to himself. Iain and Spring Thaw knew any questions about his strange mood would meet with denials. So they didn't press him. After Christmas he decided that the Widow MacKenzie must have kept his secret. Like a bedraggled dog hauling himself ashore he shook off the gloom that had clung to him.

He asked Iain what gifts they should carry for Spring Thaw's family.

"They suffer in the winter when there's so little game. But they don't want charity."

"I remember how people wanted Silent Owl to be in a photograph with them. There's a call for native portraits. If they agreed to be photographed, we could pay them."

So while thick snow still swaddled the earth, they set off with a sleigh weighed down with potatoes, dried fish, and oatmeal. Owlet was strapped to his mother's back in a wooden frame and gurgled at the swaying motion. Where the trees were close packed, Iain and Tom put on snowshoes and led Maple along the narrow tracks, following the shoreline of the lake. They took care as the treacherous hummocks of snow smudged every feature. Land, frozen lake, every rise and hollow were all smothered. Silent Owl was right, Tom thought. An ordinary map was no use in this white blankness. Spring Thaw guided them as a pilot would steer a ship through unfamiliar shallows. There was no sight or sound of life until a clearing opened up before them to reveal a cluster of wigwams. Their birch bark sides with the poles bursting from their tops scarcely seemed like human habitations. More like a natural part of the forest, a squirrel's dray or a raccoon's den.

Their hosts had heard their approach and were waiting outside the entrance flaps of their tents. Spring Thaw translated and made the introductions. There were about twenty people there, including children. Tom noticed the gaunt faces, sunken eyes, and hacking coughs while he struggled to follow Spring Thaw's description of the relationships between them all.

"And this is Silent Owl's wife, Dark Otter."

The slender woman beside her nodded. She was holding a baby in her arms while a toddler clung, wide-eyed to her leggings. Tom stared, beyond speech or movement. Everyone else was busy unloading the sleigh or walking to the largest wigwam. Tom floated helpless as flotsam as eager children pulled at his hands. Inside the space smelt of wood smoke and resin from the pine branches spread across the floor. Hands pressed him down onto a soft sealskin mat near the fire. He bent his numb legs and sat, head down while excited voices whirred around him.

"It's not so different here from when I was a boy. Sitting on the earth fire and pickled by the smoke." Iain spoke loudly, to cover up Tom's silence.

Steaming clay pots of meat arrived, waterfowl, squirrel, and venison. Everyone else blew on their bowls before pulling out chunks of tender meat. They smacked their lips and let the juices trickle down their chins. Tom, though, swirled a piece around his mouth, fearing to swallow it in case he choked.

After the meal was over, they all lay back and a long pipe of carved wood was passed around. A cautious puff left Tom spluttering for breath. It was even more pungent than the tarry stuff the old sailors used to smoke. He kept coughing while the young men rose to dance. He had no intention of joining in. Iain, though, was up on his feet stamping and whooping outside. Tom was unaware of the small children who reached out to stroke his hair. Somehow he endured the eternity of time until everyone settled down to sleep and he could move into a smaller wigwam with the single men. The whole time he had refused to look in Silent Owl's direction.

Early the next morning, Tom crept out to relieve himself. He turned back to find Silent Owl stalking him.

"You knew I was married. You saw my canoe the first time we met." Tom looked blank. "A man and wife always build a canoe together."

Tom scowled and walked away, but Silent Owl caught him by the shoulders. "How could I stay a barren twig? So many of us have died of white men's diseases."

"You should have warned me." Tom broke away.

"I told him to ask you here," a voice whispered behind him. It was Spring Thaw. "You can help us. One day soon white men will take this forest, rip out the trees and make the red earth bleed. They will drive us away. Iain told me how his tribe over the sea were pushed off their land. But they came here like wolves and took ours instead."

"What do you expect me to do?"

"Show us how to buy this land."

"It won't be cheap." Tom turned to Silent Owl, "What about your share from our trip?"

Silent Owl shuffled and looked away. His sister lunged to

poke him in the chest. "You used it to buy firewater didn't you?"

"No, I'm keeping it safe."

"Liar!" she shouted, kicking him on the shin.

Tom enjoyed Silent Owl's shame for a moment before saying, "We must think about how you can make more money. Let's all sit down again with that smelly old pipe. Again." He punched Silent Owl on the arm.

Chapter 39

Cape Breton Island, 1865

"We could sell pictures of your family. It's the fashion back in England to take photographs of natives, Eskimos, South Sea Islanders, headhunters, and so forth. Meanwhile I'll find out who owns the land."

Spring Thaw translated and they all nodded. They seemed to trust him. He recalled with a pang his old gift of winning over sailors and islanders. But what about Silent Owl? He seemed able to lead two parallel lives without a qualm. Tom could endure months of separation if he had to. Seafarers learnt how. But now that he knew Silent Owl returned to his wife's embrace for half the year, Tom felt the rip and tug of jealousy. Was there a map for men like him? Men who led a double life? He remembered married masters at school who seemed to be impersonators, shrugging on family life like an ill-fitting overcoat. Silent Owl though felt no shame or jealousy in sliding between his two lives.

"How can you split yourself in two?" Tom asked him later.

"I go away in the summer and stay with my family in the winter. Everyone is satisfied."

Not me, thought Tom, but if I want to keep his affection I have to accept his rules. He couldn't endure being alone again.

When he returned home, he made enquiries about the forest. It belonged to Malcolm Buchanan, a reclusive man who had moved to Cape Breton over twenty years earlier. He lived alone on a small cabin on the edge of his woods. There was plenty of gossip about his secretive ways but little information.

"I could visit him," Tom suggested. "It might be he has no wish to sell."

"We'll come with you," said Spring Thaw, looking at her husband and brother. "This man needs to know that it's us who are buying his woods."

As so often, Tom was taken aback at her directness. He had been given information about Buchanan's whereabouts but there was no sign of any path through the ranks of trees. Tom scratched his head.

"How would you have done on your own?" Silent Owl asked, slapping Tom on the back.

They had to thrust and hack their way through low branches and undergrowth. Silent Owl led them, stopping often to look and listen. He found a length of twine behind a rock, close to some overhanging sticks bound together to form a roof. As he pointed it out they heard a crash. Something huge and urgent hurtled toward them. Tom pushed Spring Thaw behind him, cursing that he had no rifle. Silent Owl crouched down, knife in hand as a snarling head with glistening teeth leaped at him. But instead of striking it he dropped his arm and made clicking sounds in his throat. The creature whimpered and lay down, its feathered tail swishing.

"Take us home," Silent Owl whispered in its ear.

It stood and padded ahead along a narrow track up to a homestead. It looked abandoned with its sagging roof and bulging walls. But a thread of smoke spooled out from the chimney. The grizzled dog whined and scratched at the battered door. It swung open to show a man with long, tangled hair, wearing a fur waistcoat.

"What do you want?" He spat out a plug of tobacco.

"Mr. Buchanan? May we speak with you?" Tom held out his hand. The old man glared at it. A second sticky pellet splattered in front of Tom's feet.

Spring Thaw stepped forward. "We want to buy your wood," she said, her dark eyes fixed on the old man's rheumy blue ones. He opened his mouth and Tom braced himself for a roar of fury. The dog's ears twitched and a growl rumbled in his throat. Silent Owl felt for the knife in his belt.

But it was a rumble of laughter that erupted. "I've been expecting you," he said and showed them inside into a warm but bare room. He kept staring at Spring Thaw, "Aye, maybe I've got the second sight."

Was he simple minded? Tom wondered. Had living as a hermit rotted his brain?

It was Spring Thaw who recovered first. "We need somewhere to live. Somewhere that can't be taken away from us. Our ancestors helped yours when the first white people came. They saved them from starving. They didn't know that hordes more would come and drive us off our land."

What was she doing? Tom thought. That kind of talk would only vex the old man, but he seemed bewitched by her.

"And how much money do you have to reclaim the Garden of Eden?"

Tom intervened, "So far only £100 as a deposit."

But Malcolm wasn't listening. His parched eyes drank deep of Spring Thaw's face, drawn toward her like a neap tide to the moon.

"You're so like my wife in her youth. 'Bright Star' she was called, a chief's daughter. You have her bearing."

"How did you meet her?"

"I came out to work for the company up north at the end of Boney's war. It was like the Garden of Eden then, a cold one." He paused as his laugh turned into a wheeze. "In those days we got on well with the natives, well enough to marry them." He spoke only to Spring Thaw. It was as if the others were invisible.

"What went wrong?"

"Greed. That was the serpent. Greed and trickery. Too many furs taken. Indians given drink that made them crazy. The women used to hide all the weapons when their menfolk were on the whisky. So they tried to kill each other with their bare hands."

"But what became of Bright Star?"

"Dead these many years and our children died young." She

came close, hugging him and putting her head on his chest.

"I couldn't bear to stay up North any more. I bought the woods here to clear them but I couldn't do it. Too much gone already." He loosened her arms and tilted her chin up. "I've had men with money sniffing around here but I set the dog on them."

"Would you let us have it?" she asked.

The only sound in the room was the dog panting,

"I've no one to leave it to. So you shall have it. I've been waiting for you to come."

Chapter 40

Cape Breton Island, 1865

"Did that really happen or was it a dream?" Tom asked as they turned homeward. "I'm not sure he's of sound mind."

"Sound enough to do what was right," Spring Thaw replied.

"Who cares? We won!" Iain yelled, throwing his cap high in the air. It blew off the back of the buggy, but Silent Owl somersaulted off the back and caught it. Iain whipped up Maple so that she cantered too fast for him to climb aboard again.

"Come on boys, behave yourselves." Tom tried to sound stern, but a smile was in his voice. Spring Thaw caught his eye and sighed.

"You want back on, do you?" Iain pulled on the reins to stop the horse.

Once they were home the doubts began to circle again, pointed fins around an open boat. The business of getting the legal papers drawn up would bring unwelcome attention. So Tom approached a lawyer in Halifax to arrange the sale rather than a local man from Sydney.

He made the appointment by letter. Mr. MacGregor's face was a study when they all sauntered into his office. His jaw hung open like an unlatched gate and his eyes almost burst out of his head as Spring Thaw and her brother appeared in full native dress. Disbelief, apprehension, and disdain scudded like wind-driven clouds across his face. Then the lawyer steadied his features back into professional composure. He drew up the papers, still looking stunned and had them delivered to Mr. Buchanan. After an anxious delay MacGregor sent a letter to Tom. It explained in stiff legal prose that the terms had been read aloud to Mr. Buchanan who signed them with a cross.

"I would like to have been there when they fought their way

to his cabin and braved that dog," Tom said. "No wonder Mr. MacGregor's fees are so steep."

It had been agreed that Mr. Buchanan would continue to live in his home. So nothing had visibly changed. Tom began to trust his weight to their good fortune until the afternoon when Iain came hurtling in from a trip into town, pulling in cold air behind him.

"Look at this in *The Chronicle.*"

Virgin forest sold to Indians

Tom ran his eye down the report:

The land near Bras d'Or lake was sold to Mi'kmaq natives by Mr. Malcolm Buchanan who acquired it after leaving the service of the Hudson's Bay Society. The sale was expedited by Mr. John Robinson on behalf of his daughter-in-law's native relatives. Mr. Robinson used to rent premises in Sydney for use as a photographic studio and was well-known for the unusual displays of native photographs that adorned his windows. Mr. Stephen Miller and his business partners had been planning to buy the forest themselves to turn it into farmland.

There is a desperate need for new farms and we are disappointed that this land is going to remain unproductive. It's well-known that Mr. Buchanan is an elderly and somewhat reclusive gentleman. We can only assume that he was willing to sell his land to the natives and was not misled in any way.

Tom thrust the paper away. "They're suggesting that Mr. Buchanan was tricked out of his land but just skirting clear of libel. It's a pity that Stephen Miller's involved. I don't want to upset that family even more."

"They can't harm us. We can always set Silent Owl and the others on them. I'd like to see tubby wee Fraser running away with his backside full of arrows."

Tom smiled but the old jumping at shadows was back again. Skittish as a jack rabbit, ears swiveling and eyes straining he dreaded the swoop and snatch of teeth from behind or claws from above. He tried to shrug off his fears by thinking about the summer expedition. He had wondered about traveling to New Brunswick this summer to see the famed tidal surge in Fundy Bay, but he longed to go even further west, to the plains that were being opened up. He wanted to capture the tribes there before their way of life was too tainted by contact with settlers.

He decided to go into Sydney to buy supplies for the journey. A watery sun had broken through the gun-metal sky. As he hitched up Maple to the buggy he saw Spring Thaw taking a rare rest from her work, leaning against the cabin door with her eyes closed. She looked weary and on an impulse Tom invited her to accompany him. Her eyes widened in surprise before she smiled and agreed.

"It would be good for the baby, too. He's in pain with his new teeth. The ride will soothe him."

They were all cheered by the journey. After stowing the provisions in the buggy, Tom suggested a walk along the shore. He pulled faces to make Owlet laugh. Looking up he saw a family group coming toward them. As they drew closer his heart slumped as he realized it was Mrs. MacKenzie with her daughter Eliza and son-in-law. There was no avoiding them. Tom felt awkward and exposed. He remembered the comment in the newspaper about "unusual displays of native photographs." Was he ashamed of being seen in public with Spring Thaw? No, not any longer. It was the fear that Mrs. MacKenzie would never forget this latest affront. He straightened his back and forced his mouth into a smile. The matriarch and Peter looked as fleshy and bustling as usual but what had become of Eliza? He could barely recognize her in this hollow-eyed woman with the yellowish complexion.

"How do you do, today?" he asked, doffing his hat.

"Very well, thank you kindly," was the stilted reply from Mrs. MacKenzie while her companions nodded, their faces tense. Spring Thaw gazed at Eliza.

"You're not well."

She touched her arm. Eliza flinched.

"It's your womb isn't it? I know some herbs that could help you if. . ." Her words scattered in empty air as Eliza shrieked, "Let go of me, you savage."

Her husband rushed forward to push Spring Thaw out of the way at the same time as Tom reached to draw her back. For a moment the two men glowered at each other before Miller scurried away, wafting his hands at the women.

"Disgraceful! Fancy a white man living with savages," Mrs. MacKenzie shot over her shoulder.

Tom walked away, squeezing his lips together. Had she forgotten how eager she had been to have him as a son-in-law? He shuddered as he thought about the hatred in her eyes. She was dangerous and vengeful. Spring Thaw's face was unreadable. He squeezed her hand, as much for his comfort as for hers. They drove home in sombre silence and spattering rain. The baby caught their troubled mood, grizzling and wriggling in his mother's lap.

Chapter 41

Nova Scotia, Summer 1865

Silent Owl dismissed Tom's idea of traveling to the plains. "The tribes will be jumpy if white men are taking their game. They would kill us both without a second thought."

He hoped that Emma would be more encouraging.

I can understand why you want to use art in the service of philanthropy. It reminded me of Mama showing me one of those medallions of Mr. Wedgewood's that Grandmama had made into a bracelet. Do you remember? It showed a man in chains with the inscription, "Am I not a man and a brother?"

I know that artists have sold paintings to help the cause of the natives. There was an American gentleman called Catlin who opened an Indian gallery about twenty years ago, first in London and then in Manchester. Fred and I went to see it on one of the rare occasions he managed to escape from the demands of his patients. There were all sorts of objects displayed, weapons, costumes, skulls even but what impressed me most were the portraits. What fierce noble faces! And of course, there were some live Indians there, a troupe of men and boys. I believe they were from Canada. I read later that some of them died and Catlin's own wife succumbed to pneumonia.

Would your idea of an exhibition of paintings and photographs be successful, I wonder? Fashions change. Pictures of exotic places are still popular. There are plenty of ladies like me with time hanging heavy on their hands who are willing to run charity committees. However, there are so many worthy causes that I doubt if helping dispossessed Indians would be a popular one. If people think about them at all, it is as rather bloodthirsty savages. Of course there is always a call from the Churches to convert the heathen, but I sense that you don't want to see them turned into well-behaved Christians in European dress.

Tom scrunched up the letter. Iain had told him now that Spring Thaw was expecting a second child, he wanted her to rest more from the farm work. The wind was blowing against his westward adventure from every direction. It would have to be New Brunswick instead. At least he could pretend for a few precious weeks that he and Silent Owl were in the Garden of Eden. No that was wrong. There was no Fall. They were free of religion and convention. How far he had traveled from the rules of his past life. His old self was a tiny, distant figure seen through the wrong end of a telescope. By the time they came back, the fuss about the land sale would have burnt out. But he could blow on the embers of the summer memories to keep him alive through the lonely winter.

Again they were feted at every village. Why was everyone so keen to be photographed? A photograph told them that their lives mattered, even if they lived in the wilds. But the camera could only captured an instant of their lives. That moment was preserved, a sort of photographic taxidermy, an illusion of life. They were drawn to the beam of the camera as if it could illuminate their lives. But photographs were so fragile. They faded and crumbled away like the gossamer wings of a dead butterfly. And what about the photographer himself? He created a mirage of immortality for others but stayed invisible. Tom would never appear on the other side of the lens because his image could betray him.

People he photographed told him their stories. Many like Iain had left behind poverty and misery in their homelands although some had welcomed the chance of adventure and reinvention. Others had been exiled twice over, their ancestors forced to flee northward because they had stayed loyal to the Crown in the American wars. A photograph was a certificate of survival.

As always, once they turned homeward Tom felt the warning blast of losing Silent Owl again to his wife, but he braced himself against the blizzards of jealousy. Better to be together and complete for some of the year than not at all, he kept telling himself. How could they live and love together all the time? Tom had to act the part of the steady citizen, the quiet bachelor approaching middle age. He couldn't risk the dangers of scandal seeping out among his neighbors.

They let the horses amble at their own pace once they were back on the island. Tom drank in every detail of his companion's being as they rode side by side, his supple legs and muscular chest, ripened brown by the sun, the delicate softness of his ear lobes and the ridges of old scars on his arms, like rows of rough stitching.

Silent Owl turned his horse's head several miles before home, leaving Tom to ride on by himself. But Iain was waiting for him at the summit of the small hill, in sight of the farm. Surprised and pleased, Tom was about to dismount and stretch his legs.

"No, don't stop. Let's get back."

"Is something wrong? It's not Spring Thaw or the baby?"

"No, they're well. I'll explain when we're inside."

"I hope he's not worried you too much, father-in-law," Spring Thaw said once they were inside away from the mosquito patrols.

"What is it? Imagining is worse than knowing."

"Thank God you didn't get back last week," said Iain. "I was in the town when I saw that old witch MacKenzie. Talking with a stranger, too busy blethering to see me. I didn't like the look of it. So I slipped into a nearby alleyway. There was no one else about and I could hear most of what they were saying."

Tom felt dread, wind ripping a sail. "Carry on, son."

She said, "John Robinson used to rent a shop from me."

"Describe him to me if you will," the man asked.

"Not young, but not yet well into his middle years."

"The same age as me, perhaps? Yes? My height? Taller, you

say? Now what about his coloring?"

"Fair, very pale hair, almost white." Tom held back a gasp.

"Ahh, that's interesting. Do you know anything about his life before he arrived here?"

"She sniffed, 'A secretive man. I always thought he had something to hide. He claimed to have a fiancée back in England but no sign of her. Is he in trouble? A criminal?'

"The witch couldn't keep the glee out of her voice," Iain said. "The stranger kept firing questions at her."

"Did he ever talk about his previous profession?"

"If I remember rightly he said about working in a shipping office. In Liverpool?"

Iain paused, his breathing ragged.

"What happened then?" Tom whispered.

"Some people walked toward them and they moved along to let them past. I couldn't catch any more."

"But you sniffed out more, didn't you?" Spring Thaw prompted.

"The stranger was from a naval vessel, a Captain Rogers,"

Tom's heart was bolting. That was a name he never thought to hear again.

"His ship's left harbor now," Spring Thaw said, touching Tom's hand.

"Who is he? Iain asked.

"We served together. And hated each other."

"We thought he might come snooping around," Iain said, "I kept watch at night with my rifle loaded."

Tom was trying to round up his stampeding thoughts. "What we don't know is whether he came intending to hunt me down. Or did he meet Mrs. MacKenzie by chance?"

"She would have put out a line like she does for every stranger," Spring Thaw said." She's still after a husband for her second daughter."

"You're right," Tom answered, letting his shoulders drop.

"She likes to cause trouble. Surely if Rogers had really come to arrest me, he wouldn't have given up so easily?"

"And if he had come here, I'd have shot him," Iain said, in a cold voice that disturbed Tom much more than any shouting would have done.

"Well, he's left and what evidence did he have? I'm not the only man in the world with pale hair."

Spring Thaw smiled and rocked her son who had fallen asleep on her lap, but her eyes were shadowed. Tom looked at Iain's grim face and there was no comfort there either.

Chapter 42

Cape Breton Island, Winter 1866

There was nothing for it but to carry on with life as usual. The long hibernation was soon upon them. Tom asked at the docks about the naval vessel and was told that it was a survey ship mapping the eastern seaboard. It had steamed south for the winter. That suggested that Rogers' meeting with Mrs. MacKenzie was only bad luck. She of course had taken the opportunity to hole him beneath the waterline. But was the ship due to return north again in the spring? He must ask Emma and see what she could find out. It was odd that she hadn't written. He had expected to find a letter on his return. Probably some shipping delay. Iain wanted a chance to use his new horse sleigh. So he traveled to Sydney to see if there were any letters waiting collection at the post office.

"Any news?" Tom called out, as he heard the door open.

There was no reply until Iain had removed his coat and boots.

"This arrived for you," he said, holding out an envelope.

Tom took it eagerly and then almost dropped it. It was bordered in black ink. Tearing it open he was at first too shocked to take in what was written. For a terrible moment he had thought that it was Emma who had died but then he recognized her handwriting on the envelope. His eyes sprinted backward and forward, picking up phrases here and there.

Outbreak of typhoid fever at the workhouse and the poor parts of town . . . Fred determined to do his duty . . . worst of it over and he came home to rest, exhausted but in good spirits . . . dead within hours. Rest of us became ill, Thomas the worst afflicted . . . once he was over the crisis, Sophie delirious . . . never regained consciousness. I don't know why God spared me and sometimes I wish He hadn't but I have to keep struggling on for the sake of my son.

Tom stayed sitting and looking out of the window, the letter crushed in his hand. He remembered when Emma had screwed up his drawing in that hotel in Liverpool. That seemed so many years ago now. While his mind was tormented about fears that might never happen, Emma's worst imaginings had struck her down. How could he reply? He couldn't bear to suggest the consolation of religion when he no longer believed himself. What could he offer?

Then a few days later he woke in the middle of the night, bathed in a cold sweat. He had been dreaming about Rogers arriving on his doorstep with a group of sailors. He had that infuriating, smug grin on his face as he raised his hand, crooking his forefinger to summon Tom. A wave of relief washed over him that it was only a dream. But he couldn't throw off the undertow of unease. Then another thought, like the seventh wave, the strongest one, engulfed him. What if the dream was a premonition? He stayed still until the tides of panic receded, leaving furrowed rows imprinted in the sand. He had no way of finding out what Rogers planned to do. Should he leave his life behind and disappear into the wilderness for good? But he feared that Iain would act rashly if he ever came across Rogers. Would Spring Thaw be able to curb his rage? Tom got up and paced the room, tugging his hair in his torment. Finally he sat down and wrote:

My Dearest Emma,

I've just received your letter with its tragic news. I wish I was nearer so that I could offer you help in your ordeal. What can I say? How can we make sense of the deaths of two blameless people? Frederick selflessly devoted himself to caring for the sick and your daughter was just setting out in life. I didn't know her, but if she had only a fraction of the virtues of her parents she would have become a remarkable woman. If you have Christian beliefs, I hope that they will sustain you through your grief.

You have accused me, rightly, in the past of being selfish. I am going to make a suggestion for the future that I believe could greatly benefit both of us. It might be that it is too soon for you to consider what I'm proposing, but I hope that you won't reject it. When last I wrote to you I was full of plans and projects. Since then a shadow has fallen on them that I can explain more fully later. It may be that I'm unduly anxious, but I want to protect my family and I believe that is best achieved by my absence, at least for a while. I would use my time traveling more extensively in the wilder parts of Canada, photographing the natives.

Iain and Spring Thaw are trustworthy and industrious but still too young to be fully responsible for both the photographic work and the farm. I need someone older and wiser who can keep everything on an even keel. Even better would be someone who has a keen interest in photography. The right person would of course be well recompensed. Can you think of a suitable candidate? I can think of no one better than yourself. Canada is a more progressive country than England. It's not considered outlandish for a lady to be proficient in business. Thomas of course would be very welcome if he chose to accompany you.

I don't minimize the magnitude of this change for you. If you wished you could come over for a period of time and see if the arrangement suited you before making a final decision.

I await your reply with bated breath,

Your Loving Brother,

Tom

Chapter 43

Cape Breton Island, Summer 1866

Tom didn't need to wait for too long. Emma's reply came within a month. He weighed the envelope in his hand. It felt substantial. He took this as a good omen as surely a negative answer would be shorter. With a deep breath he tore it open:

My Dearest Brother,

Your idea shocked me at first, but I did as you asked and didn't reject it out of hand. I let it roost quietly in my mind and grew used to its presence there. On purely monetary grounds the notion has much to recommend it. Although Fred was a respected doctor he did not, like some physicians, spend his time cultivating wealthy patients. As a result he left me, not penniless but in somewhat straitened circumstances. Fortunately, his brother has taken on the responsibility of paying for Thomas's education.

However, money is not of course the only consideration. The more I turned your offer over in my hand the more it glistened. As you know, I've long felt constricted as an "amateur lady photographer." How marvelous it would be if I were respected as a professional and paid for my skills.

I wrestled with the idea that I was being selfish in pursuing my own desires. When I broached the subject with Thomas, he was quite adamant that he had no wish to accompany me. He wants to complete his schooling. He can stay with his uncle in the holidays and seems happy at the prospect of so doing. I still worried that I was neglecting my maternal duties in leaving him. Then one day when I was thinking about Sophie, I wondered what she would say about my dilemma. I was determined that she should have a proper education and study subjects like Latin that were denied to me. Fred was amused and puzzled by my insistence on this subject, but he put no obstacles in my way. I wanted her to have choices about the direction her life would follow. Her life was cruelly snatched away before she could make those choices but she was a clear-sighted girl and would probably have said, "Mother, why are you denying yourself the opportunities you would want me to have?" So, my mind is made up and I shall join you in this brave new world. I've booked myself a passage in May on 'The Aurora.'

Your dearest sister,

Emma

Tom was overjoyed. He could prepare for the longed-for expedition. Emma would need time to settle in, of course, before he left. But what about Silent Owl? Would he be willing to leave his family for a trip of a year or more? He frowned when Tom told him of his plans.

"I still say they would kill us both, as slowly as they can."

"It will be safe enough if we meet the Indians at a trading post."

"If they're at a trading post, they won't be the free men you're after."

But the next day he came up to Tom, grinning wolfishly, "I'll do this for you, to stop you wandering off on your own and getting yourself killed."

Tom accepted without question. He didn't want to risk scuttling his chances by asking Silent Owl why he had changed his mind.

Emma arrived. She was as resolute as Tom remembered although more gaunt. All the ballast that had settled on her hips had melted away. Her coming acted like a drawstring to the rest of them, pulling them into shape. She poured all her energies into being neighborly. Cakes were baked, acquaintances invited, and their advice sought on local customs. Knowing how people like to be consulted and deferred to, she sought their help in understanding Gaelic, growing vegetables, or asking for their recipes for scones. Sometimes he would snatch a glance of her face in repose and see the markers of grief, the hollows gouged into her cheeks, and the bleakness in her eyes. But she kept her sadness to herself. She was hospitable and friendly, more acceptable to the neighbors than the rest of them. Tom knew he was considered to be aloof while Iain came from suspect stock and was quick-tempered. Spring Thaw was only a native and one who refused to show the submissiveness expected of an Indian, especially a female one.

"Don't give too much away. Gossip spreads like a forest fire," Tom warned her.

"Watch me. I listen carefully and pretend an interest in their doings, even if I don't feel it. It's what's expected of women. Remember your story about the smugglers' boat that was hidden in plain sight? That's what I'm doing."

In the end, even Mrs. MacKenzie couldn't hold out from visiting them.

"Ah, there's the new baby," she cooed over Fawn's cradle. "Darker than her brother, isn't she? She looks so Indian."

Spring Thaw's eyes smouldered as she scooped up the baby but Emma replied, "She's a wee angel. So contented. Now tell me about how your family are faring."

So Mrs. MacKenzie did that, at some length. When she had finally stopped, she looked hard at Emma. Then she seemed to come to a decision,

"You've not heard about old Mistress MacLean's funeral?" she asked.

Emma shook her head. "I've not heard of any MacLeans staying near us."

"Well, you wouldn't. They all moved down to Sydney but the *cailleach* always said that she wanted to be buried in her parents' grave lot. So her neighbors agreed to carry her coffin the twenty miles or so."

"That was good of them."

"Hmm. Well some of these neighbors were MacLeods."

Emma looked puzzled.

"MacLeans and MacLeods have never got on."

Emma resisted asking why and waited for Mrs. MacKenzie to continue.

"Well, the eight of them had a dram or two to give them strength before they set out. Then of course they had to keep stopping for a rest."

"Yes, indeed. It must have been heavy work."

"And each time they stopped, they had another wee sup. And tongues were loosened. One of the MacLeans muttered an old insult about the MacLeods." She paused and Emma waited again. "A lot of nonsense about the skin of MacLeod's . . . er, backside."

"Meaning he talked through his bottom? We have similar sayings in England."

"Do you? Well, words led to blows. Then they dusted themselves down, picked up the coffin and staggered on up the track until they needed another wee rest."

"Did they reach the burial ground in the end?" Emma asked.

"Aye, when it was almost dark. Most of them were hobbling along by then, bloodied and bruised."

"Well, I'm glad they were able to honor the old lady's wishes."

"Hmm. What a disgrace though, having a running battle while they were carrying a coffin. They say they're going to have to appear before the judge."

"Were some of the men badly hurt, then?"

"Not really, it was more their pride."

Emma told the story to the others while they ate that evening.

"I've saved the best for last. Mrs. MacKenzie looked all around us as if someone else might be hidden in the walls before whispering in my ear, 'We've both been married women. So I can tell you.' I told her that as a doctor's wife I'm not too easily outraged."

"There were a lot of bloodied faces and sore heads but poor Donald MacLeod was badly injured. He was kicked in the fight and his tentacles were damaged, I hear. All swollen up."

The others laughed, tears coursing down their cheeks.

"Well, poor Iain MacLeod. I never knew that he was some kind of merman," Tom spluttered and started them all howling again.

When they had quietened down Tom said, "You're right Emma. We should hold our enemies close."

"She's an object of pity," his sister replied. "Her elder daughter childless, the younger one a spinster and. . ."

"I've heard her son haunts the docks after sailors," Iain added. "Why should we care about her?"

"Because a wounded animal is dangerous," said Tom. "Don't forget we're outsiders here. Folk are affable enough but they only let us into the porch of their hearts, not close to the fire."

The light-hearted mood had been doused. Emma turned the conversation to ideas for increasing business.

"We need people to order photographs for all their celebrations, weddings, christenings, coming of age."

"You're a wonder, Emma. I'm so pleased you came." Tom stopped, as her eyes welled up.

"But I can't forget what I've lost. Still I'm glad to be busy and useful. So many days in my past life time sagged like a line of sodden washing."

"Like the tedium of endless days at sea," Tom acknowledged, but the look of desolation in Emma's eyes silenced him.

Chapter 44

The Prairie, Spring 1868

Tom and Silent Owl had set off on their long journey westward in the previous summer, across land they didn't know toward frontier territory. Trappers had penetrated among the Indian bands there, scavengers beyond the reach of the Hudson's Bay Company, men who paid for buffalo hides with a barrel of rot gut whisky. Tom believed they should seek safety in numbers. They would use the company's trading forts to punctuate their journey. This meant they could find native guides and sell photographs to the traders and clerks.

Tom's burden of fear was still there, but now it had become part of him. No longer an unwieldy load on his back it had grown into his ribs and spine like a tortoise's shell. And the mystery girl? He had abandoned the stained and creased drawing in a drawer, although he couldn't bring himself to finally destroy her image. Before setting out he had visited the lawyer to settle his affairs. All he owned was to be shared between Emma, Iain, and Spring Thaw. Mr. MacGregor had shaken his head at such an irregular arrangement, but Tom felt only relief. He knew that he could support himself on what he made as a traveling photographer and any profit would go to help Indian tribes buy land for themselves.

At Lachine, beyond Montreal, they arrived at the fine stone house built across the river from the canal and warehouse that served as the headquarters of the company. They hired a canoe and followed at the tail of a brigade of company boats heading west. Tom and Silent Owl passed unremarked among the voyageurs, French, Scots and Indians, many of them a mixture of all three. By the time they straggled ashore in the evenings on watery legs, the voyageurs had already set up camp.

"Is this how the mighty English won their battles by bringing up the rear?"

"No stamina, these east coasters."

On they went up the Ottawa River, past Claudiere Falls where the Rideau River plunged down, the water frothing after a fall of sixty feet. Onto Lac des Chats, named after the catlike raccoons who lived there. The exhausting rhythm of paddling and portage continued, past Calumet Island, the rapids of Portage du Fort, Lac des Allumettes with its island, Riviere Creuse and Portage des Joachims. The voyageurs relished pointing out places where men had fallen to their deaths over a towering waterfall or were buried after succumbing to illness or injuries from a fight. Then they turned west up the Petite Riviere, a hard upriver journey before reaching Turtle Portage and the mosquito-plagued marshes beyond. When the torment of the nipping insects had become almost unbearable they saw Lake Nipissing stretching ahead like a mirage. The mosquitos disappeared as they crossed the lake. Next was the north shore of Lake Huron and after three more portages they were smothered in the clammy fogs of Lake Superior.

After a month's canoeing they bade farewell to the company men at Fort Garry. The voyagers were heading northward to Fort Alexander and Berens House on the shores of Lake Winnipeg before going on to York Factory. Tom knew that the factory was the main center for exchanging trade goods such as blankets, tools, and guns in return for pelts of beaver, otter, and wolverine. These animals were trapped farther north. So the company had turned its attention to virgin territories to the south and west. It was here that Tom and Silent Owl might find tribes still following their old ways of life.

Tom couldn't endure the thought of more traveling by canoe. So they hired horses to ride the six hundred miles along the North Saskatchewan from Fort Garry to Fort Carleton. Finally, they struck out toward the Rockies.

The first band they encountered were from the Sarcee tribe. A group of them lived in cabins on a settlement around a mission church. Dressed in shabby European clothes, they were hunched around a fire in the compound, scarcely glancing up as they approached. An angular man emerged from the church and strode toward Tom and Silent Owl. He scowled at Silent Owl in his doeskin tunic and introduced himself as Reverend Matheson.

"They're all women and children here. Where are their men?" Tom asked.

"They're not permitted to stay here. Once they've been paid for their buffalo skins, they drown themselves in whisky. Last time we hid all their weapons, but they fought each other with poles from their wigwams."

Silent Owl grinned.

"White men never get drunk? It's the traders who poison them." Tom said.

"That's why we offer the women sanctuary here."

"But they have to give up their customs."

"In return they receive salvation through God's love. And the benefits of civilisation."

Now Silent Owl's eyes were spitting fire. Tom shook his head and said, "We also want to help them. I take photographs to raise money for native tribes."

"I save souls as well as bodies."

"We too act out of concern for our fellow man."

"Well, you may take a picture or two if you make a donation to our funds. I'll gather them together."

"Do they have their own clothes to wear?"

Matheson recoiled. "No. They put on civilized garments to mark their new lives."

"Then we will not shame them by photographing them as beggars."

Tom turned on his heel and saw that Silent Owl had already stalked off. Tom ran to catch up with him. When they unhitched and mounted the horses, Silent Owl rode in front with his eyes fixed ahead, refusing to speak. The seething silence continued as they made camp until Tom could bear it no longer. Throwing down the sticks he was gathering for the fire he asked, "Why make me suffer for the faults of other men? That minister was bigoted but he offered them help. He didn't cheat them or shoot them like vermin."

Silent Owl still kept his back turned until Tom walked up to him and put his hands around his waist. "I might be the palest of pale faces but I would be happy to devote my life to helping your people."

Silent Owl turned, his eyes awash with unshed tears. "I know. You're different from most white men but the bad ones will win. I can't see a future for my own people or any other tribes. First they slaughter the beaver, the otter, and the buffalo. Then for us only a slow death of shame and despair."

"I don't know what will happen but we mustn't let hope slip through our fingers."

Later Tom woke in the night and lay on his back in his deer skin, watching the stars thrown across the sky like shining, frozen pebbles. He listened to the snuffling of the horses, standing asleep with drooping heads. Life was fragile, a pinprick of light soon snuffed out, but at that moment he felt held in a web of contentment. He rolled onto his side and trickled his hands down Silent Owl's back. How smooth and warm his flesh felt. How had he managed to stay so hot when the night air had turned so cool? Tom sighed and fell asleep again.

Chapter 45

The Prairie, Summer 1868

They rode west toward the Rockies. The mountains were scored against the vivid blue sky. An ocean of prairie land rippled southward. They had followed the winding route of a coulee, its bed cracked dry in the sun. Now they climbed through pines growing thick as quills on the high ridge known as the Porcupine Tail. Tom had smiled when he first heard the name. How different this was from his old ship. Was there any sadness left still in his heart to bail out? Very little. He felt content in this empty land of wide horizons. The next day they traced the wandering track of the Oldman River. Toward noon, they reached a canyon where the thick pelt of trees thinned a little. It was warm and they allowed the horses to amble along the river at their own pace. Stopping at a group of flat rocks for a rest Tom opened one of the saddlebags to get some oatmeal and pemmican. Silent Owl padded down to the water's edge, looking for pools where fish might be lurking. As always, Tom felt wonder at how his companion, absorbed in his task, seemed so much part of the natural world, woven into the weft of trees, river, and fish.

Suddenly the air was shredded by sharp cries. Tom leapt to his feet and ran toward Silent Owl who pointed upstream. A bend in the river stopped them from seeing the source of the noise. Then something spun into view. Something red and sodden swirling in the water. A whimper from inside it, a flailing arm. Silent Owl unhitched a rope from one of the horses. Tom was tugging off his moccasins and shirt. "Tie it round a rock." He tightened the knot around his waist and lowered himself into the water, gasping at the heart stopping chill. Before plunging in he scanned the flow of the current, hoping to intercept the bundle as it floated closer. But the waterlogged cloth sank under the water. He struck upstream and dived below the surface. The current buffeted him and rocks scraped the skin from his legs but he hardly noticed as he pushed on. Finally his bursting lungs forced him to surface. The rope was almost played out to its limit. Something brushed against his foot and he reached down, grabbing a leg. His numb fingers hauled the small body clear. It slumped in his arms. Holding it close he chafed its back with trembling hands. A splutter. The hands fluttered and nipped his face.

"I'm here."

Silent Owl had waded out to a flat rock and was perched there, a bedraggled diving bird, arms outstretched. Tom floated on his back, clasping the squirming child to his chest. Almost there. He reached out but the current was too fierce and tossed him sideways. He grasped the cloth with his teeth so that he could stretch out both his arms but as he did so he was flung back against half-submerged rocks. The back of his head struck a jutting edge. He groaned as tongues of pain licked across his skull. Blackness swallowed him.

Chapter 46

The Prairie, Summer 1868

Branches stretched upward like ribs, joining together above his head. Was he back in the forest? Everything was foggy. Where was that musty animal smell coming from? Was it tanned skins? No sound though. He must be on his own. He inched his head up.

"Keep still."

Firm hands pressed him back onto the furs. A long braid of hair brushed his forehead. He blinked, trying to focus.

"Spring Thaw, is it you?" No, the color was wrong, not raven-wing black but glowing russet. He reached out to touch it. "Richard?"

"No," It was a woman's voice.

There was that red fabric again. He tugged at the plaid shawl covering the hair and peered into the green eyes.

"It's you! Am I dead or mad?"

"Neither. You split your head open and have lain insensible for two days."

"The child?"

"My son's safe and no worse for falling in. How can I thank you? And your friend too. He's been pacing around like a hungry bear. I was so scared you had been killed." Her tears dripped down onto Tom's face.

Tom shivered.

"I've as many lives as the ship's cat. I can't believe I've found you here, living in the wilderness."

"In a tepee with savages, you mean?"

"I'd given up all hope of finding you. But I kept the sketch I drew of you."

"Why? We only met once and never even spoke."

"But you recognized me when you saw me again?"

"Of course I did. You stared at me like a man bewitched."

"I believe I was. I loved Richard and he had killed himself. I didn't know why. Then you appeared and I knew you must have the answer."

"It was the sins of the fathers that decided Richard's fate, and mine."

She told him the story of her life, with many pauses and sighs. "But I wouldn't accept my fate. I kept searching until I found a man and his people who didn't turn up their noses or talk about me behind their hands."

She smoothed her hand over his brow and left. Over the next few days Tom stumbled through his own story, his throbbing head making it hard to concentrate. He made light of his setbacks, thinking that she had suffered far more than he.

"It's odd how I went to sea to find adventure, but it was only when I left that I found it. Far more than I wanted."

Afterward, he lay back, eyes closed and mind empty, beyond thought or speech.

The next morning when he woke he raked through the embers of his conversation. She had been nameless for so long. "Catriona." He mouthed her name. Their lives were so far apart but for a brief, wild moment the same beat had linked them and they had stepped together into the dance. She had swung away from him but now they were back facing each other again.

"Don't you ever miss the company of your own kind?" Tom asked her, when she reappeared.

"Do you ever ask that question of your daughter-in-law?"

"No."

"Because she had so much to gain by marrying Iain? And for me it's different because I gave up civilized life? Did you know that when the first settlers came they felt honored to marry the daughter of an Indian chief?"

Tom nodded, ashamed. As he recovered he saw more of how

she lived. She bargained with the fur traders, insisting on a fair exchange. Thanks to her skill the tribe was paid in tools, woolen cloth, farming implements and seed, not in strong drink and shoddy trinkets. She showed her band how to cultivate crops so that they weren't hungry in the winter. At the same time she had learned all the skills of an Indian wife, healing her children with herbal potions and learning the tales handed down from the past. He could see why she was given her new name of Beaver Mother.

"My family here are like the Gaels back home," she told him. "We treasure the land and love stories." He asked her about a carved buffalo horn that hung from the roof poles.

"This holds the power of the buffalo and brings good fortune to us. The Blood people's story about the horn is not so different from the tales about the selkies who could change their form from seal to human."

"Tell me while I rest my eyes."

"Long ago, a man married a buffalo who had taken on the form of a woman. She bore a son and told her husband that he must never threaten her with fire. One evening though he was angry and forgetting her warning he picked up a blazing stick and struck her with it. At once she and their son vanished. In desperation he sought them until he found her herd. The leading bull looked toward a group of calves that were dancing and playing together, "If you can pick out your son from among them four times, your family will be given back to you."

The man looked hard at the calves and noticed that one of them held his tail high in the air. So he chose that one and he was right. The calves galloped around him a second time and the man chose the calf that had closed one of his eyes. Again he chose right. The third time his son let one ear hang down so that his father could recognize him.

The man dared to hope because he had to guess right only once more. This time his son held up one of his forelegs but a second calf was watching and thought that this was a fine new game. So he held up a leg too. What could the man do? Praying that he was right he chose one of the two calves."

"And was he right this time?"

"No, his luck ran out and the herd trampled him to death. The cow buffalo and her calf were left to mourn over his body."

"Is that the end of the story?"

"No, there is always hope left at the end of a tale. An old bull buffalo took away one of the broken bones into a sweat lodge and brought the man back to life. Then he restored the cow and calf to their human state once more and taught the family the mysteries of the Horn Society. We still follow them. They help us with hunting and save us in times of peril." She squeezed Tom's hand. "It was the Horn that brought you here to save my son's life."

Tom nodded but he couldn't meet her gaze. He was thinking of how this sanctuary would be invaded by hordes of traders and farmers. He remembered the stacks of buffalo hides piled high at the trading forts and the heaps of carcasses left to rot in the prairie.

But he held on to the tiller of hope. He told her how he raised money through his work and she nodded in agreement. So once his head cleared he began a frenzy of painting and photography. Everyone and everything. Individuals, family groups, and the whole band together. Tepees, horses, tools and the sacred horns. He was struck at how his Indian subjects sat for him. They were at ease with themselves unlike his white customers with their stiff shoulders, fretting in their Sunday best. The warriors calmly readied themselves. First they greased their long hair, arranging it so that a shorter strip pressed forward against the centre of their foreheads. Next, they threaded rows of beads through the sides and smoothed on red and black face paint. Each man had a different pattern, a text describing his prowess in hunting and fighting. The women lacked facial adornments but like the men wore tunics decorated with quills and beads. Tom took special care with his painting of Beaver Mother. She was still beautiful in a way that clutched at his heart although her hard life had scored her face.

Tom decided to leave before the winter so that the band wouldn't have to feed him and Silent Owl through the hollow months. He drew Beaver Mother aside to show her all the photographs and portraits of her family again. Her husband Brown Bear, her son Young Cub and his older sister Clear Stream. The gray tones of the photographs disguised the glowing russet hair, light eyes, and freckled skin of the children and their mother but they were revealed in the paintings.

"Are you happy for these pictures to be shown to the world?"

She nodded. He gazed at her until she replied to the question that hung heavily between them. "No, do not take them to the widow's house. If you do I will heap curses upon your head in our Blood tongue, Gaelic and English. You will turn into a pile of dust and be blown away on the winds."

Chapter 47

New York, 1872

Tom stood on the Manhattan shore looking out at the Statue of Liberty. How fortunate he had been to emigrate at a time when people were freely admitted. Would he have slipped through now, with clerks asking questions? It was a sticky July evening and he prised the collar of his shirt away from his sweating neck. The crowds around him sauntered. The humid weather had slowed down the Yankee bustle. He was content to be among his fellow men but separate from them while he savoured the unusual pleasure of being in a city with all its comforts.

"Lieutenant Masters, as I live and breathe," a booming voice rang out from behind him.

At first Tom was too stunned to move. Was he dreaming? Had his imagination conjured up the voice? He spun around, glancing in both directions for escape routes. He might be in his middle years now, but his outdoor life had kept him light on his feet. Flight would be better than using his fists. He would have a fair chance of escaping through the throng. All these thoughts sped through his mind as his eyes searched for the owner of the voice. He had always believed such an encounter would happen one day and there was a strange sort of relief in knowing it had finally come.

There he was, a narrow road's distance away, unmoving. He too was dressed in a summer suit and appeared to be on his own. Older too and heavier. Tom decided he could risk coming closer. So he advanced, stiff legged and poised for escape.

"It is you. You've kept that pale hair but it was your gait that I spotted. After years of living at close quarters I never forget a man's way of walking." The boom had softened. Tom had covered half the distance between them. He halted, his face expressionless.

"You've nothing to fear. I give you my word."

Tom still waited, undecided. It was too late to deny his identity. A genuine stranger would have looked puzzled at once. He could still run, a loose thread unspooling among the strolling groups. No, it was time to drop anchor. He waited unable to speak.

"Shall we walk a while?"

"If you wish, Captain Otter," Tom managed to croak.

"Not an active captain any longer. I've retired, and as an admiral, but I had a fancy to cross the Atlantic after the *Porcupine* did that deep water survey. You've worn well for a hunted man."

Tom was unable to stop the flush of shame swooping up his face. "I deeply regret betraying your trust."

"I'm sure you do. It was a terrible business Williams killing himself."

"But I shouldn't have fled."

"No, you were a coward." The captain's voice was stern. He hadn't changed much at all. His beard was white now, but he stood as foursquare as Tom remembered.

"I can't ask for your forgiveness. I betrayed the service but worse, I betrayed you and my shipmates. I heard you were reprimanded by the Admiralty for Richard's suicide and my desertion."

"The captain has to answer for his ship and crew. I was too lenient with you. I knew you were too close to Williams. No, hear me out," he added, seeing that Tom was about to protest. "I'm sure you weren't guilty of any unnatural practices. Both of you had kept your innocence despite all the sodomy that goes on in the Navy. But you were miserable and drinking too much. I should have tackled you sooner."

"I wish I could make amends."

"Well, you can tell me about what you've been doing as we stroll along."

Tom felt a stab of regret. Those words transported him back to the *Porcupine* when he would report to the captain as they paced the deck together.

"You look as if you've prospered. I was furious with you, of course. But when Rogers told me he had a whiff of your whereabouts I prayed he would fail to find you."

"He gave me a scare. He was snooping in Sydney while I was away on a trip upcountry."

"Hmm. He was planning to track you farther. That man was like a ferret but engine trouble put him into Montreal for repairs. I sowed the idea in his head that you were last seen in London as a penniless beggar. That news seemed to console him." Captain Otter let out a rumbling laugh.

"I can't believe you would tell a lie on my behalf."

"I surprised myself, but Rogers was altogether too gleeful about flushing you out," Henry Otter flashed tobacco-stained teeth. "As I've become older I lean more toward the forgiveness of the New Testament rather than the harsh justice of the Prophets. Now tell me about your life since."

So Tom did, especially his work for the Indians.

"That's why I'm here in New York exhibiting photographs and paintings. I've learned that the natives here in America are in an even worse plight than those in Canada." He took a deep breath. "I found my life's companion among the Indians. He was a Mi'kmaq from Cape Breton."

"Was?"

"He died last winter," Tom replied, his voice cracking.

Captain Otter nodded. "You've suffered enough. I shall tell the Admiralty I heard confirmation of your death."

"Thank you, sir." Tom felt both his voice and hands shaking.

"Well, I'm pleased you put your drawing lessons to good use. You always had a neat hand. However, my offer of announcing your death depends on one condition."

"Yes, sir?"

"That you tell me why Williams killed himself."

"You could always spot evasion. I have found some answers. The story goes back to the island of Rona."

"Well, we'll find somewhere to sit down and you can tell me while we eat."

Chapter 48

New York, 1872

"It's hard to know where to begin. It's as fantastical as those tales you used to tell the midshipmen," Tom sighed, as they settled down at a table near the open door of a bar. Both men had removed their jackets, but they still oozed sweat into the clammy air.

"Well. Keep it simple. I can always ask questions."

"I'm sure you remember Richard's funeral service in that grim chapel overlooking the sea? Afterwards I had an encounter that robbed me of my senses. That happened to Richard too, although at the time I didn't know that." He paused and cleared his throat, "It seems so incredible now, how I jettisoned everything because of a vision, an apparition. There was a young woman. Do you recall seeing her? She watched us from a distance, her head swathed in a shawl. I became convinced she had the answer to the riddle of Richard's death. And she was so beautiful, a goddess. All I cared about was tracking her down. I drew a sketch of her and carried it everywhere. I lost count of how many strangers I showed it to in the hope that someone would recognize her. I kept it until it was so creased that you could scarcely make out her features."

"I remember her standing like a sentry by the shore, but I was anxious to return to the ship and thought no more about her. You found her in the end?"

"I did. Many years later, when I had almost given up hope. But the story was more complicated than I realized."

"Get to the marrow of it, man. Start with the reason why Williams killed himself."

Stung by Otter's impatience, Tom determined to tell the story at his own pace.

"What do you know of Richard's earlier life, sir?"

"Very little, except that he was better schooled than most sailors. I dare say, like the rest of them, he was running away to sea to escape something on land."

"He ran away from the cruel man who adopted him. He knew nothing of his own blood. Richard was a solitary man by nature, hard to fathom. But he loved music, even if it was only old Billy limping along on his squeezebox. So when we anchored at Portree he went to a dance. He joined in a reel and was mesmerized by his partner. A man in a trance. She sped away after the first dance. He strove to find her, to no avail. No one would tell him who she was. They all looked askance at him. In the end a local minister explained. It was after that he took his own life."

"And who was this woman?"

"Màiri MacQueen. The name meant nothing to him, but he recognized her."

"You're talking in riddles."

"The minister told him that the woman who bewitched him, this Màiri, was in fact his mother. Many of the people there were struck by his likeness to her and guessed that he was her long-lost son."

"Good heavens. And that revelation led to him killing himself?"

"I believe so. She refused to meet him and he would have taken that hard. I've wondered since, maybe this is fanciful but . . . was he eaten alive by guilt and shame? His adoptive father always told him he was a worthless sinner. If he already felt guilty about his love for me? Rather the love we had for each other, not expressed but deemed unnatural. Then he fell in love with a woman and that would be a relief to him."

The captain nodded.

"But when he found out that she was his mother, might he not be horrified at an incestuous passion?"

Captain Otter scratched his beard, "So finding his mother left him more wretched than ever?"

"Yes. He saw a beam of light, thinking it would take him to safety but it was a will o' the wisp. It lured him on and then snuffed out, leaving him in the darkness."

"And his mother, what about her?"

"She lost her son for the second time. She ran away in a panic. Didn't know what to do. The minister advised her not to see her son again. I suspect he didn't want scandal. Immorality must be kept hidden." Tom's voice was bitter.

"So this Màiri MacQueen had borne Richard out of wedlock?"

"Yes. As a girl she worked in the kitchens of the local laird's house. She fell in love with the eldest son and he with her. You look disbelieving, sir, but it sounds as if it was a real love match and he planned to marry her. When her condition became obvious the boy confronted his father, declaring that they were betrothed. However, he was below the age of consent and his father packed him off to university in Edinburgh. The young man never saw his son who was handed over to a foundling charity soon after his birth."

"A sad tale but not an uncommon one. How did you discover the truth?"

"I met Màiri herself, not in the Highlands but by chance in Newfoundland when I came across the indomitable Widow MacKenzie again."

"Ah, I heard that she had emigrated."

"I came across her house when I was a traveling photographer. Her son was still earning his living by fishing. She had taken her lantern across the Atlantic with her, her own one, not the one from the commissioners. It was Màiri who opened the door to me. She looked so like the widow's son that I presumed she was one of the family. I asked for her to join the rest of them for the photograph. The atmosphere was very strained. She was indeed related to them but she was also their servant. Afterwards

I spoke with her and she told me about meeting Richard." Tom gulped down some beer and wiped his brow.

"And it was this Màiri that you saw after the funeral?"

"No, sir. That's what I mean about it being complicated. Shall I continue?"

"Very well."

"After Richard's death she couldn't bear to stay on Skye. She got a berth on an emigrant ship. That's where she met the widow and her family. They were all shocked to see how she resembled her brother."

"This story seems to be full of shocking encounters."

"It is. They saw what I saw when I met the family. She and her brother Murdo had the same dark red, wavy hair and blue-green eyes."

"This is too difficult for an old salt like me."

"They're brother and sister, well half-brother and sister. Widow MacKenzie's husband was by all accounts a handsome man with a roving eye. He passed on his features to his children, legitimate and illegitimate alike."

"And did Mrs. MacKenzie know of Màiri's existence before they met on the ship?"

"No, not at all, although Màiri said that she showed no surprise when she learned her identity. I dare say the Widow MacKenzie had her suspicions about her husband's nature. Anyway, she offered Màiri a roof over her head."

"An act of Christian charity, then."

Tom shrugged,

"Albeit a chilly one. She had never known anything but poverty. Brought up grudgingly by her grandparents and treated as a skivvy. She was weary of struggling and took the widow's charity.

"Children born out of wedlock have a hard time of it. They suffer for their parents' sins. Màiri though seems not to have learned from her mother's mistake. She also bore a child outside marriage."

They sat silently, both delving into their own thoughts.

"I'm clearer now about why Williams was in such a turmoil that he took his own life," said Captain Otter, eventually, as he pushed his empty glass away from him. Suddenly he reached across the table and seized Tom's wrist, "But that's not the whole story is it? Who was it that you met? And why did you desert?

Chapter 49

New York, 1872

Tom ran his fingers through his hair before meeting the captain's gaze.

"Richard and I were both bewitched. But not by the same woman. That was the key. Màiri couldn't tell me where my mystery girl had gone. I felt such a fool that I had thrown everything away for a delusion, a chimera. And I was terrified that Rogers was on my trail. Doomed to be a fugitive forever. But by the time Silent Owl and I traveled to the Rockies, I was finally at peace. Because of him but also as a father to Iain. And grateful to his wife, a young woman wise beyond her years."

Tom's lips curved into a smile as he thought about how Spring Thaw knew that he and her brother would end up forged together, two links of a ship's cable. Only the hammer blow of Silent Owl's death had severed them.

The captain waited while Tom hauled his thoughts back to the present.

"Silent Owl had been reluctant to go so far westward. He never said why he changed his mind. Since then I've wondered if he sensed he didn't have long to live, even though the consumption had barely shown itself. By that time, I had almost let go of my obsession about the young woman. During our journey we rescued an Indian child who had fallen into a river. I managed to knock myself out, like I did back at Bonawe all those years before. That time I came to and was convinced it was you, sitting by my bed and waiting to call me to account. This time I opened my eyes to see a lean face, swimming before me, a face marked by winter hunger. I was confused by the hair, long plaited tresses like the natives favor but the hair was dark red. I've never seen a native with that color hair. The figure stared at me while I rubbed my eyes. 'I recognize you, now.' It was a woman's voice that had the singing lilt of the Highlands. Then I knew it was her. 'I've found you at last.' I tried to sit up but the throbbing of my head forced me to lie back again. 'I don't understand,' I groaned. 'They call me Beaver Woman here. You were brave in saving my son. So you may ask me what you wish,' she said, in the creaking way of someone speaking in a tongue they don't use much.

"We only met once but you put a spell on me," I said.

"'That's because of who I reminded you of,' she whispered.

"I had to close my eyes again because I had been hit broadsides on. Once she said the words I saw the truth of it. How had I not understood before? I only had a glimpse of her face, but now I could see how she looked so like him, younger and with more delicate features but the same hair and eyes. How could I not have realized?"

"Looked like who? Williams?"

Tom nodded, "Yes, his younger sister, Catriona."

Otter frowned. "So Catriona and Richard are brother and sister, full brother and sister?"

Tom nodded.

"Then, Màiri MacQueen, whom you met at the Widow MacKenzie's house, is the mother of both of them? And this Catriona was living with Indians in the wilds? How extraordinary."

"Incredible indeed," Tom agreed. "She must have seen the shock on my face because she said, 'I know what you're thinking but listen to my tale before you pass judgement on me. Have you met my mother?' I nodded.

She snorted, 'And did she tell you I'm her daughter?'"

"Not in so many words." I showed her the drawing. "She told me that the young woman had carried on farther west on her own," I explained.

"Couldn't you see the resemblance between us?"

For so long it had been hidden in plain sight. I began to wonder but I didn't want to press her in case she refused to say more.

"She wouldn't tell you who I was because she was ashamed. My mother never learned her lesson. She listened to my father's lies, gave birth to my brother and had to part with him. After she lost him, she moved away from her home but not far enough away. Gossip followed her but in the end folk found fresher meat to chew over. Ten years later, my father returned home to see his parents. He had done well as a lawyer in Edinburgh. He sniffed my mother out and she, the fool that she was, didn't send him away with a curse. Listened to his false words a second time and I was the result."

"Were you sent away too, like Richard?" I asked her.

"No. He had promised to marry her, like he did the first time but he forgot to mention that he already had a wealthy wife in Edinburgh. Generous as he was," she spat out. "He gave her money for my keep. We didn't starve but everyone knew I was his lordship's bastard. It's a useful stick to beat a child with. She never told me about my brother herself but other kindly souls did." Her laugh was raw.

"Then Richard appearing and his terrible death turned their lives upside down," the Captain observed.

"With a vengeance. Tongues hissed with venom, accusing Màiri of causing Richard's death. Neither mother nor daughter could bear it any more. So they left on the emigrant ship. Màiri let the MacKenzies take her in, but Catriona despised her mother for accepting their charity. She wanted to go where no one knew about her."

"Well, she certainly did that."

"She told me that for the first time in her life she felt respected. She has achieved miracles for her adopted people, teaching them how to outwit the fur traders."

"Surely the old ways have gone. Their only hope is to become farmers."

"That's what Spring Thaw believes but many Indians, like Silent Owl, cannot endure the loss of their way of life. How much upheaval can people bear? A ship can be refitted a number of times but in the end she's only fit for the scrapyard. That's what happened to Silent Owl."

"You said he had consumption. Did low spirits hasten his death?"

"In a manner of speaking. We went back again to see the Blood tribe and by the second trip things were much worse for them. They tried to keep away from the traders but their camp was raided by some of them, along with Crees and mixed bloods. The young men wanted revenge and wouldn't listen to Beaver Woman urging caution. They galloped off in pursuit. I didn't realize at first that Silent Owl had ridden with them. They were ambushed in a canyon. Some of them were able to turn their horses back and escape with their lives." Tom's voice had shrunk to a whisper.

"But not Silent Owl?"

"No, he stayed back to give the others covering fire."

"He died bravely, then."

"It's what he chose but I had no chance to say farewell. Only to arrange his funeral. Like most Indians he had a horror of being buried. The Blood, like the other Blackfoot tribes, build a platform in the trees for their dead. They did that in his honor."

"Have you gone back since?" the Captain asked, after a long silence.

"No. I couldn't bear it. I send money to Beaver Woman. The Mounted Police have restored law and order but the band is no longer free to roam."

"And has she stopped haunting you now that you've solved the mystery of who she is?"

"Yes. But I'm still a wanderer."

"I've heard many tales in my life, but this is one of the

strangest."

Captain Otter downed the rest of his beer while Tom sat still, relieved that all the fraying ropes had been tarred and knotted together. His life was finally shipshape.

Chapter 50

Samoa, 1891

Tom came ashore from the American steamer at the port of Apia, on the island of Opolu. He had watched in admiration as the pilot nudged the vessel through the coral reefs into the narrow neck of the harbor. Captain Otter would have been impressed. It was still hard to believe that the captain, Tom couldn't get used to thinking of him as an admiral, had died fifteen years ago, his wise and generous spirit gone. Tom still silently thanked him every time he boarded a ship. He had made a number of voyages in the Pacific over the last few years and he always felt relieved not to be looking over his shoulder. What a consolation to be officially deceased with his name struck off Admiralty records.

Mount Vaea rising up through the tropical jungle had looked enticing on their approach, but as so often disembarking was a disappointment. There was the usual quay-side clutter of grubby, rusting bars and warehouses. Among them were the squat white painted houses of the foreign traders, awkward transplants from a staid Europe, ill at ease in this island of waving coconut trees and scarlet bursts of frangipani. He became more cheerful as he noticed the rounded shapes of the native houses and the Samoans themselves, handsome and muscular in their patterned skirt-like *lava-lavas*, bare chests glistening with oil. Not unlike Indians he thought but more carefree.

His first task was to arrange transport up the mountain slopes to Vailima. He approached a group of Samoans. With smiles, sign language, and jangling coins he conveyed his message. His guides coaxed the horses up a wavering path above ravines and waterfalls. The stiletto blade of memory slid in under his ribs as he recalled his expeditions with Silent Owl. All that grumbling about the burning heat, the biting insects, and his aching muscles, never thinking that one day he would welcome any discomfort if he could have his companion back.

As he neared the estate he felt a mixture of apprehension and curiosity. It was months since he had written requesting permission to photograph the Samoan workers. He had half expected to be refused. After all, famous writers looked to be photographed and fawned over, not ignored in favor of their servants. To his surprise Tom had received a warm reply:

I shall be delighted to welcome you. You sound like a fellow after my own heart with your interest in native ways of life. For a change I shall be the contented spectator rather than the nervous subject of the magic eye. Our Samoans have not yet suffered so brutally at the hands of Europeans as have the New World Indians, but most of the traders routinely despise them. Although I've had the opportunity to meet many Americans I know less about their northern neighbors except that I believe they have stayed closer in spirit to their Scottish and English forebears.

The trees reached high above them, huge banyans over a hundred feet tall, with monumental trunks. Then suddenly there was the house, in a clearing in the jungle. Like the Widow MacKenzie's house on Rona this building too was unexpected. Both houses seemed to clasp tightly to their surroundings, one perched on the rocky beach, the other erupting from lush jungle. This house though, unlike the widow's, was brightly colored. Its wooden walls were painted a vivid blue and topped by a dusky red corrugated iron roof. It had two storeys, with a veranda on both levels along the north side. Large enough to be a mansion or a summer palace, it was much more imposing than Tom had expected. His apprehension grew as they halted in front of the building and dismounted. A gangling figure strode toward him, arms outstretched and face grinning.

"Pleased to meet you at last. Mr. John Robinson, I presume? Robert Louis Stevenson at your service," he said, his voice deep and resonant for such a frail body. His head nodded, a heavy

249

bloom on a drooping stalk.

"How do you do?" Tom replied, extending his hand.

The handshake was unexpected too, solid and firm, even though the wrist poking out from the shirtsleeve was as twiglike as a sickly child's. Tom thanked his guides and paid them while Louis watched, his dark, glittering eyes missing nothing. He showed Tom into the house, holding back a hanging mat suspended from the doorway for there were no doors. They entered a large hall that made Tom want to gasp in surprise. It was clad in shining planks of redwood like a luxurious ship. Paintings and photographs were clustered on the walls but there was no chance for Tom to examine them as Louis rushed on.

"I'll show you the family seat while the servants take your luggage," he said, over his shoulder. "Vailima is my wife's pride and joy. The name means 'Five Waters'."

As Louis strode through to the dining room, Tom had to lengthen his stride to keep up. There was an incongruous fireplace, silk curtains in shimmering streams of yellow and silver, and an antique sideboard.

"Now you can meet the family in the family seat."

The people sitting in the well-worn leather seats around the table fell silent and turned to stare at the stranger. They were clearly waiting for lunch and Tom felt as if he were the goose being carried in on a serving platter.

Louis introduced Tom to the three people there. "Joe Strong, my son-in-law," he said indicating a figure dressed in a sailor's shirt and cap.

As he stood up Tom saw that he wore a *lava-lava*, knotted around his waist and strangely, trouser bottoms visible underneath the hem. Tom ducked at a sudden swooshing sound behind him. There was a blur of flapping wings. A gaudy blue parrot swerved into the room and landed, squawking, on Joe's shoulder.

"Captain Flint," said Tom, with a nervous laugh.

Joe groaned and rolled his eyes. "No, just Peter."

Joe's wife, Belle, was small and neat with a hesitant smile, quite different from her brother Lloyd Osbourne, a tall fair man whose chilly blue eyes glinted behind wire-rimmed spectacles.

"That's my whole family, apart from Fanny and my mother who you'll meet later," Louis said. "I'll get one of the servants to show you to your quarters. We've put you in the small cottage where we lived before we built the big house. Then join us for luncheon if you wish."

"Thank you but I'm tired after the journey. Maybe I could join you later?" replied Tom, wanting to escape. He could hear the drawling American voices start up again once he and Louis left the room with its discordant furnishings.

"There's a banquet tonight. When there's a ship in port, I like to invite the officers," Louis said and Tom nodded, trying not to stiffen. "Americans, they're more fun than the English ones," Louis added. "Not a universal rule, of course." Tom grinned in relief.

Louis was right. They were agreeable company. Five of them, all cheerful and talkative and not too curious about an aging English man living in Canada. Tom was amused to see the servants' special livery of striped jackets and *lava-lavas* in Stewart tartan. Like the fireplace, a sort of misplaced Scottish baronial fantasy.

The meal was astounding too. Tropical fruit he had expected but not in such variety, fried banana, pineapple soaked in wine, coconut cream baked in leaves, and tarts made from cape goose-berries. The other foods were lavish, too—fish, prawns, pigeons, roasted pig, and sweet potatoes.

"We lack none of the trappings of civilisation," Louis said, as coffee and more wine was brought in. "That's why I have to work my fingers to the bone writing." It was said lightly, but Tom noticed how Fanny glowered.

"I grow much of the fruit and vegetables," she said.

"Of course you do my dear and you must show Tom your

garden tomorrow."

"I should be delighted," Tom said, but his heart sank at the prospect of having to spend time with this odd, dumpy woman who was dressed in a sort of voluminous striped nightdress. She had an air of barely controlled ferocity, like a chained guard dog.

"Of course we weren't complete pioneers," she told him the next morning, as she showed him her vegetable garden. All the plants jostled and twisted upward, straining for light. "When we arrived we found some ancient banana and papaya trees half strangled by the jungle. I brought seeds from Australia, melons, tomatoes, and pineapples—No boy! Don't dig a hole there. Wait until I tell you what to do," she shrieked at one of the sweating Samoan laborers.

"They won't listen, think they know best and then wonder why I won't keep them on," she grumbled, bustling ahead and swiping at the undergrowth with a stick.

Tom couldn't resist turning back and winking at the young man who was scowling at her back. As they walked back to the house, Fanny continued her litany of grievances.

"I have to keep everything running smoothly and watch over Louis's health as well. All these visitors are sucking the life out of him. Then off he goes for a gallop on Jack and leaves me fretting that he'll suffer a fall."

"Well, I certainly don't want to add to his burdens, Mrs. Stevenson. My plan is to slip away and take some photographs of the servants."

She grunted and fell silent. They returned to the house to find a substantial lunch being prepared: duck, chicken, baked yams, and taro pudding. The American sailors were still in residence, as convivial as the night before. Tom watched Louis reveling again in his role of a tropical Highland chieftain. He pressed everyone to eat their fill, topping up their glasses and hooting with laughter at their jokes as his family munched silently. Louis spurted energy. He was the beam that dazzled all the passing vessels. Tom shivered as he thought how that light could suddenly be quenched. He remembered the time as a young boy when he found a bewildered pheasant bumbling into their garden to escape the guns. It seemed unharmed and he had brought it some of the chickens' feed to peck at but when he returned later it was lying on the ground, its burnished plumage ruffling in the breeze. The creature was stone dead, its heart stopped by shock.

"Now, let me find you some subjects to photograph," Louis said, wrapping an arm around Tom's shoulder as they all rose and staggered away from the table.

"No, don't let me interrupt your writing," Tom replied. "I'll find the Samoans I saw earlier."

"Do you ride? Take Jack. He needs the exercise."

Tom was glad to take the horse and let him trot up into the hills. Although the air was humid, it was fresher than the fevered atmosphere in the house. Tom found the men he had met before. They were glad to stop work and pose for him. They had an easy grace and needed little direction. He touched the arm of the young man he had winked at earlier to move him into position and as he did so he marveled at the smoothness of his skin and the supple muscles underneath. It was a similar sensation as the first time he had touched a snake. He had expected something slimy and flaccid but instead was surprised by its dry, firm surface.

The men enjoyed being photographed in the same way as the Indians used to. Tom supposed that it was because the process gave them dignity. They parted with much laughter and back slapping. Reluctantly turning Jack's head back down the hill, he resolved to bid farewell to his host the next day and return to the port, even if it meant he had to wait there for a steamer. As it was his last night in the house, he decided that for once he would take a glass or two of wine with his dinner.

"Well, Mr. Robinson, did you take your pictures of our

Samoan boys? I'm surprised you didn't want portraits of all of us, too. Usually visitors can't wait to photograph us." Fanny's voice was peevish.

"Well, the purpose of my travels is to take pictures of native peoples. To record their way of life before it vanishes."

"Does that matter? The Samoans' way of life when white men came here was a very idle one." Lloyd's pale eyes had a hostile glare as he turned to Tom.

"Well, of course Nature is more bountiful here than in Canada. Indians in North America have a harder struggle against the climate."

"Pah," Lloyd sneered and looked at his mother. "We don't find Samoans to be willing workers."

Louis watched them, his dark eyes unfathomable. Feeling uncomfortable Tom changed the subject. "While I was photographing them something odd happened. A strange sight emerged from the jungle. A middle-aged man, dressed like the other Samoans except for his head. As he walked toward us I could see him smoothing down the starched tail of a white widow's cap that streamed down his back. Once he was satisfied with the lie of his headdress, he smiled at me in a gracious manner. Then he sat down straight-backed for me to take his picture."

"He's a thief. It's another of their faults." Fanny glared at her husband. "It's all very well for you to laugh. They worship you. Tusitala, the teller of stories, they call him," she said, turning to Tom. "You indulge them like children and leave it to others to instill some discipline."

"Well, well, well. Mother has been complaining for weeks about how her caps keep disappearing when she sends them to be laundered. I think our friend here has solved the mystery. They're trophies. Magpies like glittering objects while Samoans collect widow's caps," Louis said, wiping his eyes with a handkerchief.

"That proves my point about them being unreliable," said Lloyd.

Exasperated, Tom decided to challenge him. "Did you follow horticulture before you came here? Or another profession?"

"He would have become an engineer like so many in my husband's family. But his eyesight prevented him," Fanny said in a tone that brooked no dissent. "He devotes himself to managing the estate. He has the thankless task of overseeing the outside boys while my daughter Belle supervises the inside staff."

"We're all working like niggers on this god-damned estate," added Joe Strong. His parrot had been clinging to the curtain rail, its head tucked under its wing. Now it woke up and screeched at the sound of his voice. "That's right, you tell the fellow it's none of his business, coming here, pointing his lens everywhere and asking damn questions."

Louis listened, tight-lipped, his eyes swiveling between the speakers.

"Hi, everyone. I hope I'm not too late, "a jovial voice rang out from the doorway.

"No, of course not, Lieutenant Barker," Louis replied with a smile. "There's plenty still here to eat. We were talking about different professions. You remember Mr. Robinson from last night? He's been photographing our Samoan workers."

"Sure. You're from Canada, sir? But you came out from England?"

"And you haven't told us what you did there?" Lloyd's tone was sharp.

Lieutenant Barker raised his eyebrows. "I would guess you were in uniform once, sir, like me. The Navy? You've the bearing of an officer."

Now everyone was scrutinising Tom, the American smiling, Louis quizzical, Fanny and her family suspicious.

Tom paused to slow his breathing. "I wish that were true. I've always been drawn to the sea and ships but the nearest I got to them was working for a shipping company. Until I crossed the Atlantic."

"And you chose the northern wilderness rather than the States," Barker laughed, tapping Tom on the arm to show he was joking.

"Neither country is as beautiful as Samoa though," Tom said, "And I'm very grateful to our kind host," he added, raising his glass in Louis's direction.

What did it matter? He would soon be leaving. He wasn't a fugitive any more. Still caution made him push his wineglass to one side. He said little as wine, laughter, and loud opinions flowed freely. Although Louis's tongue seemed to have loosened as much as the others, Tom sensed the author's eyes probing him. As soon as he decently could Tom made his apologies, blaming a full day for his tiredness. As he left the room he could feel their eyes pricking him.

He walked back to the cottage and pushed aside the flimsy mat hanging limp in the humid night air. He would have preferred a door to close behind him.

Chapter 51

Samoa, 1891

The unaccustomed wine made Tom restless. Eventually he fell into an uneasy sleep until a sound startled him. He lay rigid in the dark. He had no idea of the time and he could feel his heart battering against his ribs. Easing himself into a sitting position he could sense rather than see a figure in the doorway. Tom sprang to his feet.

"What is it?" he croaked, through cracked lips.

No reply. He shuffled toward the figure. His groping hand touched an arm,

"Come outside, so that I can see you."

Whoever it was backed out willingly enough until Tom could see his face in the moonlight. It was the young Samoan he had winked at that morning. Now he stood smiling uncertainly and shifting from foot to foot.

"What do you want?" Tom whispered, although he knew the answer. The young man leant forward and clasped his hands around Tom's bare, sweating back. Tom groaned as his body signaled its readiness. He kissed the soft wide mouth, sliding his hands down the young man's spine to the curve of his buttocks.

"No." He jerked his hands away and pressed the palms against the Samoan's smooth chest. "I've resisted since Silent Owl died."

The young man frowned, understanding the action but not the words.

"Wait." Tom went back inside and returned with a fistful of coins. "Take these and use them well," he said, ramming the money into the Samoan's hands.

As the young man padded away into the darkness Tom heard a shriek. That bloody parrot. Was its owner out in the moonlight?

If so, he was up to no good. Tom felt too jarred to go back to sleep again. So he lit a candle, tugged on his clothes, and stuffed his belongings into his bag. He would go to the main house as soon as it was light, find something to eat in the kitchen and leave. It would be rude not to bid anyone farewell but no matter. He couldn't endure this place any longer. If he stayed he would be suffocated, like the banana trees in the jungle.

He was creeping past the dining room, carrying a plate of fruit when he heard footsteps behind him. There was Louis himself descending the stairs.

"An early breakfast?" he asked, "Or an early escape? I spent the night reclined in my study. Won't you join me for a short while? We writers are vultures, plucking meat from other men's lives and I'm sure there are fine pickings from yours."

This was said with a boyish grin and to his surprise Tom found himself nodding and smiling back. He followed Louis upstairs into a library whose walls were covered in hundreds of books, their spines shining as if they had been polished.

"I have to get them varnished or they would rot away in this climate. My study's through here." He indicated a monastic cell, with a narrow bed and shelves crammed with books. Although cramped it had two windows, one facing the sea toward the port of Apia and the other looking out on Mount Vaea.

"It's like a cabin," Tom exclaimed.

"What more could a man want? The sea and the hills." Louis pulled out a chair and offered it to Tom while he flopped down on the camp bed. "Look at this. Isn't it ingenious?" He pulled a cord that lowered a small table down from where it was suspended from the ceiling. "I can write in comfort without rising from my bed. I wish I could have had this when I was a child. Now we won't be disturbed. I'm sure you've led an adventurous life, even though you pretend you haven't. I can see it in your face. The man who hides behind the cloth to take pictures but never appears in them himself."

Seeing Tom's eyes widen in alarm he added, "Have no fears. I will turn and twist what you tell me. No one will recognize you when they read the story." He reached into a cupboard for a bottle of wine and two glasses.

Although still wary, Tom was seduced by Louis's manner, guileless and complicit at the same time. Why not? This would be very different from talking to Captain Otter all those years ago. That had been a confession. This was a chance to become immortal. So over several hours his life story poured out, sometimes in a spate, at others a sluggish trickle or a looping meander turning back on its self.

When he ended, Louis said, "Despite everything you've achieved, you still skulk on the fringes of society like a renegade Jacobite."

Tom bridled.

"I don't intend any offence. I'm only surprised that you can't forgive yourself for a youthful error of judgment. Look at me. I was a colossal disappointment to my father. Refusing to join the family business. He disapproved of my writing and my morals. Yet, despite his disapproval he never cut me off. In that respect I've tried to follow his example with my own children, well stepchildren, as best I can."

"Of course," Tom replied not knowing what else he could say as he thought about Louis's parasitic relatives and compared them with his own family.

Iain was middle-aged now, a respected citizen and businessman. His half-breed children had turned out well. They had inherited their mother's toughness and were able to straddle both the white and the native worlds as she did. And Emma, of course, the only sister he knew and whom he loved dearly, despite her tendency to disapprove. A little slower now but always hospitable and capable she was the one who anchored them to the community. Even his dreadful old landlady, Mrs. MacKenzie had been tamed by her relentless kindness. One or two widowers had sought Emma's hand but she was too independent to be hobbled by matrimony.

Louis's sigh interrupted his reverie. "Maybe I didn't escape the lighthouses after all. Books send out a light over the waters, too. My father would have snorted at such a fanciful idea. Maybe an old sailor would too?"

Tom smiled and shook his head.

"I've been living in the South Seas for a number of years now. I shall never return to Scotland, but I would like to visit it again in my imagination." Louis's tone was wistful.

But how much longer can your stock of oil last? Tom wondered, when you are blazing so fiercely, consuming your fragile body?

Louis spoke, almost as if he could read Tom's thoughts, "I keep thinking about Widow MacKenzie on her remote island, tending her lamp for all those years."

Tom waited, expecting him to finally refer to his stay there as a child.

Louis's face flushed. There was a fevered expression in his eyes,

"Are you feeling unwell?" Tom asked.

"No, but there's something tugging in my memory, a sail flapping in the wind. I feel I know this lady and her island, but how? I would only have been a wee boy when my father was building the lighthouse on Rona."

"Did he ever take you with him on his visits?" Tom asked.

"Not generally. My mother wouldn't allow it because of my health."

Tom was too much a respecter of secrets to probe further. He waited while Louis frowned, his gaze turned inward.

"I do remember kindness there. And being ill, lying under a counterpane and hearing stories. And being on a ship."

He glanced up and Tom couldn't stop his face stretching into a smile.

"You? You were the sailor. Are you home from the sea?" Louis muttered.

"Pardon?"

"It's from one of my poems. I can't remember writing it. It's lived in my mind forever." He shook his head, as if to rid himself of trapped thoughts, buzzing and bumping on the edges of his mind.

"My home is in Samoa now. How about you? Is Cape Breton your home?"

"I believe it is. It's only now that I'm so far away that I know where my home truly is."

"So you will return there. To a safe anchorage."

They shook hands and Tom left to start his long journey homeward.

.

Note to Reader

Thank you for buying *No Safe Anchorage*. I hope that you enjoyed reading it as much as I enjoyed writing it. If you have a few moments, please feel free to add your review of the book at your favorite online site for feedback. Also if you would like to know about other books that I have coming in the near future, please visit my website www.lizmacraeshaw.com or e-mail me at lizmacraeshaw@outlook.com for news on upcoming works.

Sincerely,

Liz MacRae Shaw

Glossary

bodach—old man
cailleach—old woman
dùn caan—flat-topped hill on the island of Raasay
Eilean an Fhraoich—Heather Island
eilean tigh—island with a house
Garbh Eilean—Rough Island
isean—chick, term of endearment
Loch a'Bhraige—Loch of the Upper Bay
machair—meadow above the beach
sasannach—Englishman
Sgeir nan Eun—Bird Skerry
sgitheanach—Skyeman

**TOP HAT
BOOKS**

Historical fiction that lives.

We publish fiction that captures the contrasts, the achievements, the optimism and the radicalism of ordinary and extraordinary times across the world.

We're open to all time periods and we strive to go beyond the narrow, foggy slums of Victorian London. Where are the tales of the people of fifteenth century Australasia? The stories of eighth century India? The voices from Africa, Arabia, cities and forests, deserts and towns? Our books thrill, excite, delight and inspire.

The genres will be broad but clear. Whether we're publishing romance, thrillers, crime, or something else entirely, the unifying themes are timescale and enthusiasm. These books will be a celebration of the chaotic power of the human spirit in difficult times. The reader, when they finish, will snap the book closed with a satisfied smile.
If you have enjoyed this book, why not tell other readers by posting a review on your preferred book site. Recent bestsellers from Tops Hat Books are:

Grendel's Mother
The Saga of the Wyrd-Wife
Susan Signe Morrison
Grendel's mother, a queen from Beowulf, threatens the fragile political stability on this windswept land.
Paperback: 978-1-78535-009-2 ebook: 978-1-78535-010-8

Queen of Sparta
A Novel of Ancient Greece
T.S. Chaudhry
History has relegated her to the role of bystander, what if
Gorgo, Queen of Sparta, had played a central role in the Greek
resistance to the Persian invasion?
Paperback: 978-1-78279-750-0 ebook: 978-1-78279-749-4

Mercenary
R.J. Connor
Richard Longsword is a mercenary, but this time it's not for
money, this time it's for revenge...
Paperback: 978-1-78279-236-9 ebook: 978-1-78279-198-0

Black Tom
Terror on the Hudson
Ron Semple
A tale of sabotage, subterfuge and political shenanigans
in Jersey City in 1916; America is on the cusp of war and the
fate of the nation hinges on the decision of one young
policeman.
Paperback: 978-1-78535-110-5 ebook: 978-1-78535-111-2

Destiny Between Two Worlds
A Novel about Okinawa
Jacques L. Fuqua, Jr.
A fateful October 1944 morning offered no inkling that the
lives of thousands of Okinawans would be profoundly
changed—forever.
Paperback: 978-1-78279-892-7 ebook: 978-1-78279-893-4

Cowards
Trent Portigal
A family's life falls into turmoil when the parents' timid political dissidence is discovered by their far more enterprising children.
Paperback: 978-1-78535-070-2 ebook: 978-1-78535-071-9

Godwine Kingmaker
Part One of The Last Great Saxon Earls
Mercedes Rochelle
The life of Earl Godwine is one of the enduring enigmas of English history. Who was this Godwine, first Earl of Wessex; unscrupulous schemer or protector of the English? The answer depends on whom you ask...
Paperback: 978-1-78279-801-9 ebook: 978-1-78279-800-2

The Last Stork Summer
Mary Brigid Surber
Eva, a young Polish child, battles to survive the designation of "racially worthless" under Hitler's Germanization Program.
Paperback: 978-1-78279-934-4 ebook: 978-1-78279-935-1 $4.99 £2.99

Messiah Love
Music and Malice at a Time of Handel
Sheena Vernon
The tale of Harry Walsh's faltering steps on his journey to success and happiness, performing in the playhouses of Georgian London.
Paperback: 978-1-78279-768-5 ebook: 978-1-78279-761-6

A Terrible Unrest
Philip Duke
A young immigrant family must confront the horrors of the Colorado Coalfield War to live the American Dream.
Paperback: 978-1-78279-437-0 ebook: 978-1-78279-436-3

Readers of ebooks can buy or view any of these bestsellers by clicking on the live link in the title. Most titles are published in paperback and as an ebook. Paperbacks are available in traditional bookshops. Both print and ebook formats are available online.

Find more titles and sign up to our readers' newsletter at http://www.johnhuntpublishing.com/fiction

Follow us on Facebook at https://www.facebook.com/JHPfiction and Twitter at https://twitter.com/JHPFiction